# Cage of Deceit

## Book 1
## Reign of Secrets

### By:
### Jennifer Anne Davis

THIS book is a work of fiction. Names, characters, places and incidents are the product of the author's imagination or are used fictitiously. Any resemblance to actual persons, living or dead, business establishments, events or locales is entirely coincidental. NO part of this book may be reproduced, scanned, or distributed in any printed or electronic form without permission. Please do not participate in or encourage piracy of copyrighted materials in violation of the author's rights. Purchase only authorized editions.

*Cage of Deceit*
Copyright ©2015 Jennifer Anne Davis
All rights reserved.

ISBN:978-1-63422-098-9
Cover Design by: Marya Heiman
Typography by: Courtney Nuckels
Editing by: Cynthia Shepp

"I was completely captured by this story. An outstanding and riveting read."
~CAMEO RENAE, BESTSELLING AUTHOR OF THE HIDDEN WINGS SERIES AND AFTER LIGHT SAGA

"Twists and turns, danger and drama--this book has it all! Heart-dropping moments that literally had me holding my breath and an ending that demands book two be available NOW!"
~MELANIE NEWTON FROM NERD GIRL OFFICIAL

"I thought Jennifer Anne Davis's True Reign series was one to rave about, but Cage of Deceit has topped it, and has completely blown me away! I love this book! I cannot wait for the sequel! Davis will forever be on my MUST-READ list. A Good Choice for Reading!"
~DAMARIS DELGADO FROM GOOD CHOICE READING

"Cage of Deceit is a wonderful blend of fairy tale and fast-paced, thrilling adventure. With a kick-ass heroine princess, this novel will not only get your heart racing, but leave you clamoring for book two."
~LIZA WIEMER, AUTHOR OF HELLO?

"An amazing fantasy that is a thrilling adventure from start to finish. I totally found myself loving the world that Jennifer Anne Davis has written in Cage of Deceit. This was a real gem to read."
~GRACE FROM BOOKS OF LOVE

"This is an edge of your seat start to a great series and will keep you begging for more once you close the book. I am anxiously awaiting the follow-up. Ms. Davis's writing has turned me into a forever fan!"
~ ANGELLE LEBLANC FROM CAJUN BOOK LOVER

"*Cage of Deceit* is a masterfully woven tale of royal responsibilities mirrored with the desire for freedom and adventure. This confliction is personified with Alyssa, the teenaged daughter of Darmik and Rema. When she meets Jarvik, the infuriating squire for Prince Odar, the word play is as sharp as their swords. A thoroughly enjoyable read that satisfied both my inner romantic and adventurer!"
~Kelly Risser, Author of Never Forgotten

"Jennifer Anne Davis knows how to weave a story that pulls at your heartstrings. She makes you want to take the sword and run it through the evil characters. Davis is an outstanding storyteller and on my must read right now list."
~ Jan Farnworth from J.R.'s Book Reviews

"We have flawed, judgmental characters who feel truly human. There's political intrigue and deceit so thick you can disappear inside of it. And threats that gleam like a blade in the night. Welcome to the Cage of Deceit, where even a princess isn't all she's cracked up to be."
~ Leah Alvord from Vitality Reviews

"In this enchanting spin-off Jennifer Anne Davis brings the world she created in the True Reign series to a whole new level. There's plot turns and twists, action and suspense. And a dash of romance, as expected from Jennifer Anne Davis's previous books."
~ Rebecca van Kaam from GotToReadThoseBooks

*For Allyssa*

For more information about our content disclosure,
please utilize the QR code above with your smart phone
or visit us at
www.CleanTeenPublishing.com.

*Cage of Deceit*
is the first book in a series.
Therefore, if you expect a happily ever after
and a neat, tidy wrap up at the end of this book,
you will be disappointed
because I enjoy leaving people hanging from cliffs.
If you have the spirit of an adventurer, flip this page.
~I DARE YOU!~
After all, embarking on a tumultuous journey
is far more rewarding in the end.
By turning the page, you understand that you are
entering book one of the series
*Reign of Secrets*
and anything can happen.

# The Mainland

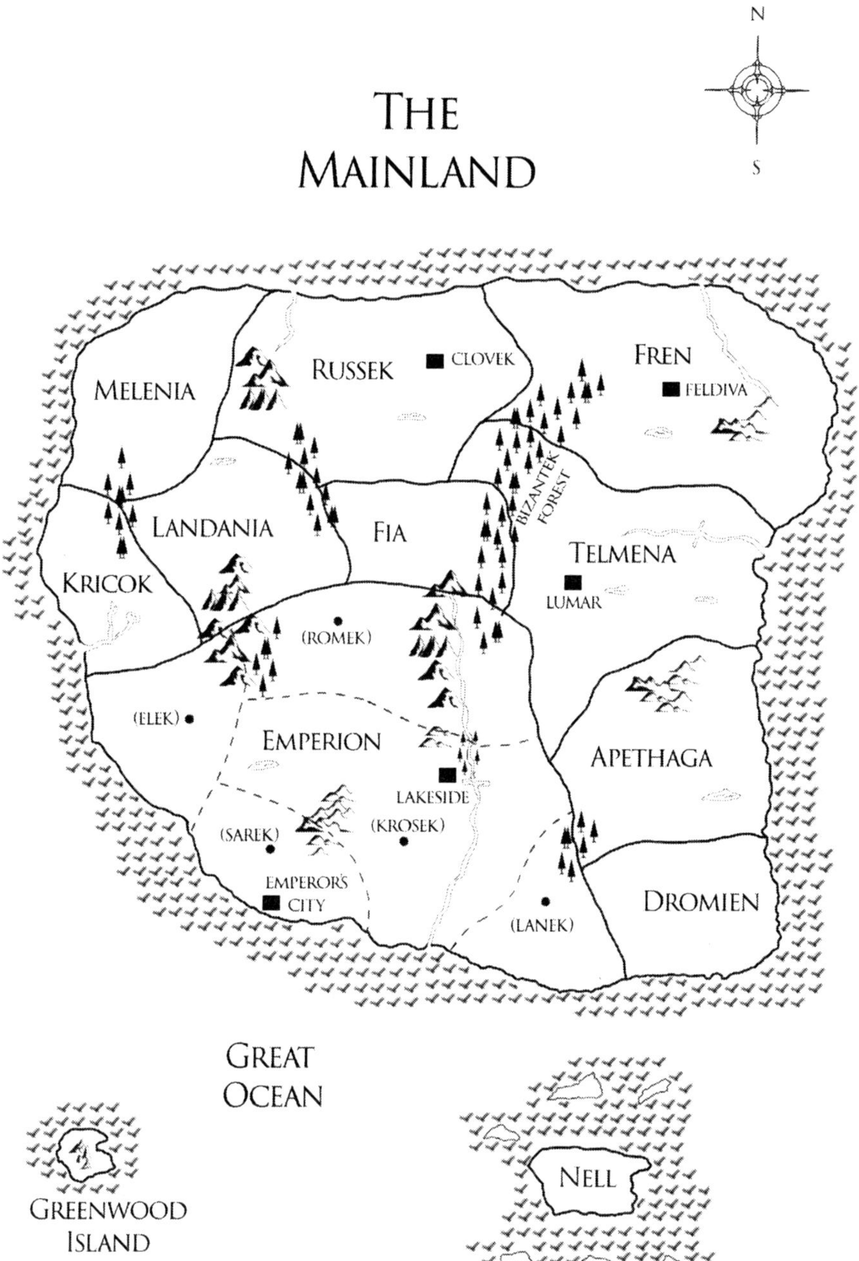

# Chapter One

Running along the edge of the rooftop, Allyssa kept an eye on the man below. He was three blocks ahead of her as he sprinted down the street, clutching a bag of coins. Allyssa jumped the two-foot gap to the adjacent rooftop, not wanting to lose sight of the thief. He slowed and turned a corner into an alleyway. With any luck, he'd hide there and she could catch him by surprise.

Allyssa couldn't believe she was the one running on rooftops after him. Grevik had insisted only she could do such a thing because she was smaller, lighter, and more agile. She suspected her friend was just too much of a pansy to do it himself.

There was one more building to go. Unfortunately, the next one was much further away. If she had to guess, it was a good eight to ten feet. Keeping her breathing steady, she steeled her resolve and ran a bit quicker. She pumped her legs faster and faster, the edge of the rooftop rapidly approaching. Twenty feet to go. Why did she agree to this? *Focus*, she scolded herself. Now was not the time to think about it. Ten feet to go. *Here goes nothing*.

Her right boot hit the edge of the roof. Using all her strength, she pushed off, flying through the moonlit night. Her arms waved and her legs ran on air as she

hurtled toward the adjacent rooftop landing with a jolt. Starting to fall forward, she tucked her head, rolled onto her back, and somersaulted. Crouching low, her heart beat frantically. *Blimey.* A smile burst on her face. That was fun. Not that she was about to do it again, though.

Jumping to her feet, she glanced over the edge of the two-story building, searching for the thief. Sure enough, he was right below, hiding in the alley. Allyssa pulled out her dagger and slid onto her stomach. Peering over the side, she carefully aimed her weapon at him. As long as the thief stood still, striking him would be relatively simple. She counted to three and threw her knife, watching it zoom down thirty feet and whack the man dead center in his right shoulder. He screamed, dropping the bag of coins as he looked frantically about for his attacker. The hilt was facing straight up and hopefully wouldn't give away her position.

If only Grevik would hurry and catch up. Shortly after they had started pursuing the thief, a rowdy crowd of about twenty men spilled out from a tavern, blocking the street as a fight broke out. Since Allyssa and Grevik didn't want to lose the thief, he told her to climb the building so she could follow him. She hoped Grevik had made it through the crowd without incident.

Standing, she scanned the adjacent streets, not finding her friend anywhere in sight. The thief still stood in the alleyway, not making an attempt to run. It was up to her then. She climbed down the ladder attached to the side of the building. Taking a deep breath, she stalked around the corner.

The man stood in the middle of the dark alley, clutching his shoulder. "Stay back or I'll gut you!" he screamed.

"Funny coming from an injured lowlife who steals," she answered, trying to use a deep voice.

The man laughed. "Go back home where you belong, little girl," he said, shaking his head.

"That's no way to speak to someone who's about to wallop you." She plucked her knives free and held them low. "Now give me the bag of coins you stole from the baker and maybe, just maybe, I won't kill you."

The man yanked the dagger out of his shoulder, stifling a scream. When his head tilted up, his eyes gleamed with malice. Based upon the way he held his body, prepared to fight, he had to have some skill. Nothing she couldn't handle, though. Not wanting to risk the weapon cutting her, she threw her knife at the dagger he held, hitting it hard enough that he dropped it, the metal clanging on the stone street.

"What are you waiting for? Scared?" the man taunted.

Allyssa meandered toward him as she tossed her cape behind her shoulders, freeing her arms and legs. "Yes," she whispered when she was only three feet away. "I am scared. Scared I'll kill you when you really deserve to be rotting in a jail cell." And with that, she spun and kicked his head, sending him to the ground. Much faster than she expected, he sprang to his feet and swung his fist at her. She stepped out of the way and was about to hit him when he punched her cheek. Stars exploded across her vision. *Blasted.* That would leave a mark.

"You did not just hit me," Allyssa said, seething with rage.

The man had the audacity to laugh at her. She flung her last knife into his thigh. He screamed. *Wimp.* Using a front kick, she struck his chest and he went flying to the ground. Just for good measure, and because he'd hit her

face of all places, she went over and kicked his groin. He had the decency to curl into a ball and surrender.

A man ran into the alley behind her. She spun around and came face to face with her friend, Grevik. "It's about time you showed up." She smiled sweetly at him. "You missed all the fun."

He went over to the man lying on the ground, making sure he was knocked out cold. "While you were jumping over rooftops like a gazelle, I was stuck in that brawl outside the Snakeskin Tavern." He stood and turned to face her. "I can't believe you took this man on without me, Lilly."

The first time she met Grevik all those years ago, she'd told him her name was Lilly so he wouldn't suspect her true identity.

"I couldn't wait for you," she said with a shrug. Now that she could see Grevik in the moonlight, she noticed his knuckles were cut and bleeding. "Are you all right?" she asked, pointing to his hands, hoping he hadn't broken a bone.

He nodded. "It was easier to punch a few of the drunks to make my way through the brawl." Grevik scanned the rooftop. "I guess we can add jumping buildings to your ever-growing list of skills."

"It was bloody fun," she said, unable to suppress her smile.

Grevik shook his head. "You're unbelievable. Only you would think leaping through the air thirty feet off the ground over alleys is fun."

"You told me to do it so we wouldn't lose the thief." She picked up her daggers and sheathed them.

"Blame it on me," he teased, wrapping his arm around her shoulder, tugging her closer to him. Allyssa stiffened before forcing herself to relax. This was the sort of thing friends did. "Come on," he said. "We need to drop this bloke off to my contact in the City Guard so I can go home. It's later than usual, and I don't want Mum to wake up and find me gone."

"I need to go home, too," Allyssa said. If she didn't arrive before daylight, she would be in severe trouble.

"Wake up," Mayra hissed. "Your mother is on her way. She'll be here any minute."

Allyssa groaned and snuggled further under the warm blankets. It was too early. She wasn't ready to wake up and face the day. Her body ached from running on the rooftops and fighting a grown man last night. Just a few more hours—that was all she needed. Mayra yanked the blankets off her. "You are cruel!" Allyssa chided her friend. Grabbing her pillow, she smothered it over her face, shielding out the bright light.

"Didn't you hear me?" Mayra tried again. "Your mother will be here in less than five minutes. It is already mid-morning. If she arrives and finds you in bed, you know what will happen."

Mayra was right. Allyssa needed to climb out of bed and dress before her mother arrived. Otherwise, she'd never hear the end of it. She threw the pillow off her face and stretched.

Mayra's eyes widened at the sight of her, and she gasped. "What happened?"

"I'm tired is all." Allyssa yawned and sat up. "I want an easy dress to put on without a lot of frills."

Mayra shook her head, her eyes wide with horror.

## Cage of Deceit

"What is it?" Allyssa asked as she slid off the bed and moved to the tall mirror in the corner of her room. She expected to see a tired face looking back at her. Capturing thieves was no easy task. Staring at herself in the mirror, she hissed. "That son of a harlot!" she cursed. The entire side of her face was a deep, raging purple, the color of eggplant. She growled. She'd forgotten the thief had hit her last night.

"I'll get the dusting powder," Mayra said, running to the dresser. "Madelin," she called over her shoulder. "Find something purple for Allyssa to wear."

There was no way they were going to be able to hide this before her mother arrived. *Blimey*. Rushing into her dressing closet, she ran her hands over her long, brown hair, trying to tame it. She could feign an illness, but then she'd have to stay in bed all day with people fussing about her. The mere thought made her want to vomit.

Madelin plucked lavender fabric off a hanger and shoved it at her. Allyssa grabbed the material and yanked it over her head, shimmying into the outfit. Mayra rushed in, carrying the tray of powder. As Madelin cinched up the back of the dress, Mayra dusted Allyssa's face, trying to hide the nasty bruise.

Mayra shook her head. "If you had come to me right when this happened, I could have made a paste of herbs to lessen the swelling." She dabbed her brush into more powder and applied a thick second coat.

A knock resounded through her bedchamber. Her mother was there. Allyssa's hair wasn't even done.

"Keep your head slightly forward," Mayra instructed. "Try to hide the side of your face with your hair."

Allyssa nodded, looking at herself in the mirror. Even with the powder on, her face had a hint of purple to it. The sleeves and skirt of her lavender dress were adorned with thousands of small beads. With the color of the fabric and the shiny beading, it merely seemed as if the dress were reflecting on her face. *Brilliant.* She hugged Mayra and Madelin. "Thank you."

"No need to fuss," Madelin said, hugging her back.

"Now hurry," Mayra added, giving her a small shove. "It's not wise to keep your mother waiting."

Allyssa exited the dressing closet and entered the sitting area of her bedchamber. "Hello, Mother," she said, trying to keep her head angled so her hair covered her bruise.

Mayra and Madelin came up behind her. "Your Majesty," they said in unison, bowing before the empress.

Empress Rema quickly dismissed the royal guards and Allyssa's ladies-in-waiting. Once the door closed and they were alone, Rema's eyes narrowed. "Did you just awaken?" she asked, a hint of disbelief coloring her voice.

"No," Allyssa lied. "Why do you ask?" She prayed her mother didn't notice the bruise.

"I haven't seen you today. And you seem a bit… thrown together. Are you feeling all right?" Rema came over, gently clutching her daughter's arms as her eyes roamed over her body, inspecting her for some sign of distress or illness.

Allyssa stood there, knowing her mother was only concerned for her wellbeing. Since her twin brother died shortly after birth, and Rema hadn't been able to conceive another child, Allyssa was all she had. If her mother wanted to fuss, the least she could do was let her. She smiled, trying to reassure her, but had to stifle a yelp since her face was sore from being punched. "Yes, Mother. I'm all right," she forced herself to say, trying not to wince from the pain.

There was no way Allyssa could tell Rema that she snuck out of the castle at night to aid the City Guards in tracking down criminals. The empress would never understand or allow it, especially since Allyssa was the crown princess and the only heir to Emperion.

"Very well," Rema said, releasing her daughter. "I've come to tell you that a small ball will be thrown in honor of Prince Zek of Fia tonight." She moved to the window, gazing outside.

Allyssa wondered if the boring prince from the tiny kingdom of Fia was ever going home. He'd already been there a fortnight, and she'd been forced to sit alongside him at dinner on more than one occasion. She couldn't take much more of his idle chatter.

"He's requested an audience with us tomorrow," her mother continued. "You will be there when he speaks."

Allyssa stood in front of the hearth, allowing the fire to warm her. She suspected Prince Zek would ask for her hand in marriage at the meeting. Although her parents had insisted she be present when such declarations were made, they hadn't pushed her into marrying. Yet.

So far, all the princes or high-ranking nobles who had come hadn't interested her. Rema and Darmik told the gentlemen that their daughter was simply too young and in no hurry to marry. But she could only put off the inevitable for so long. She dreaded the day when she would have to choose who would live in this cage with her, who would rule by her side, and who would be her companion for life. Granted, it had worked out for her parents, but their story was far from usual. They were the lucky ones. Rema and Darmik had managed to choose each other and weren't forced into an awkward arranged marriage.

"Care to join me in the Throne Room for the weekly proceedings?" Rema gently asked as she turned to face her daughter with sympathy in her eyes.

Allyssa most certainly did not want to join her mother in that stifling place. However, she knew it really wasn't a question. "Of course."

Rema smiled and came over to her, linking their arms together as they exited the room. "Want to go riding with me later today?" she asked, kissing the top of Allyssa's head.

"I would love to," she answered. Riding with her mother was one of her favorite things to do. "But I'm going to have to decline. I'll need the time to prepare for the ball." In reality, she needed to rest. Her muscles were sore, and there was no way she could mount a horse—not after the events of last night.

"I understand," Rema said, patting her daughter's hand.

"Tomorrow?" Allyssa suggested, hoping she'd feel better by then.

"I look forward to it." The empress led them out of the Royal Chambers and to the corridor where their royal guards surrounded them.

"I forgot to tell you that the Legion of Emperion was thoroughly impressed with your handling of the meeting yesterday," Rema said, her eyes flickering with amusement.

Allyssa had to stifle her laugh. The Legion was made up of elderly gentleman. Her mother had told her to make sure she smiled but maintained control at all times by not letting anyone speak over her.

"Your father and I had a bet," Rema whispered. "He

thought you'd lose your temper and yell at the lot of them."

Allyssa snorted. "And you didn't?" she asked, surprised.

"That's not to say I don't think you'll lose it in the future, but I knew you'd be able to remain composed the first time."

Allyssa laughed.

"Thanks to you, I won a new horse." Rema smiled.

"You bet a horse?"

"You know your father," Rema mused. "He jumped at the chance to acquire a new stallion. Too bad he lost."

Sitting in the Throne Room for hours, listening to the representatives from each of the five regions in Emperion drone on and on about the state of their land, nearly drove Allyssa to tears with boredom. She didn't know how her mother and father sat there listening to this once a week.

At least when she snuck out with Grevik, she was making changes for the better by helping citizens and ensuring criminals were put in jail. It felt like everyone who came to see the empress and emperor wanted or needed something from them. It was utterly exhausting, yet Rema managed to sit there with a kind smile, listening. Allyssa's father, Darmik, at least appeared a little antsy. He preferred managing the army to politics.

When it was finally over hours later, the royal family stood and strode down the aisle. Allyssa mimicked her mother and smiled at the representatives, who all bowed. The second she exited the room, she moaned.

Her father's eyes sliced over to her. "There are still

courtiers lurking in the hallways," he mumbled so only she could hear. "Behave."

She rounded her shoulders and plastered the never-ending smile back on her face. "Of course," she said. "Forgive me."

He raised an eyebrow.

"I'm going riding," Rema announced. "I have a new horse I need to become acquainted with."

Allyssa knew her mother needed to break free from this place on occasion as well.

"I'll accompany you," Darmik said, taking his wife's arm and escorting her down the hallway.

Sighing, Allyssa headed toward the Royal Chambers, wanting nothing more than to crawl in bed for a few hours. She needed to have enough energy to not only make it through the ridiculous ball tonight, but also to meet Grevik afterwards. If she didn't have the chance to leave the castle for a bit, she'd go stark raving mad.

Marek, the head of her personal guard, stepped next to her. He wore his light armor with his gleaming sword strapped to his waist. "Care to spar for an hour before you dress for the ball?" he asked.

She fought a smile. He knew she loved to fight. After all, they'd grown up together sparring, especially since his father and hers were best friends. As tempting as his offer was, her body couldn't withstand the physical exertion right now.

"Are you sure you're ready for me to beat you again?" she teased.

He chuckled. "I let you win."

"As much as I would enjoy the opportunity to trounce you, I have too many things to do before the ball this evening," she said. "However, I do believe I will have

some free time tomorrow?"

"I look forward to proving you wrong. Again," Marek said, smiling at her.

The head of her guard was rather handsome, she supposed. She'd grown up with him and his younger sister Mayra. Both of them had dark hair and eyes. Mayra was small and slim like her mother Ellie, whereas Marek was tall and lean just like his father Neco.

When Allyssa caught sight of a group of courtiers up ahead, she stiffened. She hoped the powder still concealed the nasty bruise on her cheek. Marek hadn't said anything to her about it, but then again, he knew better. Holding her chin high, she glided down the corridor. The pristine leaded glass windows allowed the sun to shine brightly through. As she approached the group, everyone bowed. Allyssa kindly smiled at her subjects. She was the heir to the throne, and they were supposedly beneath her. Yet … yet … she felt like a child playing at a game she knew nothing about. These people had been navigating court for years. They each had an agenda, wanted or needed something, and they were all here for a reason.

Allyssa kept walking, not wanting to give them the opportunity to talk to her. When she rounded the corner, she finally relaxed her shoulders.

A BALL WAS NOTHING UNUSUAL SINCE SEVERAL WERE held each season. Rema insisted it was good policy to please the nobility. Allyssa had grown up attending these functions. At first, she'd been bedazzled by the glittering chandeliers, the fine clothing, and the ornate flowers. But after attending so many balls, they began to lose their appeal. However, at every single one, she made sure no one knew how she really felt. She smiled at, danced with, and listened to her subjects. Her parents had groomed her well.

Her father took her hand, leading her to the dais at the front of the room. That was when she caught sight of the decorations. "Are the flowers from the main courtyard?" she asked, stifling a laugh.

"I believe so. We didn't have time to have them brought in."

"Hopefully, no one will notice. We wouldn't want to offend the prince from Fia," she sardonically replied.

Darmik patted her hand. "Care to tell me what happened to your face?" he asked under his breath. Without a pause, he expertly led her through the throng of people who parted and bowed as they passed by.

Of course he'd notice. "It's silly," she replied, keeping a smile on her face. "An accident."

"Really?" he said, playfully pinching her arm. He knew she was lying. Being Commander for the army had taught him to notice such details and had made him far too observant.

"I assure you, it's nothing." She smiled up at him. If she didn't convince her father, he'd send one of her guards to stand inside her bedchamber to watch her at all times. As it was now, having four guards posted outside was more than enough. Having someone actually inside her room would be beyond stifling. "It's embarrassing," she muttered.

"Sparring with Marek?" he asked, amused.

She allowed her face to redden, as if ashamed. Darmik chuckled, and Allyssa let him believe the lie. With any

luck, he wouldn't question Marek about it. "Please, let it go," she begged.

Her father patted her hand again when they reached the dais. Allyssa stood at the front of the room while he left to escort Rema inside. When her parents made their entrance, the room went utterly silent. Everyone loved the empress. She had ascended to the throne at the age of eighteen and managed to take a kingdom devoted to war and turn it into the most prosperous and peaceful kingdom on the continent.

Allyssa hoped she could be half the ruler her mother was.

She peered down at her red gown. Rema had insisted she wear red—the color of Emperion. She didn't mind, actually. It set off her long, chestnut hair and blue eyes, which almost made her look pretty. Almost. She'd never be beautiful like her mother, though.

After her parents joined her on the dais, Prince Zek from Fia was announced. He was too tall and skinny for her liking. His face was pleasant enough—light brown hair with soft brown eyes. The prince bowed before her and asked for the first dance, as was custom. Of course, she smiled and obliged. His sweaty hand took hers, and they danced.

Surprisingly, he was a good dancer. The problem came when the prince opened his mouth. He never had anything interesting to say—he always discussed his kingdom's spice trade, or the weather, or the fact that he was in line to inherit the throne of Fia.

Thankfully, the song ended and a noble courtier immediately swept in and asked for a turn. She danced for about an hour with various partners, each conversing about his land, wealth, and what he could offer the crown. Once she'd had enough, she claimed she needed to rest. Allyssa slipped out of the side door, hoping no one noticed.

Marek came up behind her. "Already retiring for the night?"

"Yes," she said, faking a yawn. "I'm exhausted."

He silently escorted her to the royal wing where Mayra and Madelin were dutifully waiting in her bedchamber.

"Did you even dance?" Madelin asked.

"Of course I did," Allyssa replied.

"If I were you," Madelin continued, "I'd dance with every available man." She spun around the room, dancing with an invisible partner.

Mayra shook her head. "It's a good thing she's not you, then. She's a princess, not a barmaid."

Madelin stopped in front of Mayra, placing her hands on her hips. "Excuse me?"

"Girls," Allyssa said, exasperated. She needed to hurry up or she would be late. "My gown."

Both immediately came over and helped her remove the dress. After Allyssa was in her nightclothes, her ladies-in-waiting left. Knowing her guards stood watch just outside her door, she quietly changed, pulling on wool pants and a tunic.

Grabbing her cape, she tied it on, making sure the hood concealed her hair and face. Satisfied with her disguise, she opened the laundry chute and climbed in. After closing the small, wooden door behind her, she slid down in complete darkness, landing in a pile of clothes and bed linens at the bottom. Carefully peering around, she made sure no one was about at this late hour. Certain it was clear, she climbed out and hurried from the room. Allyssa exited the castle via the servants' entrance.

She was free. Finally free.

# Chapter Two

Cool air whipped around her body, and the moon shone brightly above as she walked along the street to the tavern where she was supposed to meet Grevik. She loved it here. Loved the bustling city, loved the people scurrying about, and loved the smells and sounds. All the chaos drove her mother crazy sometimes. Rema needed open land, which was why the empress relocated the capital from Emperor's City near the Great Ocean to the town of Lakeside in the middle of Emperion. Even though this city was significantly smaller, there were still hundreds of shops and plenty to see. Her mother had chosen this location because it was surrounded by low, rolling green hills and a forest about a mile away. It reminded Rema of her home, Greenwood Island. Often times, Allyssa would find her mother standing on top of the castle late at night, staring out at the open land.

Allyssa, on the other hand, adored Lakeside. She was thankful the castle had been built right next to it, and that every front-facing window had a clear view of the city.

Before entering the tavern, Allyssa quickly made sure her hair was combed back the way commoners wore their hair. She'd already removed all her dusting powder and smeared some dirt on her face. Opening the door to the Boar's Head Tavern, she immediately spotted Grevik sitting at a table in the center of the room with two cups of ale in front of him.

"Lilly, where have you been?" he asked.

She slid onto the chair across from him and rubbed her face. "Sorry I'm late. I got held up."

He shook his head. "You're always held up." He shoved one of the mugs toward her. "Luckily for you, I'm used to it." He wiggled his eyebrows and flashed a smile before taking a drink.

"What's on the agenda for tonight?" she asked. He clasped his hands around his mug, no longer looking at her. "What is it?" she demanded.

Grevik sighed. "I got my orders today. I got my first choice—City Guard."

"Oh." Orders. She'd forgotten that since he was sixteen, he had to choose his profession. Allyssa looked at her dear friend, remembering the first night she'd ever snuck out of the castle. She'd been twelve years old at the time and had wanted to escape from the sniveling, conniving, back-stabbing girls at court. She hated them all. They only pretended to be her friend because of her position.

Donning a servant girl's dress that Allyssa had found in the laundry room, along with a knit hat that hid her hair, she had gone into the city. She had never been outside the castle's outer wall on her own before, but she'd been out plenty of times with her parents and guards. Having a general idea of where the market and most of the businesses were located, she headed in that direction, wanting to blend in with the shoppers. As she passed a dark alley, a man stepped out from the shadows with a nasty gleam in his eyes. He approached and demanded she hand over any money she had. A City Guard was patrolling the street only a few feet away from her. She called out for his assistance, and he rushed over, scaring the man off. The guard asked if he could escort her home, and she started crying, afraid her parents would discover what she'd done. When he couldn't calm her down, he took her home to his wife so she could help locate her parents. Since no one expected the princess to be roaming the streets on her own at night and she was disguised as commoner, no one recognized her.

When Allyssa walked into the small, cozy apartment, she met a boy about her age—Grevik. He asked her to play a game of cards and she stopped crying, gladly accepting the challenge. The guard went back to work, and the mother allowed the two children to play. Allyssa beat Grevik twice. When he questioned her about her parents and where she lived, Allyssa lied. She told him her parents owned a small business nearby.

Grevik made her promise to come back—he'd never lost to a girl before and he wanted the chance to beat her. She agreed to return, and she started sneaking out of the castle every evening after supper to visit her new friend. She would slip into Grevik's apartment, and they'd stay up all night, playing cards and talking.

But everything changed when Grevik's father was murdered.

He was on duty one night when he came upon two men fighting. He shoved his body between the men, separating them. One of the men withdrew a dagger and plunged it into his back. The two men ran away while Grevik's father died on the street with only an elderly woman as a witness.

Grevik swore he'd join the City Guard one day in order to put criminals, like the ones who killed his father, behind bars. Allyssa thought he'd make a fine guard, but she had an idea for something they could both do until he was old enough to claim his profession. It was she who suggested they track down thieves at night. They were almost thirteen years old and if they worked together, there was no reason they couldn't capture criminals and make a positive change now. Luckily, Allyssa already knew how to fight, and Grevik had some basic skills his father had taught him. Together, they made a formidable pair. So it was on that horrible night, the night Grevik's father was murdered, that the two friends swore an oath to fight side by side in an attempt to make a difference in the city.

Rubbing her temples, Allyssa tried to force herself to focus on the present instead of the memories of the past. When she looked over at her friend sitting across the table from her at the tavern, she gave him a reassuring smile. Grevik had worked hard for this position—he'd gone to school, took his exams, and passed all the physical trials. Not many were lucky enough to have their first choice of professions, especially when it came to the coveted jobs of the City Guard.

"You must be excited," she said, trying to sound happy for him.

"I'd be happier if you'd gotten in with me." He scooted his chair closer to hers.

Ignoring the fact that he was now invading her personal space, she said, "I'm proud of you. Congratulations. You certainly deserve it. Your mother must be proud." She tipped her cup back and finished off her drink.

"She is." He leaned on the table closer to her. "What profession did you choose?" he asked.

Allyssa had told him she didn't go to school—even though it was free for all children, regardless of class—because her parents needed her to help work at their shop. He'd asked on more than one occasion where their store was located, but she'd always been vague and quickly changed the subject. "I chose my family's business," she said. She hated lying to her friend but didn't know how he'd react if he found out she was the crown princess, and the family business she was running was the entire kingdom of Emperion.

"Why are you sitting so close?" she asked.

"If you were in trouble, you'd tell me, right?"

"Of course," she replied, totally offended he was even questioning her in the first place. "We're best friends. If something was wrong, you'd be the first to know."

Grevik nodded. "I just have the feeling that, sometimes, you keep things from me."

She playfully nudged him. "Are we going out tonight or are we going to just sit here gabbing like sissies?" She needed the freedom of running through the city. There had to be a thief out there who deserved to be in jail. It was her duty as Grevik's best friend and the heir to the kingdom to make a positive difference. And this was her way of doing it.

How much longer would Allyssa be able to do this? In a few weeks, her friend would be an official City Guard. Where would that leave her? She couldn't track down thieves on her own. And one day, when she married, she'd never be able to slip out of the castle. She shivered, hating the idea of growing older, having responsibilities, and not being able to do whatever the bloody hell she wanted.

"You sure you're okay, Lilly?" Grevik asked, his eyebrows pulling together with concern.

"I'm fine," she assured him, curling her hand into a fist. While she appreciated him caring, she wished he would leave it be.

He chuckled. "Are you mad because your parents wouldn't let you apply for a position in the City Guard?"

"Sod off," she snidely said.

He laughed and then finished his drink, slamming the mug down on the table. "Rumor is that a supply wagon carrying expensive fabric arrived early this morning. Two men, both in their thirties, robbed it, stealing almost everything inside."

Excitement coursed through Allyssa. This was the part she loved. The thrill of the hunt. "Let's go," she said.

Most likely, the thieves were in one of the seedier taverns, trying to lay low. The two friends headed to The Lion's Den in search of their newest targets.

"Ready?" Grevik asked as he shouldered the wooden door open.

Reaching down, she made sure all her weapons were in place. "Yes," she answered.

"Remember the plan." He gave her a pointed look.

"What?" she innocently asked. "What happened the last time we were here wasn't my fault."

"Regardless," he said as he headed to the bar, "I'd prefer not to fight everyone in this tavern tonight. Stick together, find the thieves, follow them, and when the chance arises, we take them down together."

"Which won't be a problem as long as no one touches me."

Grevik looked at her with raised eyebrows. As a

princess, no one ever touched her—especially strangers. How was she supposed to know the man was simply patting her shoulder as he squeezed behind her? If she'd known, she never would have attacked him—and most of the patrons who came to his aid. She and Grevik were lucky to have gotten out of that scrape alive.

Grevik ordered them two mugs of ale since they couldn't be at a tavern and not have a cup in hand. Allyssa turned and leaned against the counter, surveying the room. There were several games of cards going at different tables. If the men had already sold the stolen goods, they'd have money to burn.

One of the tables had a larger pile of coins in the center. She nudged Grevik and tilted her head in that direction. Since she was female, she couldn't join a card game played only by men without garnering undo attention. Allyssa furtively handed him a bag of coins, and he made his way over to the table. She watched him speak to the men as he tossed his bag of coins on top of the pile. One of the men nodded, and Grevik pulled a chair over and joined the game. Allyssa studied the one who had nodded—most likely he was in charge, which meant he was one of the thieves.

She stood there, growing tired, while Grevik played a couple of games, purposely losing each one in order to rouse the other men into boasting. When he ran out of money, he stood and came over to her.

"Well?" she asked, holding the mug in front of her lips so no one could see her talking to Grevik.

"The tall, thin guy with black hair," Grevik mumbled, pointing out the one she'd suspected, "is one of the thieves. Don't know who the second is, though."

Observing the other tables, she didn't notice anyone

who appeared out of place or suspicious. "Anything else?" she asked, hoping the man had told Grevik something useful.

"He said he was only passing through. Plans to leave first thing tomorrow."

They didn't have time to figure out who the second thief was then. They had to take this one to their contact in the City Guard tonight. "Very well," she uttered. "One is better than none."

Grevik chuckled. "Sometimes you speak so ... formal. It makes me laugh."

"Glad I can be of amusement."

"Me too."

They made their way to an empty table near the back where they could watch the thief without being noticed. After a couple more rounds, he collected the money piled high in the middle of the table. This was Allyssa and Grevik's cue to leave. They exited the tavern and slid into the shadows, watching. When the thief left, they silently followed him until they came to a deserted street.

The two friends had done this so many times they didn't even have to talk to one another. Grevik left her side and ran a block ahead to cut the thief off. Allyssa remained trailing the man. When she saw Grevik step into the middle of the street up ahead, she unsheathed her daggers. While the thief's attention was on Grevik ahead of him, Allyssa silently strode up behind the man and struck him across the back of his head with her dagger. He dropped to the ground.

When she glanced up at Grevik, his eyes widened at something behind her. She knew someone was there. She spun and kicked, her foot nicking her attacker. He lunged with his sword and she stepped to the side.

Bringing her arm up, she hit his sword arm. His weapon clanked to the ground. Grevik managed to strike the man's head with the hilt of his own sword, and he fell to the ground, unconscious.

"I take it this is the second thief?" Allyssa said, panting.

"Doesn't matter," Grevik replied. "We're taking them both to my contact, regardless." His contact in the City Guard ensured anyone they delivered to him was secured in prison. This particular guard had been good friends with Grevik's father, and he was eager to help.

# Chapter Three

ALLYSSA GLIDED INSIDE DARMIK'S OFFICE. HER PARENTS and Prince Zek sat at a small, round table waiting for her. She had planned to arrive early so she could talk to her parents before the prince showed up, but it had taken even longer today to conceal her bruised face than it had yesterday. It actually hurt to smile. As gracefully as possible, she took her seat between her parents.

She'd attended enough of these meetings by now to be able to determine the seriousness based upon small subtleties. The low fire in the hearth, the absence of fresh flowers, and the fact that her father wore his commander uniform instead of his royal tunic and crown indicated that her parents didn't consider the prince a potential suitor. However, there was definitely something of importance they wished to discuss—otherwise, they wouldn't have even bothered to meet with him.

Darmik motioned for the remaining guards to exit and shut the door, leaving the four of them alone. "You wanted an audience with us," he said to the prince. "What would you like to discuss?"

Prince Zek cleared his throat. "I wish for your daughter's hand in marriage."

Allyssa had heard similar declarations before. Many

wanted to marry the crown—no one actually cared for the person wearing it.

"You and every other prince on the continent," Darmik bluntly answered.

Allyssa wanted to kiss her father. She tried desperately not to laugh at the look of shock on the prince's face.

"Why don't you save us both a lot of time and get to the point?" Darmik said. He leaned back on his chair, crossing his legs.

"My country is in need of Emperion's protection," Prince Zek declared, trying to regain his composure.

Allyssa admired the fact that he was willing to marry her in order to protect his kingdom. It showed loyalty, duty, and a sense of honor on his part—something she hadn't learned listening to him drone on and on over the course of the past few weeks. However, she wondered what Fia needed protection from. The ten kingdoms on the mainland had lived in relative peace for the past decade. She'd heard whispered rumors that Russek was bullying its neighbors, yet that was nothing new or worth being concerned about.

Rema folded her hands on her lap. "You come from the small kingdom of Fia, which has little to offer us. Why would we allow you to marry our daughter?" She kept all emotion from her face, but Allyssa knew her mother well enough to know she was leading the poor prince right into a trap.

"Russek has invaded the kingdom of Melenia," Prince Zek stated. "My parents fear Russek will invade us next."

*Russek invaded Melenia?* Allyssa opened her mouth to question Prince Zek when Rema shook her head. Allyssa withheld her question and sat there silently, waiting for her parents to respond. Since neither of them appeared to be shocked or outraged, this information wasn't new to them.

Darmik stood and paced about the room, appearing deep in thought. Allyssa tried not to roll her eyes. Her parents were master negotiators and planners.

"I have a proposition for you," her father began. "Your kingdom is in need of protection. We will give you the resources you seek." Darmik stopped walking and turned to face the prince. "If Fia joins the Emperion Empire."

"What?" the stunned prince asked, his eyes wide.

Darmik smiled. "Fia will become a region within Emperion. Your parents will retain their titles and land. However, they will pay taxes to Emperion. Their army will join with my army. That is what I'm offering you. No need to marry my daughter."

Prince Zek sat there, fumbling with the edge of his cuff, not looking at anyone in the room. If his parents deemed him capable enough to come here to Emperion, the largest kingdom on the continent, and seek her hand in marriage, thus securing an alliance, surely he could speak on their behalf regarding this matter.

"I'll, uh, need to discuss it with the king and queen," he answered.

Rema abruptly stood. "You do that. Until then, we wish you well." She was dismissing him. He was no longer welcome in their castle under their protection.

The prince stood, his chair scraping against the stone floor. After he exited the room, Allyssa sank back against her chair, sighing.

"Interesting move on his part," Darmik said, folding his arms and staring out the window.

"How so?" Allyssa inquired.

"He didn't even attempt to negotiate," Rema

answered. "It makes him appear weak."

"Do you really think his parents will agree to it?" Was the threat from Russek so severe that the king and queen of Fia would willingly join the Emperion Empire?

"I do," Darmik answered.

"Why didn't you tell me Russek invaded Melenia?"

Before either of her parents could respond, Neco, Darmik's best friend and Mayra and Marek's father, entered the room.

"Your Majesty," he said, bowing to Darmik, which seemed oddly formal for him. Usually, there was an unspoken casualness between her parents and Neco. "Our spies have returned," he said, clasping his hands behind his back and not once looking Allyssa's way. "Russek has established control in Melenia. The king and queen were publicly executed after being forced to watch the executioner decapitate their three children."

Rema squeezed her eyes shut as Darmik said, "Allyssa, out of the room."

Her parents had never been so quick to dismiss her before. "King Drenton of Russek did this?" she asked, a chill overcoming her.

Darmik's attention snapped to her, and his eyes narrowed.

"Sorry," she muttered as she stood. "I'm leaving."

"One more thing," Rema said as Allyssa headed to the door. "I want you to give the weekly report this afternoon. Alone."

Allyssa froze. She'd never addressed the people of their kingdom without her parents at her side. "Is this because of Russek?" she asked.

"No. It's because you're sixteen now," Rema answered. "We'll be increasing your duties so you'll be ready to rule

Emperion when the time comes."

"That's years away," Allyssa said. She wasn't supposed to ascend to the throne and become empress until she was thirty.

Rema's blue eyes flashed, instantly looking hard and unyielding. "I pray that's the case. However, sometimes life has a way of turning out quite different than we expect it to. I've learned it is better to be prepared." Darmik gently placed his hands on either side of Rema's face and kissed her nose.

Not knowing what else to say, Allyssa simply nodded and left, closing the door behind her. She couldn't get that intimate image of her parents out of her head. It seemed as if they shared a secret—one so big that they couldn't even reveal it to their daughter.

Taking a deep breath, Allyssa stood before the closed double doors, listening to the cheering crowd outside. Glancing behind her, Allyssa noticed Mayra and Madelin smile encouragingly. Of course, they had nothing to worry about—they weren't the ones going out there. Alone. How could her parents do this to her? She'd never publicly spoken to the people before.

"Ready?" Marek asked, clutching the hilt of his sword, which was strapped to his waist. Since he was head of her personal guard, he'd be on the balcony with her, but only in the background as protection. He couldn't help her if she stumbled over her words or forgot what to say.

Facing the doors once again, she wiped her sweaty hands on her dress. At least she looked the part, donned in a simple, yet elegant, red gown etched with gold

embroidery. Squaring her shoulders and holding her head high, she refused to be intimidated. She would do this, and she would do it well. "I'm ready," she announced.

Her ladies-in-waiting came up behind her, placing a heavy cape bearing the royal family's crest upon her shoulders. Allyssa tried not to hunch forward from its weight. Marek flung open the doors, revealing an additional four heavily armored guards on the balcony.

The crowd roared as Allyssa strode out to greet everyone. The sun shone brightly overhead. She went to the railing and waved, smiling at the packed courtyard below. The crowd got even louder as they cheered for their crown princess. Her arm shook slightly, so she lowered it, not wanting anyone to see how nervous she really was.

The people quieted down, eager to hear the weekly address. Luckily, her father had told her exactly what to say.

"My dear people of Emperion," she began. "Thank you for coming this afternoon. It is with great honor that I am speaking to you today. The empress and emperor wish you well. They requested I update you regarding a situation brewing in the north." Allyssa paused here, just as Darmik had instructed. "Russek has invaded Melenia," she said with a strong and determined voice. A murmur rippled through the courtyard. "The dukes from the five regions of Emperion—Romek, Elek, Sarek, Krosek, and Lanek—will arrive within the next couple of days in order to discuss the situation in Russek. As a precaution, we are sending additional troops to ensure our borders are secure." Many of these people had family members in the army, and Darmik believed it was best for everyone to know the state of the continent at all times. "I assure you that Emperion is strong," she bellowed. "Not only are we the largest kingdom, but we have the most proficient army. We will maintain peace. Of this, I am certain."

The crowd burst into applause and cheers. She raised her hands, and they quieted down. "My people," Allyssa said, her voice echoing in the courtyard. "Thank you for your loyalty to the crown. *I* serve *you*." She bowed and strode off the balcony, the crowd roaring their approval behind her.

When the doors closed, she could finally breathe again.

"That went well," Mayra said as she removed Allyssa's heavy cape.

"Except that you forgot the entire part about Emperor's City," Madelin said with her hands on her hips.

"I know," Allyssa admitted, upset with herself for having forgotten at least half of the speech.

"It doesn't matter," Mayra said, shaking her head. "You went out there and addressed them on your own."

"Yes, I did," Allyssa said, smiling. "It was invigorating to speak before so many people, all cheering for the crown and what it represents. I'm lucky to be part of this legacy."

ALLYSSA ENTERED THE GREAT HALL WHERE TWO LONG tables were set for supper. A third table, set slightly apart, was situated straight ahead for the royal family. She walked toward it, passing between the other two tables where nobles and courtiers sat watching her.

After taking her seat, she saw Neco and Ellie sitting nearby, their heads bent together in quiet conversation. Ellie kept glancing her way, and Allyssa knew they were

talking about her. Perhaps they were discussing her speech today, or Prince Zek's proposal.

A small group of musicians played a simple melody, setting a joyful atmosphere. The tables were lined with large vases filled with fragrant flowers. While everything appeared perfect, hardly anyone in the room was talking and everyone kept glancing furtively at her.

Allyssa clasped her hands together on her lap, forcing a pleasant smile on her face. Something was wrong. If her parents didn't arrive soon, she'd leave to find them and demand to know what was going on. Right when she was about to stand, the guards stationed near the doors announced the empress and emperor. Rema and Darmik entered, arms joined together as they walked toward Allyssa. Once her parents were seated, the food was brought out and conversation resumed.

"I hear you did a decent job addressing the citizens," Darmik commented as he took a bite of his potatoes.

She noticed the way he said *decent* and not *good*. Since people were around, she couldn't roll her eyes or make a snarky comment, so she simply replied, "Thank you, Father. Your approval and kindness is astounding."

The corners of his mouth lifted as he fought a smile. Allyssa took a sip of her wine, trying to catch bits of the conversations going on in the room.

"We need to talk," Darmik said, taking another bite of potatoes. "I just can't decide if I should discuss the matter with you when there are people around, or when we're alone." He chuckled.

Allyssa clenched her fork. She'd only thrown a fit in public once, and she had been five at the time. The king and queen from Dromien had been visiting with their eight-year-old son. When no one was listening, he'd called her a skinny, ugly runt. So Allyssa punched him in the stomach and started yelling at him.

"I believe you've just made the decision for me," he said. "When we're alone then, since you have difficulty...controlling yourself." He lifted his goblet and took a drink, signaling for her to keep her mouth shut on the matter.

Allyssa peered around Darmik to her mother. Rema didn't say anything. Instead, she sat there, moving her food around her plate and barely eating. Darmik reached over and patted Rema's leg, comforting her. Allyssa wanted to demand to know why her mother was upset. Was it because of the situation with Russek? Or was something else bothering her? And what did Darmik wish to discuss with Allyssa? But she couldn't make such demands. It wasn't the time or place to behave in such a way. Contrary to what her father had said, she *could* control herself. He had no idea how much control she was exhibiting right now. Sitting there, she ate her food while making boring, unimportant conversation. She wanted to scream.

When dinner was over, Darmik and Rema glided out of the Great Hall with Allyssa behind them. They usually retired to the Royal Chambers, which consisted of the family's private sitting room and bedchambers. However, Allyssa needed to cool off before she faced her father for whatever it was he wanted to discuss. She decided to go to the library until her temper was reigned in. Besides, her tutor had requested she read a book on the history of Fren.

The entrance to the library was on the lower level at the east end of the castle. After parting ways with her parents, she headed in that direction with her guards

trailing close behind. Given the late hour, most of the servants should be gone for the night, but as she went along the hallway, she encountered a dozen or so dusting the furniture, straightening the tapestries, and scrubbing the stone floor.

"What's going on?" she asked Marek.

He took a large step so he was walking alongside and not behind her. "It appears the castle workers are preparing for something," he answered.

Two maids bowed to Allyssa as they rushed by, carrying large bouquets of flowers.

"What are they preparing for?" Allyssa demanded, stopping to face Marek.

"I haven't been told what specifically." He clasped his hands behind his back and kept his focus just above her head, not meeting her piercing gaze. If they were alone, she would have punched him in the stomach for his ridiculous formality.

"Take a guess," she said, putting her hands on her hips, her temper heating up instead of cooling down. She was the crown princess. He had to answer her truthfully.

His eyes flickered to hers momentarily before staring at that blasted spot above her head again. Marek cleared his throat and said, "Someone of importance is arriving. That's all my father said."

Allyssa started tapping her foot. "He didn't tell you anything else?"

Marek shook his head. Allyssa resumed walking. When they had received word that Prince Zek of Fia was coming, her parents had barely done anything to prepare for his arrival. Of course, he was of little consequence. So whoever was coming now had to be of great significance to warrant so much preparation. But why keep her in the dark? Unless this was what her father planned to discuss with her. Given the fact that he wanted to talk in private because of her temper, this must have something to do with her. Something she might not take kindly to. She stormed into the library.

A fire roared in the massive hearth, casting a soft glow throughout the four-story room. She went straight to the section where the histories of the kingdoms were and immediately located the book her tutor had assigned. Since her guards were waiting patiently at the library's entrance for her, she made her way to her favorite section. Trailing her fingers over the spines, she found the next book in the series she was reading for pleasure about a girl from a foreign continent who had magic and used a bo staff to wield that power. Allyssa was eager to learn if the girl defeated the evil king.

Fairly certain she could remain calm when she spoke to her parents, she headed to the royal wing, discreetly observing the people still awake and moving about. She had never seen this much activity at night. One sentry was meeting with a handful of guards, waving his arms about as if giving instructions. Several kitchen workers were carrying baskets of food to the kitchen. Dozens of servants were still cleaning.

When she reached the Royal Chambers, her parents had already turned in for the night. As Allyssa went to her bedchamber, she was filled with a sense of dread. Things were about to change. She just knew it. Thankfully, she was about to leave the castle and spend some time with Grevik. Chasing thieves through the city would help ease her nerves. At least, that was what she hoped.

# Chapter Four

Allyssa wished they were roaming the streets. She hadn't snuck out of the castle to just sit in a tavern for hours and not do anything even remotely productive. They only had a couple of weeks until Grevik became an official City Guard, and they couldn't track down criminals together anymore.

"You look more agitated than normal," Grevik teased, poking her in the ribs.

She shot him a look of annoyance. "Why are we sitting here?" she asked.

He leaned back on his chair, observing the patrons eating and drinking. Now that she was paying attention, she saw several groups of people huddled close together talking. No one was playing cards. *What is going on?*

"Did you hear the news?" he asked, leaning forward on the table and lowering his voice. She shook her head. "My friend Vardin's sister works at the castle. She told him another prince is on his way to ask for Princess Allyssa's hand in marriage."

Based upon the way Allyssa's father was acting and the state of the castle, she'd suspected as much.

"People are saying the threat from Russek is worse than the royal family is letting on," Grevik added. "The empress probably wants to align with another kingdom to strengthen our army."

"We won't go to war," Allyssa said, unable to believe he was talking about her family without even knowing it. "Especially against Russek. They're small and insignificant."

"That may be," Grevik answered. "But they are vicious. I heard they raped and murdered all the women and children in Melenia."

Bile rose in the back of her throat. How could any man behave in such a cruel and evil manner? "Luckily, we don't share a border with them," she absently said, thinking about Prince Zek of Fia.

Grevik shrugged. "You never know, Lilly. At least we have the princess to ransom off to the highest bidder. I'm assuming it's Telmena."

She almost spit out her drink. "The prince from Telmena is an old croak."

"I hardly think thirty is old," Grevik mused. "And it doesn't matter. He could be sixty for all I care. The point is we have an eligible princess who will strengthen our kingdom through marriage."

Allyssa whacked her friend's arm. "We don't need Telmena," she vehemently replied. "We're strong enough without them." Under no circumstances would she marry a man twice her age—even for the good of her country.

Grevik took another swig from his mug.

Straining to listen to those sitting at nearby tables, Allyssa couldn't catch any of their conversations. Was this how her people saw her? A bargaining chip to be ransomed off to the highest bidder? She rubbed her hands over her face.

"You never talk of marrying," Grevik said. "Why is that?"

## Cage of Deceit

Irritation coursed through her. Just because she was a girl didn't mean she had to be enamored with the idea of marrying. "You don't talk of marriage either," she snapped.

He pursed his lips, staring at her.

"Are we just going to sit here?" she said louder than she intended. "Or are we going out? I, for one, need some fresh air." Before she clobbered someone.

"Not tonight. The City Guard is having an emergency meeting. I spoke with our contact, and he told me to lay low."

Unable to sit still another minute, she shoved her chair back and stood.

"Where are you going?" Grevik asked, finishing off his drink and wiping his mouth with the back of his hand.

"Home," she lied. "I'll catch you tomorrow."

Wrapping her cloak around her, she exited the tavern and headed to a nearby alley. When no one was near, she climbed the ladder on the side of the building and made her way to the center of the rooftop, laying down on her back and staring up at the stars. The smell of baking bread wafted in the cool air.

She loved her kingdom dearly, but she would not marry some old geezer just to keep peace. There had to be another way. Emperion's army was strong. Surely, they could keep their borders secure. All her life, she knew she'd most likely have an arranged marriage—she just didn't realize it would come so soon and be so... so unappealing. A tear slid down her cheek, and she punched the rooftop. She would not cry like some silly girl. She was better than that.

Growing up, her parents were always happy. Even if they were dealing with a nasty political issue, they always had one another for comfort and support. She knew her parents loved each other and that they were best friends. Allyssa desperately wanted the sort of marriage her parents had—one of mutual love and respect.

Gazing up at the stars, she found the biggest and brightest one. "I wish to marry a man who possesses all my heart's desires and who is the prince of a great kingdom that can complement and strengthen Emperion."

Taking a steadying breath, Allyssa released the bow string and the arrow sailed through the air, landing with a small thud directly in the bull's-eye. She nocked another arrow, aimed, and released. Again, a direct hit.

Her father had taught her everything she knew. When she was only four, Darmik showed her how to defend herself. She learned how to shoot a bow and arrow by the time she was six, could accurately throw daggers from a long distance by the age of eight, and had been sparring for as long as she could remember.

Mayra, who stood beside her, raised her own bow and attempted to hit a much closer target. She released her arrow, and it struck the outer ring.

"Lower your left arm when you aim," Allyssa instructed.

"That's what my father always says," Mayra answered, nocking another arrow. "I'll never be as skilled at archery as you."

"You don't practice enough."

"I'd rather be studying another language than doing archery," she replied with a wry smile, releasing the arrow and hitting the outer ring for a second time.

Mayra had always been interested in other languages and cultures. In fact, she had quite the ear for linguistics, so good that Neco had sent her on a few missions as a spy.

"Gah," Madelin said as she stomped her foot, her target still empty. "What is the point of us shooting?" she asked from the other side of Mayra. "This is tedious. Shouldn't we practice dancing instead of archery?" She set her bow down and folded her arms.

Allyssa chuckled, ignoring her friend. Madelin complained every time they did this.

"If you'd like some help," Marek said, stepping forward, "I could be of assistance."

"That would be lovely," Madelin cooed as she bent over, picking her bow back up.

Mayra rolled her eyes. "Really, brother? Aren't you supposed to be guarding us? Not flirting?" She released another arrow, hitting the outer ring, again.

Marek whacked his sister's arm. "I'm guarding the princess, not you," he chided.

"I hardly think helping Madelin shoot is guarding the princess," Mayra replied.

"It's fine," Allyssa said, not wanting them to fight. She honestly didn't mind and had suspected Marek and Madelin had feelings for one another for quite some time. Besides, there were half a dozen soldiers guarding Allyssa right now, and they were still on the castle grounds. If Marek wanted to spend a few moments with Madelin, he could.

Allyssa took another arrow from her quiver and nocked it. The skirt of her dress swayed to the left from the gusty wind. Adjusting her aim accordingly, she released the bow string. Direct hit. She really should request the targets be moved further back. This was far too easy.

"I don't think Father would want the two of them courting," Mayra mumbled to Allyssa.

"Why?" she asked. Allyssa didn't think Marek and Madelin were courting—flirting definitely, but it hadn't progressed beyond that.

"Marek works here. It's unprofessional for the head of your personal guard to show interest in your lady-in-waiting." Mayra put her bow on the ground.

Allyssa set her bow down next to Mayra's. "Weren't both your parents servants when they met?" Rema had told her Marek and Mayra's father, Neco, was in the elite guard with Darmik and their mother, Ellie, was Rema's chambermaid years ago on Greenwood Island before Rema overthrew the illegitimate king.

"Yes, but that was different."

"I don't think so. I'm sure your parents would be fine with Marek courting Madelin. Besides, your two families are close."

Allyssa peered over at Marek and Madelin. Marek stood behind her, his hands on her arms, angling the bow properly.

Mayra rolled her eyes.

"Oh come on, it's sweet," Allyssa said. She suspected her friend was probably just jealous.

"No," Mayra said. "It most definitely is not. It's gross. He's my brother."

One of Darmik's stewards approached, clearing his throat. "Princess Allyssa, His Majesty bid me to deliver this." He handed her an envelope closed with her father's seal.

She tore it open and read the hastily written letter. Her father wanted her to arrive at the Throne Room in

two hours' time. A dress had been laid out for her in her bedchamber. She turned the paper over, looking for more. That was it. Very strange.

"I'm assuming you heard the news about Prince Zek?" Mayra asked after the steward left.

"I haven't heard a word." She needed to go to her bedchamber to change; however, she wanted to give Marek and Madelin a few more minutes alone.

Mayra whispered, "He was seen leaving this morning. I overheard my father say that your parents insisted he be gone before sunrise."

As relieved as she was to hear the boring prince had finally gone home, it only confirmed Grevik's gossip that someone of more importance was coming.

# Chapter Five

Staring at herself in the mirror, Allyssa ran her hand down the red material of her dress. She couldn't help but admire the exquisite fabric and attention to detail her personal seamstress had taken in making the gown. The outer material was softly woven silk, while the top skirt had a slit down the middle, allowing the underskirt to be seen with its intricate embroidery. The edges and square-shaped neck were lined with diamonds. It was utterly beautiful, elegant, and classy—something befitting of an empress.

Mayra finished loosely braiding Allyssa's hair.

"Why all the fuss?" Allyssa whispered. She still hadn't had a chance to speak with her father.

Her lady-in-waiting sighed, not answering her. She picked up the crown and placed it atop Allyssa's head. "There," she said, "you're ready to go to the Throne Room."

Allyssa raised her eyebrows, waiting for Mayra to offer additional information. Mayra started tidying up the dressing room, studiously ignoring her.

Knowing her friend's keen ear for gossip, Allyssa asked, "Is the prince from Telmena coming?" If she had to entertain the idea of marrying a thirty-year-old goat of a man, she'd consider running away until he found someone else to wed."

Her lady-in-waiting froze. "No," she whispered. "Although, I did hear an interesting rumor about his sister, Princess Jestina of Telmena. Since the crown passes through the female line, Telmena wanted Princess Jestina to marry the Crown Prince from Fren, uniting their two great kingdoms. However, the prince from Fren refused to marry her. To prevent their countries from going to war, the prince's younger brother, Prince Kren, married Princess Jestina instead."

"Why do you think this information is of use to me?"

Mayra shrugged. "I guess you'll have to wait and see."

If the prince from Telmena wasn't coming, then it had to be the Crown Prince from Fren. Otherwise, Mayra wouldn't have bothered sharing that bit of information. Allyssa abruptly turned and exited her bedchamber, her guards falling in position behind her. As she neared the sitting room in the royal wing, she heard her parents talking to Neco. Unable to stop herself, she paused in the hallway, listening.

"The royal convoy just entered the city," Neco announced.

It was wrong to eavesdrop, but she wanted to know if her suspicions were correct. Thankfully, Marek wasn't on duty; he'd have made noise to ensure she was discovered. She waved her four guards back, and they dutifully, and quietly, obliged. Allyssa peered around the corner.

Darmik rubbed his face while Rema stood and went to the window, looking outside.

"I've dreaded this day would come," the empress said. "I'll go and talk to her."

"I'll go with you," Darmik added. "After all, this was my idea."

Neco cleared his throat. "With all due respect," he said. "It's the only feasible option. She'll understand that. Her tutor has done an excellent job ensuring she understands the politics of the continent."

"I certainly hope so," Rema said, "because if she doesn't, we'll have a bloody war at our doorstep. I promised to protect the people of Emperion, but it can't be at the expense of my daughter."

"Before we make any decisions, we need to meet the prince to make sure he's suitable," Darmik said.

"I agree," Rema uttered.

"From all the reports I've received, he's more than adequate," Darmik assured her. He went over and embraced his wife. Neco bowed and left.

Holding her head high, Allyssa entered the sitting room. "Care to tell me what is going on?" She sat on the sofa, patiently waiting for her parents to explain why the prince from Fren was due to arrive at any minute.

Darmik took a step toward her, as if approaching an injured animal. "It has all happened rather suddenly," he said.

She laughed. "Suddenly? You've had enough time to prepare the castle for our special guest."

Rema looked at her with red eyes. "Honey," she said, "I need … no, we need you to be on your best behavior for this prince."

"I'm always on my best behavior."

Darmik snorted and folded his arms.

"What I mean is," her mother continued, "that there's a lot of political turmoil going on right now throughout the continent. We need to feel Prince Odar of Fren out to determine where his kingdom stands."

"We've never had anything to do with the kingdom

of Fren," Allyssa carefully said.

Darmik sat down next to his daughter on the sofa. "Fren is a powerful kingdom with a strong army," he said. "I think it's time we establish relations with them."

Were things really so dire that her parents would seek out someone they barely knew for their daughter? "Have you discussed the possibility of marriage with him?" Allyssa asked.

Her parents exchanged worried glances. "Not specifically," Rema answered. "However, our letter to Fren inviting the prince to come here to meet you certainly implied a union is possible."

Emperion invited Fren here—not the other way around.

"But we're not talking about marriage right now," Darmik assured her. "All we want is for you to meet the prince and keep an open mind."

"Be kind and cordial," Rema added.

It suddenly became difficult to breathe. Allyssa had to go outside for some fresh air before she started arguing with her parents and became even more frustrated. "Fine," she answered as she stood and left the Royal Chambers, her mother calling out for her to come back and discuss the matter in greater detail with them.

Allyssa made her way to one of the castle's inner courtyards. She tried to walk slowly and elegantly around the gardens, like a princess should. When she passed courtiers, she smiled as they bowed to her. She needed to maintain the appearance of grace when all she really wanted to do was tear something apart and break free from this cage.

After a few minutes, her ladies-in-waiting arrived, falling in step beside her. "Where have you been?" Allyssa asked.

Madelin's face turned pink, and Allyssa knew her friend must have been off with Marek somewhere. Mayra, on the other hand, said she had been speaking with her father.

"Do either of you know anything about Prince Odar of Fren?" Allyssa asked. They stopped near a red rosebush and she surreptitiously glanced around, making sure no one could overhear them.

Madelin shook her head. "I haven't heard a thing. I even asked my parents, and they said they knew nothing about him."

Allyssa looked to Mayra, but her friend wouldn't meet her gaze.

"Marek," Allyssa called over her shoulder. He'd brought her ladies-in-waiting to the courtyard and was now standing with the rest of her guards. He obediently came over.

"What do you know of Prince Odar?" she demanded.

Marek bit his lip and started fidgeting with the hilt of his sword.

"It wasn't a request," she said. She hated to pull rank, but she needed information.

"I'm sorry, Your Highness," he said, purposely using her title, "but we've been instructed to keep our mouths shut on the matter. Your parents don't want rumors or gossip floating around."

Both her ladies-in-waiting nodded, affirming what Marek had said. "Very well," Allyssa snapped, turning and heading back into the castle. She would not cry; they were simply following orders.

Mayra hurried to catch up. "I'm sorry," she whispered. "But we were given strict instructions."

"It's fine," Allyssa lied. This was why she hadn't told her ladies-in-waiting about sneaking out of the castle at night. Because when all was said and done, her parents outranked her and could make her ladies tell them anything they wanted to know. The staff's loyalty was to the crown, not her. She was a symbol and a bargaining chip.

As if in response to her agitation, the crown atop her head shifted, suddenly feeling heavy. *Blasted.* If only she could practice on her hitting dummy right now. She laughed. Dressed in the finest gown she'd ever worn and all she could think about was punching. How very unprincess-like.

ALLYSSA HURRIED TO THE ANTECHAMBER OF THE Throne Room, where she found her parents talking with Neco and Ellie. She stood in the doorway, not saying a word. She silently observed them, no one noticing she'd arrived.

"This is a real opportunity for Emperion," Darmik said. "If only Allyssa would cooperate."

"The princess is strong-willed, that's for sure," Neco said. "But she always does her duty. She has Emperion's best interest at heart."

"I agree," Rema said. "But Allyssa doesn't understand the precarious position we're in. We need this alliance."

"She's just so young," Darmik muttered.

"No, she's not," Ellie said, speaking for the first time. "Think of what you accomplished at her age. She's old enough, and more than capable."

Neco came up behind Ellie, wrapping his arms

around her waist. "I agree with my wife," he said, kissing her cheek.

Darmik sighed. "Who knew having a daughter would be so ... difficult." He turned to face Rema. "It's up to you," he said.

"Let me meet Prince Odar. Then I will decide how to proceed."

A steward came up next to the princess. "The convoy is here," he announced to the people in the antechamber.

Rema noticed her daughter standing there, so she came over and hugged Allyssa. "I don't know how much you heard," she whispered, "but we will talk later. Please, just keep an open mind and don't jump to conclusions." She released her, took Darmik's arm, and entered the Throne Room.

Neco and Ellie remained in the antechamber. "From all my spies' accounts," Neco said, "Prince Odar is a shrewd military leader, much like your father. We just need time to assess the situation and to speak with him."

"Why is he officially here?" Allyssa asked.

"To discuss Fren's situation with Russek."

She knew there was a lot more going on than she was privy to. She gave a curt nod to Neco and Ellie. After all, the least she could do was keep an open mind. Taking a few deep breaths, she put a smile on her face and entered the Throne Room.

Both sides of the aisle were filled with people eager to greet the mysterious prince from Fren. Out of all the kingdoms on the mainland, Fren was the one she knew the least about. The kingdom kept to itself, choosing to remain isolated. She couldn't imagine a marriage contract would be enough to lure the prince here. *No*, she thought, *there is definitely more going on*.

Allyssa glided down the aisle, head high, while everyone bowed. Her parents were already sitting on the dais, her mother in the center, Darmik to her right. Allyssa took her place on her mother's left. Light poured in through the windows, lining the right side of the room. Everyone present wore their finest clothes, and perfume wafted in the warm air.

The horns sounded and all heads turned toward the doors at the end of the aisle, eagerly awaiting the prince's entrance. Allyssa was mildly curious to meet him. How old was he? Twenty? Forty? Was he boring like the prince from Fia? Arrogant like most of the lords and nobles of her own kingdom? Was he ugly? Did he have a beard? Was he here to establish a relationship with Emperion? Did he seek Allyssa's hand in marriage? Perhaps he simply wanted to implement a trade agreement between their kingdoms.

The doors flew open, and four Fren soldiers clad in shiny armor entered. Behind them came two men dressed in solid black, carrying the flag of Fren as they marched down the aisle to the dais where they stopped and faced inward, clicking their heels together. Half a dozen men dressed in finery now entered the Throne Room. These must be the prince's lords-in-waiting. Allyssa squeezed her hands together to prevent her eyes from rolling at the pompous arrogance being displayed. This show of wealth was a bit excessive. Granted, Fren was one of the larger kingdoms and rumored to be well off. Apparently, the prince wanted to make sure everyone here knew it. Four more men entered, wearing fine tunics, indicating they were stewards or pages. If this display was any indication of the type of person the prince was, then he was just like every other bloke who'd come vying for her hand, and she was *not* impressed.

A collective murmur arose as the prince finally entered. He stood in the doorway a moment and flashed a smile before sauntering down the aisle. *Blimey.* He had dark hair, blue eyes, and a cocky smile that made him utterly handsome. The worst part was that he knew it and was flaunting it at her court. If she had to guess, she'd say he was about her age. The prince was dressed in a flamboyant white shirt and a dark embroidered tunic that was well suited for a ballroom and not traveling. He had to have changed after he arrived. No one could possibly be that vain. Strapped to his waist was a fine-looking sword. She was sure he'd never used it in battle. He'd probably never even seen a day of fighting in his life. She desperately tried not to laugh as his attention landed on her, his eyebrows lifting in what she could only assume was approval. This prince was even more arrogant than all the previous suitors combined. He was going to drive her utterly mad.

He stopped before the dais.

"Prince Odar of Fren," one of his squires announced. The prince regally bowed, showing his respect. The empress and emperor stood and went to officially greet the pretty prince. Yes, that was going to be Allyssa's name for Prince Odar. She supposed she should greet him too. She stood and moved forward. His hand took hers and he gently pressed his warm lips to the top of her fingers, his eyes locked on hers the entire time, making every effort to be seductive.

From the corner of her eye, she noticed his squire, the one who'd announced him, watching her intently. Maybe he also served as an advisor.

After pleasantries were exchanged, Darmik

announced, "People of Emperion, in honor of Prince Odar, a great feast will be thrown tonight. Everyone is invited. Afterwards, there will be lively music and dancing."

The people clapped, and the prince nodded his head in approval.

"Prince Odar," Rema said in a soft voice so only those closest to the dais could hear. "Please join the emperor and myself for drinks. We have much to discuss."

Darmik gave orders for Neco to show the visitors from Fren to their rooms. Then Rema and Darmik left, the prince with only his squire right behind them.

Allyssa went to follow, but Marek gently took her arm. "I have instructions to escort you back to your rooms."

She was relieved she didn't have to sit in a private room with the prince and attempt to carry on a conversation with him. As she walked along the corridors, she tried to keep an open mind about the prince, but she couldn't. He was an absolute joke. Allyssa had no interest in a man who cared more about his appearance than the people of his kingdom.

She froze in the middle of the corridor, Marek almost slamming into her.

"Are you okay, Your Highness?" he asked.

She was going to have to sacrifice herself for her kingdom. And that was something she wasn't prepared to do just yet. What value did her parents see with aligning Emperion with Fren? Her life flashed before her eyes—married to the prince while he flirted all day with women and threw parties. Her life would be lonely and unbearable. Squaring her shoulders, she continued walking down the corridor, her hands shaking.

# Chapter Six

Allyssa despised sparring in a dress. However, that was the way her father had taught her to fight. He said if someone attacked her, she would be in a gown, so she had to be able to maneuver in heavy fabric.

"Faster," Marek instructed. "You're not focusing."

She wanted to growl because he was right, she was too distracted. Putting all thoughts of the pretty prince out of her mind, she gave Marek her full attention. He swung his sword, hitting hers near the hilt, making her drop it. Not intending to lose their match so easily, she twisted and came in close to him. When he went to grab her, she rammed her elbow into his stomach. He hunched over and she yanked him down, slamming her knee into his face.

He dropped his sword.

"I win," she declared.

Catching his breath, he wiped his forehead. "You seem to have gained a few new moves." Not a question.

"Perhaps," was all she said in reply. The training room was lined with her personal guards. She knew her father didn't want her practicing—he'd rather she prepare for the ball. But in order to make it through dinner and dancing, she had to release her anger and frustration.

Marek took their wooden swords and put them back on the rack.

"I'm not ready to return to my rooms." She still felt off balance and unsettled.

He glanced to the door where Mayra and Madelin were waiting for her. "I need to go over some security details with my father," Marek stated.

"Then go." She waved him away. "I'll only be a few more minutes."

He briefly spoke with the guards before he said, "Your Highness," and left.

As soon as he was gone, she put leather gloves on and went to the hay figure secured to the wall. Taking a deep breath, she started punching it, imagining the dummy was the prince. Smiling, she started hitting it harder and faster, allowing all of her aggression to evaporate.

Someone started clapping, and she spun around about to yell at whoever had interrupted her.

Prince Odar stood there with a smirk.

"What are you doing here?" she demanded, wiping the sweat off her forehead with her arm. He was accompanied by two of his soldiers and the squire she noticed earlier in the Throne Room.

He clicked his tongue. "A testy remark from someone so delicate and lovely."

Her eyes narrowed. She was dirty, smelly, and certainly not the picture of a princess at the moment. The squire clasped his hands behind his back, staring daggers at her. He must not approve of a woman who could take care of herself, knew how to fight, and who dared to sweat. She hated him almost as much as she hated the prince.

"I'm sorry, Your Highness," she said, trying to keep

the detest from her voice. "Please excuse me, I must prepare for this evening."

Mayra rushed forward and placed a cloak upon Allyssa's shoulders. The princess yanked the hood up, concealing herself so no one from the court would see her all sweaty. She swept out of the room, not looking back. She could have sworn she heard the prince chuckling as she hurried down the corridor.

"Why didn't you use the opportunity to speak with the prince?" Mayra asked, trying to keep up. "He obviously sought you out."

Allyssa's eyes sliced over to her lady-in-waiting. "Because," she snapped, "I don't want to talk to someone who flatters with pointless words."

Mayra laughed. "He is rather charming."

"He appears to be exactly as a prince should," Allyssa said. "And I have no interest in princes."

"Aiming a bit higher?"

"No," Allyssa replied. "I'm aiming for someone a bit more real."

ENTERING THE ROYAL CHAMBERS, ALLYSSA WALKED straight through the sitting room without stopping. She knew what was there—flowers, jewelry, letters, and gifts from every available suitor who deemed themselves an acceptable match. Nobles from all over the kingdom, all desiring the wealth and notoriety of her position. All they saw when they looked at her was a crown and the power that came with it. She despised the tradition that dictated suitors send gifts before a ball or party to make their intentions known.

Just as she was about to turn down the hallway leading to her bedchamber, a small, wooden box caught her attention. It was made from simple oak, and it was the size of her hand. She stood staring at it. Everywhere else in the room, on every single surface, were gaudy flowers and ornate boxes. This one was completely out of place. Grabbing it, she took it with her.

The royal guards remained outside Princess Allyssa's rooms and only Mayra and Madelin went in with her. Both girls hurried to the dressing closet to start preparing Allyssa's gown. She plopped onto her bed, staring at the simple box. Oak was found in the Bizantek Forest that stretched from the northernmost section of Emperion, to Fia, through Telmena, and into Fren. There were no carvings or markings to suggest where the box had been made. The smoothness of the wood indicated someone had skillfully carved it.

She lifted the lid. Inside was a simple, hand-carved wooden ring. Upon closer inspection, there were several words engraved in a language she didn't recognize. Allyssa traced her finger over the foreign words. Perhaps Mayra would know what it said, but Allyssa didn't want to show the gift to anyone.

It was beautiful, and on a whim, she slid the ring on her finger. It fit perfectly. There wasn't a note or letter accompanying it. Where did the ring come from? Who had given it to her? She opened her bedchamber door, and her soldiers snapped to attention.

"Find out who was on duty this afternoon. I want to know who delivered this box." Her guards nodded, and she closed the door. Removing the ring, she gently placed it back in the box and set it on the table near her bed.

"Well?" Madelin asked, smiling proudly as she stood next to Mayra, both observing Allyssa. "What do you think?"

Allyssa just stared at herself in the mirror. The gown was the most elaborate dress she'd ever worn—even more so than the one she'd had on in the Throne Room to greet the prince.

"It's heavy," was all she said. She feared if she bent her knees, she'd actually collapse from the weight of the fabric. "Will I even fit through a doorway?"

Mayra shook her head. "You look exquisite, so stop being sullen and moody."

Allyssa laughed. "You're right, I'm sorry. Thank you for making me look beautiful." Turning away from the mirror, she faced her friends. "Are you two coming?" she asked. Since her father had opened the invitation up to the entire court, her ladies-in-waiting were officially allowed to attend.

"We are." Madelin beamed.

"Then you better hurry and change. Stop fussing over me." After Mayra and Madelin left to dress for the ball, Allyssa went over to the table where the box sat and opened it. She couldn't help but stare at the simple ring. Wearing it on her finger would be completely inappropriate; however, perhaps she could string it on a chain and use it as a necklace. Then she could tuck it under her dress where no one would see. She slammed the lid closed, wondering why she was indulging herself with thoughts of a simple, wooden ring.

Allyssa joined her parents in the sitting room.

"You have quite the admirers," her mother cooed.

"Whatever will you do with all these gifts?"

"What I always do," Allyssa replied. "Donate them to the poor."

Her parents looked at each other. Allyssa didn't know what they were thinking, but she always gave the jewelry to shelters for the homeless. She never kept anything. The wooden box was the first item she'd ever even touched.

"The prince had this delivered," Rema said, holding out an ornate silver jewelry box. "Care to open it and see what's inside?"

Her mother knew she didn't, which meant Rema wasn't really asking, but requesting her daughter open the gift. Etiquette required her to wear one of the items, indicating who she would dance with first, but she couldn't do it. She wasn't ready for what it meant. If she opened the prince's gift and wore it, she'd be announcing to the world that she was initiating marriage negotiations with him.

"It's okay," Darmik said. "If you're not ready, we understand. Maybe next time?"

She nodded. "Next time. I promise."

Rema set the gift down. "All we ask is that you dance with the prince. Try to become better acquainted."

"I can do that," Allyssa replied. "In return, I'd like you to be completely honest with me as to why he's here and why we need this alliance."

"Very well," Rema answered, taking Allyssa's hands and holding them tightly. The lines around her eyes softened as she spoke. "Your father and I haven't decided on the best course of action yet. Right now, I want to see if you and Prince Odar are compatible. Having you married to someone from another kingdom—someone with wealth, power, and a strong army—is beneficial to Emperion. I'm trying very hard to be a good mother and a good ruler. Sometimes, it's not as easy as you might think. I hope you can understand that."

Allyssa nodded, wanting to squeeze her hands out of her mother's firm grip. Whenever the word *marriage* was used, it made her want to go running the other way.

Darmik placed his hand upon his daughter's shoulder, holding her in place. "We didn't tell you about Prince Odar coming ahead of time because we were afraid of your reaction."

"If we had told you the first real potential suitor was arriving to make your acquaintance, you probably would have run away," Rema said.

If her parents had told her about Prince Odar's arrival, she probably would have run away. After all, that had been her plan when she thought the prince from Telmena was coming.

"Is there anything else?" Allyssa asked, trying to conceal the ire in her voice. Just because she was only sixteen didn't mean her parents had to shield her from politics and the unpleasantries that came along with it any longer—especially if they felt she was old enough to marry.

Darmik squeezed her shoulder and released her. "For now," he said.

"I don't want you worrying," Rema added, letting go of Allyssa's hands. "Simply become acquainted with the prince and we'll go from there."

Allyssa groaned. "Fine. I'll dance and attempt to make conversation with him."

"And you'll be nice," Darmik added.

At that, she rolled her eyes. However, she would be

the perfect princess for her parents' sakes. They wouldn't request something of her that wasn't necessary.

"We need to be on our way," Rema said.

"Shall we?" Darmik asked, holding out his arm for his wife. The empress took it and they exited the suite, Allyssa not far behind.

One foot in front of the other—that was all she could focus on right now. If Allyssa allowed herself to feel, she'd drown in her emotions. She just had to make it a couple of hours. Then, like she always did, she'd leave early and escape from this suffocating cage.

OVERDOING IT WAS AN UNDERSTATEMENT. HER PARENTS had gone all out, transforming the Great Hall into a lavish room adorned with flowers and candles. Plates were piled high with food, wine was being passed around, and hundreds of guests seemed to be enjoying the feast. Allyssa was seated between her father and Neco to show she was valuable, watched, and guarded. She was thankful she wasn't forced to sit next to the prince.

When supper was over, everyone went to the adjoining room for dancing. It, too, was extravagantly decorated with hundreds of lit candles and flowers hanging from the ceiling. A large group of musicians played a lively tune. Darmik claimed Allyssa for the first song. With so many nobles present, she was going to have to stay later than she usually did. She sighed. It was going to be a long night.

As Darmik spun her around the dance floor, she caught a glimpse of her mother dancing with Prince Odar.

"Smile," Darmik murmured as he dipped his daughter.

"I'm trying," she replied through gritted teeth, forcing herself to grin.

He chuckled. "Come on," he said. "This isn't so bad. You act like we're torturing you."

She looked pointedly at him.

"Prince Odar is by no means ugly, and all accounts claim he is an intelligent man. At least give him a chance. He might surprise you."

"The only thing that would surprise me would be if he actually turned out to be intelligent."

"Allyssa, watch your tongue."

She laughed. "You can't tell me someone who looks like that has a genuine thought in his head."

Darmik squeezed her hand. "You can't tell me my daughter is so conceited and haughty to not even give him the benefit of the doubt." He spun her around again. "All I'm asking is that you make an attempt to speak with him a couple of times. That way you can acquire a feel for his disposition."

She stared into her father's warm brown eyes. He'd never asked her to become acquainted with a man before. She had known this day would come; yet, she wasn't ready for it. Responsibility, duty to her kingdom, money—it was all overrated. Still, she loved her family, loved Emperion, and was in a position of power. She needed to take it seriously.

Darmik leaned closer, speaking into her ear. "Prince Odar has requested the next dance."

She'd figured as much. "I would be honored to dance with someone so handsome and charming."

He kissed her cheek. "Try not to overdo it—it's not very becoming."

Allyssa chuckled. For her father, she would be the perfect princess and speak cordially to the pretty prince. If only she could be herself, if only she could say what she wanted to instead of what she should, if only.... She sighed.

The prince bowed next to her, a pleasant smile on his face. Darmik handed her over to the prince like a piece of property, and she tried not to cringe. She was a princess, elegant, refined, and all that the position implied. At least, that was what she kept telling herself. Because, truth be told, she hated being stuck in this castle, playing this game.

Prince Odar took her hand and placed his free one on her lower back. A new song began, and they moved together to the beat. She kindly smiled, not in the mood to make pointless conversation. She was certain the prince was an expert in that area and didn't need to practice with her.

After a few moments, Prince Odar broke the silence. "Your castle is lovely," he commented, his eyes sparkling in amusement.

"Isn't it?" Allyssa crooned. "I simply adore this home. We have several, all larger than this one. But I'm sure you already knew that."

He blinked several times before replying. "Yes, I did know that."

He spun her around, and she glimpsed several female courtiers staring at Prince Odar. They all batted their eyelashes at the young prince, hoping to entice him with their beauty, money, or position. But none of them came close to offering the prince what Allyssa did, and so his focus remained solely on her. Whoever she married would become emperor to this great kingdom, and thereby, the most powerful man on the mainland.

"Is something the matter?" he asked.

Shaking her head, she wanted to kick herself for her own stupidity. She needed to stop being a selfish child and act like a princess. The fact was she had to marry, and she would not marry someone unworthy of ruling by her side. Her subjects deserved a just prince who would one day be an exceptional emperor.

"What brings you to Emperion?" she asked.

"I thought you knew."

"I want to hear your version of events."

He stared at her a moment, as if deciding what to tell her. He finally answered, "My parents asked me to pay you a visit. It seems we have a mutual enemy."

"Do we?"

He nodded, his smile faltering.

"And tell me, my dear Prince Odar, what do you want from Emperion?" The music ended and she stopped dancing, waiting for his answer.

The prince opened his mouth to respond when another gentleman approached, ready to claim her for the next dance.

"Another time perhaps," was all she said before turning to her new partner. The prince already had a line of ladies eagerly waiting to dance with him.

After two dozen songs, Allyssa had had enough. Hoping to slip away unnoticed, she quickly made her way to the side door. She was almost there when Prince Odar's squire pushed away from the wall where he'd been standing alone all evening.

"Leaving so early?" he asked as he approached her.

"I'm tired," she lied, faking a yawn.

"Yes, it must be exhausting to dance with so many

eligible men."

Was he making fun of her? No one in the castle ever spoke to her in such an informal manner. And she didn't care for his degrading tone either. "Is there something you want?" she demanded, in no mood to deal with him.

He stood there with his hands clasped behind his back. "Prince Odar asked me to dance with you." His lips curled as if the mere thought of spending any time with her was detestable.

If he didn't like her, perhaps he wouldn't be careful with what he said, and she could obtain vital information from him. "Very well." She gave him her hand. "I'll dance with you." She felt his calloused palm against hers as he led her back to the dance floor. He must spend a lot of time with his sword.

"What is your name?" she asked.

"Jarvik," he answered. "I'm His Highness's loyal squire."

He swung her around to face him, and they began dancing. Jarvik appeared to be a year or two older than she was. He wasn't nearly as tall as the prince, but he was still taller than she was. Jarvik's hair was dark, almost black like the night. He had broad shoulders, brown eyes, and freckles on his nose. Not handsome, but there was something interesting about him. They danced in silence, Jarvik making no attempt at conversation. They remained toward the edge of the dance floor, and Allyssa was grateful. She'd be able to easily reach the exit from there.

"I suppose the prince wants your opinion of me?" she asked, breaking the silence.

"He does," Jarvik answered, his eyes keenly aware, dissecting every inch of her face.

"Does he rely heavily on those around him to form his opinions?" She knew she shouldn't be so forward, but she couldn't help it.

The squire bristled. "He listens to the opinions of those around him," Jarvik answered in a clipped tone, "but he makes up his own mind on matters."

She smiled, certain she had offended him. This was the first conversation she'd enjoyed all evening. Jarvik didn't want to be there any more than she did. It was time to get down to business. "Was Prince Odar sent here to acquire a bride?" she asked.

His eyes narrowed, assessing her. "You're rather bold," he declared.

"You have no idea." The dance was a slow one, allowing them to easily converse.

"I have some inclination. Not many princesses know how to use a sword and defend themselves. But I suppose you've learned because of your father's background." His tone was casual, not condescending.

Although, he still hadn't answered her question. Now he seemed to be baiting her. Allyssa smiled. "I learned to fight because I am going to be the empress of Emperion. That means I will be the leader of the greatest army. A competent ruler knows how to fight in order to lead his or her people effectively." He spun her around a little too fast for her liking. "You didn't answer my question."

Jarvik huffed. "Prince Odar is here at Emperion's request."

"Why did he agree to come?"

He studied her a moment before replying. "We would like to forge an alliance with Emperion. Fren is on the verge of being invaded by Russek, and the prince will do what needs to be done to protect his kingdom."

"Russek is threatening Fren?" she inquired. "I thought you had a larger army than they do. I didn't realize you needed Emperion's assistance."

Jarvik's eyes flashed with anger, and he stopped dancing. "What game are you playing?" he demanded, holding her tightly.

She shoved him away, and he let her go. "I'm not the one seeking an alliance to save my kingdom."

"You're not?" he asked, raising his eyebrows. "If Russek invades Fren, Landania and Fia won't be far behind. Then there won't be any stopping Russek. They'll crush your kingdom so fast that you'll wish you weren't so arrogant and pompous."

"Me?" How dare he say such a thing to her?

He pointed at Allyssa. "You're a spoiled little brat," he declared. "A typical princess."

She started laughing. He had no clue. He'd made assumptions about her based on what he saw, and that wasn't who she was at all. She was simply playing a part, and he had fallen for it.

"You know nothing," she said, seething with fury. "Now be gone before I make a scene in front of everyone here."

He smiled like he expected her to throw a tantrum. She wanted to wipe the degrading smirk off his face. What an arrogant bastard. Leaning forward, she whispered in his ear, "If you ever disrespect me again, I'll kill you."

She spun around and came face to face with Marek. "Is everything all right, Your Highness?" he asked, staring daggers at Jarvik.

"It is now," she said. "Please escort me back to my bedchamber. I've had enough dancing for one evening."

He took her arm and led her from the room. She

could have sworn she heard Jarvik laugh.

"You're shaking," Marek commented when they were in the hallway.

"Only because I hate that insufferable man," she said.

"The squire?"

"Yes." She hoped she didn't see him any time soon because if she did, she would probably punch him.

"I thought perhaps you were referring to Prince Odar."

"Why?"

He shrugged. "When you danced with the prince, you had a fake smile. Then with the squire, you seemed yourself. When I saw you losing your temper, I came over as quickly as I could without tearing across the room."

They reached the Royal Chambers. "Did you have a chance to dance with Madelin?" she asked.

His face reddened. "No. I'm on duty and not permitted to partake in the festivities."

"I'm sorry." Her hand rested on the door handle to her bedchamber.

Marek shook his head. "Don't be. We all make sacrifices for our kingdom. Some are steeper than others."

This conversation had turned too heavy for Allyssa's liking. "I'm going to turn in for the night." And with that, she went into her room, closing the door behind her.

"Can you believe this?" Grevik said, indicating the Fren soldiers in the tavern.

No, Allyssa most certainly could not believe the pretty prince had brought so many men to Emperion with him. If they were all staying at the castle, then why

were they here in this tavern of all places? She hoped no one recognized her.

"Have you tried talking to your parents?" Grevik asked, abruptly changing the subject. He leaned forward, closer to her.

She raised her eyebrows, wondering what he was specifically referring to.

"Your profession," he clarified.

Allyssa smiled. If only he knew. She took having to go into the family business to a whole new level.

She was just about to reply when Grevik said, "I was at the weekly announcement."

Allyssa gulped. He'd heard her speak? Did he suspect she was the princess? She couldn't even look at him. If her identity was known, she'd never be able to sneak out to see Grevik again.

"The princess is a pretty, young thing," he continued. "Her hair was all done up fancy around her crown, she had beautiful eyes, and her dress probably cost more than my mum makes in a season."

It was amazing what elegant clothes and some dusting powder could do to improve a person's looks. "Let's go," she said tersely, wanting to end this conversation and leave the stuffy tavern along with the Fren soldiers. Until this day, she'd never come this close to having her identity discovered.

Grevik finished off his drink, and the two of them left the tavern. They headed toward the south end of town, keeping their eyes and ears open for trouble. Given the late hour, they were bound to run into something.

Allyssa tugged her cloak around her, trying to ward off the cold air.

"When I start working for the City Guard, and I

can't go out at night with you anymore, what will happen to us? Will you still visit me?"

Allyssa wished she could see Grevik's face, but it was hidden under his hood. "I don't know," she admitted. "I want to still make a difference."

Grevik grabbed her arm and stopped walking. "Lilly, you better not do this alone. That's how my father was murdered."

"Don't worry," she said. "I won't. Besides, I'll be getting married one day and I doubt my husband will approve of my nightly escapades."

"Or you visiting another man, even if we're only friends." Grevik released her arm, and they resumed walking.

Grevik was Allyssa's one true friend. Someone who valued her for her person and not her position. She couldn't imagine him not being in her life.

"Until the time comes when we're married, you are welcome to visit me. And I'd like the opportunity to come and see you. I know you say your parents won't approve, but maybe if we told them—"

"Grevik," Allyssa said, interrupting him midsentence. "Who's that?"

A man was leaning against the building about twenty feet in front of them. He was dressed in a long cloak, his low hood concealing his face. He had a long sword strapped to his waist, the metal gleaming in the moonlight. Only soldiers and guards were permitted to carry swords in the city, and this man wasn't dressed in the uniform of either. He pushed off the stone building and walked down the street, away from them, disappearing from their sight.

"I don't know," Grevik mumbled. "But whoever that

was gave me the creeps."

Allyssa nodded in agreement. "Let's go this way," she said, indicating the opposite direction the man had gone.

A block later, they passed a dark alley. Allyssa heard grunting noises. In the dim moonlight, she saw two men robbing an elderly person. Without having to say a word, Allyssa headed toward the shorter of the two men, Grevik going to the other one.

She ran and charged, doing a flying side-kick and hitting the thief. He landed on the ground with a thud. Jumping on top of him, she pinned his arms behind his back. Glancing over her shoulder, she watched Grevik duck, narrowly missing the punch the thief threw toward his head. Grevik wrapped his arms around his opponent, tackling him to the ground. After grappling with the man for a minute, Grevik finally had the upper hand.

"It's about time," Allyssa declared.

"My thief was larger than yours."

"You're bigger than me. What's your point?"

Grevik shook his head, mumbling something unintelligible.

Now that the situation was under control, Allyssa dug her knee into the thief's back, freeing her right hand. She felt under her cloak, locating a piece of rope. Pulling it out, she used it to secure his hands together.

"Thank you," the elderly man said, his voice shaking.

"Are you all right?" she asked. He nodded.

Grevik searched the thieves and returned the elderly man's possessions. The man left, eager to return home. Allyssa and Grevik dragged the thieves to their contact in the City Guard. Afterwards, they parted ways and Allyssa headed back to the castle.

Going in through the servants' entrance, she pulled

her plain hood low, pretending to be a worker reporting for duty. No one paid her any heed since she did this almost every single morning, using Madelin's name if questioned. Passing the kitchen, Allyssa noticed there were only two servants up at this hour, preparing the fire in the ovens and cutting vegetables for breakfast. Her boots silently moved over the stone flooring as she made her way to the laundry room. Climbing on top of the dirty clothes and bedding, she raised herself up until she could grab onto the end of the laundry chute and pull her body up into it. She shimmied up the four floors, lifted the wooden door, and stumbled into her bedchamber, ready to climb into bed and fall into a blissful sleep.

# Chapter Seven

"I'm sorry, Your Highness," Marek said as they walked down the corridor. "No one saw the wooden box you inquired about being delivered."

"The Royal Chambers have guards posted at all times. Surely, someone would have seen a person enter the sitting room carrying it, especially since it looks so different from all the other gifts that arrived."

He gave a curt nod. "I already reported the incident to my father, and we're increasing security measures. Thankfully, the box is harmless."

The thought of someone being in her family's sitting room without her guards' knowledge was frightening. What if that person had meant her or her parents harm? Would it be easy to attack the royal family? After all, she snuck in and out of the castle every night without notice. If she could do it, surely an assassin could as well.

"I've changed my mind," Allyssa declared. "Instead of going to the Dining Hall, I want to go to the library."

"Shall I have your breakfast brought to you?" he inquired.

"Yes."

Entering the library, Allyssa headed to the section containing books about trees, certain the ring meant something. After pulling down all the titles that had the word *oak* in it, she set the books on a table in an alcove at the back of the library. Allyssa had no idea where books about jewelry would be so she sought out the librarian, Albek. He was a short, plump, elderly man who loved reading and preferred not to be disturbed.

Entering his empty office, she quickly wrote him a letter requesting that he locate books about jewelry made from wood. She left the note on his desk, knowing that once he found the books, he'd leave them on the table she regularly used.

Sitting down in the alcove, she scanned the books she had chosen. Several confirmed that the heaviest concentration of oak trees came from the Biztanek Forest, which she already knew. Other books discussed the various uses for oak, but none mentioned jewelry.

Marek quietly set a plate of warm bread, eggs, and fruit in front of her before returning to his post near the entrance.

Allyssa slammed the last book shut. Why a ring? What did it symbolize and why oak? Even though she didn't have many answers, one thing was certain—the gift was no coincidence. It meant something, she was sure of it.

Madelin burst into the library. "Your Highness," she gasped, out of breath. "You're late."

"Blimey," Allyssa cursed. She'd completely lost track of time. "Is everyone there?" she asked.

"Yes," Madelin replied. "They're all waiting for you."

Shoving everything into a pile, she closed the curtains so no one would disturb the books. Walking as fast as a respectable princess could, Allyssa hurried to the meeting room. When she entered, the entire Legion of

Emperion and the dukes were sitting at the long table waiting for her. She tried to pretend that she wasn't nervous, late, or out of breath from practically running there.

"Princess Allyssa," her father's steward announced. All the men stood and bowed.

"Take your seats," she commanded everyone. "It's time to start."

The empress and emperor were situated at one end of the table, Prince Odar and his squire at the other end, everyone else in the middle. Allyssa headed toward the empty chair next to her parents.

As she passed by Prince Odar, Jarvik said, "Nice of you to finally arrive," so softly that only she and the prince could hear.

Allyssa was about to say some witty remark, but thought better of it. Taking her seat, she personally greeted each duke, making sure to smile and appear confident, friendly, and kind.

Darmik took control of the meeting. "Our spies have confirmed Russek has invaded and established control in Melenia. Prince Odar has eye witness accounts that Russek's army is also stationed along Fren's border. As a result, I've extended offers to Fia, Landania, and Kricok inviting them to join Emperion." There was a collective murmur around the room. "Everyone from those kingdoms will retain land rights and titles, but will now pay taxes to us, and we will gain control of their armies. Telmena has expressed their... dissatisfaction with this move. They plan to block any union between us and the kingdoms to our north."

Jarvik cleared his throat. "If I may," he said, asking the emperor for permission to speak. Darmik nodded, and the squire stood. "The king and queen of Fren are not opposed to the unifications of the kingdoms. They don't believe Emperion to be a greedy, power-hungry nation. They understand you seek such a union for survival. However, Prince Odar's younger brother is married to Crown Princess Jestina of Telmena, which means Fren has a solid and verifiable peace treaty with Telmena, and that cannot be broken. So while the king and queen do not oppose Emperion's expansion, Fren must stand with Telmena."

Allyssa's eyes narrowed. Jarvik seemed well versed in his kingdom's politics. She glanced at Prince Odar, who sat there staring at her with that beautiful smile of his. She wasn't sure he was as aloof as he appeared; otherwise, he wouldn't have such an intelligent squire speaking on his behalf.

"Which is what brings us here," Rema said, speaking for the first time. Jarvik took his seat. "We do not wish to acquire Fren under our empire; however, I am proposing a union between the kingdoms of Emperion and Fren. Both Princess Allyssa and Prince Odar are heirs to their respective thrones and both are first in line. A marriage will supersede Fren and Telmena's treaty. As a result, Telmena will be forced to stand with Fren."

"Not only that," Jarvik added, "but Telmena is worried about Emperion becoming too large and powerful. If Prince Odar marries Princess Allyssa, Telmena's concerns will be put at ease as long as Prince Odar sits on the Emperion throne and Fren doesn't become part of the Emperion Empire until after the death of the current king and queen. We would also need your word that Emperion will honor Fren's treaties with Telmena as your own."

Everyone started talking at once. Allyssa sat back on her chair, thinking over everything that had just been revealed. Her parents needed the marriage in order to acquire the three kingdoms separating them from Russek. If Emperion combined the armies, Russek would be no match for them and would have no choice but to leave Emperion alone. Fren needed the marriage because Russek was ready to invade them. They required Emperion's powerful army to keep Fren out of enemy hands.

"It is time to vote on the matter," Darmik said, raising his hand. Everyone quieted down.

The prince no longer watched Allyssa. Instead, he scribbled something on a piece of paper in front of him. Jarvik, on the other hand, was staring at her. And he seemed mad.

"All those in favor of opening marriage negotiations between Emperion and Fren, raise your hand."

Allyssa suddenly found it hard to breathe. She didn't realize they were going to vote on the matter today. Her parents had asked her to keep an open mind; they never said it was already decided upon.

The dukes and Legion members unanimously voted to enter into marriage negotiations. Not once did anyone ask her opinion on the matter.

"I have a basic contract here," Darmik said. "Let's begin discussing terms."

A little voice in the back of her head kept repeating the word *marriage* over and over again. She needed to leave the meeting room. There was no way she could sit there and listen to these men discuss the terms of her marriage. She glanced to the doors. Marek stood guard, watching her. She tried pleading with her eyes, begging him to figure a way to get her out of there. He pursed his lips, and she knew he understood.

Marek slipped out of the room, and another one of her guards took his place. Allyssa prayed he had a plan. A few minutes later, servants entered carrying trays of food and drinks for everyone. When one of the servants approached, she stumbled. The tray she carried fell on the princess, spilling food all over Allyssa's dress.

"Forgive me, Your Highness," the servant said as she bent down to pick up the tray.

"It's fine," Allyssa answered. "Accidents happen."

Two additional servants rushed over and started removing the food from her dress. "Your gown is ruined," a servant said. "I am so sorry."

Allyssa stood. "It is fine," she assured the girl. "I will go and change. If everyone will please excuse me." As she glided from the room, Jarvik's eyes narrowed. She could have sworn he knew she'd set up the incident to leave the meeting. She couldn't help but smile.

However, instead of feeling victorious and free, shame overcame her. What would her mother say if she knew the truth? Rema never shied away from what had to be done or her obligations. Yet, here Allyssa was, running away. She hurried to her room to change so she could return to the meeting and at least give the appearance that she cared about her own marriage treaty.

STANDING IN THE MIDDLE OF THE FLOWER FIELD, Allyssa closed her eyes, breathing in the heady, fragrant smell. The sun warmed her face, and a bird cawed from somewhere above. Peace coursed through her. She felt

free.

"A true smile," Prince Odar said.

Allyssa jumped. She hadn't expected anyone to find her out here. Her guards stood a respectful distance away, giving the prince and princess privacy. Did Prince Odar wish to speak with her? Was he even capable of carrying on a conversation? "Good afternoon," she politely said.

He smiled the devilish grin of his that she was sure made many women swoon. "I am here to become better acquainted with you."

He stood next to her amongst the burgundy flowers that filled the entire northern area outside the castle. It was astoundingly beautiful. Her hand reached down, grazing the tops of the petals. The prince brushed the pollen off his sleeves and sneezed.

Raising her eyebrows, Allyssa asked, "What would you like to talk about?"

"You. Tell me about yourself."

She wasn't letting him off that easily. "What exactly would you like to know?" she countered, picking a flower and twirling it between her fingers.

"Do you enjoy attending balls?" he asked. "You looked lovely last night."

"Thank you. I enjoy dancing," she answered. He smiled at her agreeable answer. "And you?" she inquired.

He sneezed again. "Oh, I love parties and balls."

Of course he did. "Do you hunt?"

He nodded. "Jarvik and I go all the time."

Releasing the flower, she gazed into the prince's blue eyes. "There is something I'm curious to know." He nodded for her to continue. "If you're the eldest son, and the younger one is married to the crown princess of Telmena, who will rule Fren if we marry and the king and queen of Fren are dead?"

"Someone will be appointed to rule—similar to the situation you have with Greenwood Island." Prince Odar glanced back to her guards. "I don't want to discuss politics with you," he said, putting his hand gently on her arm.

She wanted to yank it away because the gesture felt too intimate, but she didn't. Forcing herself to remain standing there among the red flowers, she faced the prince. If she was indeed to marry him, she needed to become better acquainted with him. "I think it's wise for us to talk about politics if we're to marry, don't you agree?"

He shook his head. "There will be time to discuss wars and armies later, but not now. I'm too tongue-tied by your beauty," he said, smiling that dazzling smile of his.

She couldn't help but roll her eyes. If the prince wanted to act like a typical courtier and had no inclination to be honest and truthful with her, then she had no desire to waste her time with him. "I came out here to be alone," she stated. "If you don't mind, I need a few moments to myself."

His eyebrows drew together in confusion, as if he'd never been dismissed by a girl before. "I understand," he finally said. Trailing his fingers down her arm, he lifted her hand, bringing it to his lips, where he softly kissed it. "Until next time." He released her and left.

Allyssa sighed with relief. Tilting her face toward the setting sun, she closed her eyes, taking in its warmth. She put all thoughts of Prince Odar and him kissing her hand out of her mind. He may be devastatingly handsome, but that was all he had going for him.

# Chapter Eight

Entering the library, she found it gloriously empty. She headed straight to the back wall where the private alcoves were located. The one on the end—the one she always used—still had its curtains drawn shut, so she flung them open and found the table stacked with books, just as she'd left it. Sliding onto the cushioned bench, she noticed two additional books about wooden jewelry. The librarian must have left them for her. She peeled back one of the covers and flipped through the pages, looking for some clue about the wooden ring she'd received.

"Princess," a gruff voice said.

"What?" Allyssa snapped. Chiding herself for her nasty tone, she said, "I'm sorry." Schooling her face into a mask of calm, she turned to whoever had interrupted her thoughts. "Yes?" she regally asked.

Jarvik stood there, staring at her. "I'd like to have a word with you."

Allyssa froze. What did the squire want with her? Perhaps he came to reprimand her for dismissing the prince so easily the other day. She hadn't spoken with Jarvik alone since the ball. Taking a deep breath, she prayed she could remain calm and not lose her temper.

She motioned to the bench on the other side of the table, inviting him to join her.

He sat down and peered at the books lying on the table. "What are you reading?"

Slamming the book shut, she placed it on the bench next to her. "None of your business," she answered.

His eyes narrowed. "You know, if you and Prince Odar marry, you and I will be working together quite often."

Interesting choice of words. Not *when* she and the prince married, but *if*.

"I would prefer to work closely with the prince, not his lackey." She folded her arms and leaned back against the wall, awaiting his response.

"I don't care what you prefer," Jarvik said, contempt in his voice. "The fact of the matter is, our kingdoms face war with Russek. We must do things we might not *want* to, in order to ensure the safety of our subjects." He leaned forward on the table, as if challenging her to disagree with him.

"What is it you came here to discuss?" she asked, ready to be rid of the surly man.

"Prince Odar would like you to join him for a private dinner tonight."

She sat there, staring at Jarvik, not sure how to respond. There was no way she was going to sit through an entire meal all alone with the prince, at least not until she absolutely had to.

"Can we be frank with one another?" Jarvik asked, his eyes darkening.

"I thought we already were." Around the squire, she found she didn't have to watch her words like she did with members of her court.

Jarvik glanced at her guards, who were far enough away they couldn't hear. "Do you already have a lover?" he questioned.

Her eyes widened and her mouth dropped open. *A lover?* "Why?" she demanded. He had no right to ask her such a thing.

"Prince Odar is my primary concern," he said, his voice low. "If you are in love with another man, he has a right to know before he enters into a marriage contract with you."

Unable to help it, Allyssa started laughing at the absurdity of the conversation.

"This isn't funny," Jarvik spat.

"No, it's not," she said, becoming serious. "It is ridiculous. And not that it's any of your business, but no, I do *not* have a lover."

"Then why aren't you interested in the prince?" he asked, scratching his head.

Leaning forward to invade his personal space, she said, "I'm going to rule an *empire*. I need more than a pretty face by my side. I want a man who's intelligent and determined. Unless the prince can prove that to me, I have no reason to be interested in him. I want you to leave before I have my guards drag you out. I'm done with you."

He abruptly stood. "Trust me, the feeling is quite mutual."

She waved Marek over. "The squire was just leaving," she said. "Please help him find his way out of the library."

Marek reached for Jarvik, but the squire brushed him off. "I don't need to be escorted, thank you very much." He stormed away.

As much as Allyssa loved her father, spending time with him, and training together, she absolutely despised these runs. When Darmik insisted she go with him, it meant she got no sleep at all since he required they leave before sunrise.

Allyssa was already drenched in sweat and could barely breathe even though they'd only gone five miles. Unfortunately, Darmik was just getting warmed up. *Blimey*. At least he let her run in pants. Both of them had on the training outfits worn by their soldiers. She'd even braided her hair and wrapped it around her head so if anyone saw her from afar, they would never know she was the princess.

"Let's pick up the pace," Darmik said. "You're a bit slow today."

*Blasted.* She didn't think she could run any faster. Her father took off and she sprinted harder, trying not to fall too far behind him.

They ran their usual route, the royal guards trailing them as they headed around the lake and entered the small forest to the east of the castle. This was her favorite part and the only reason she hadn't been moaning and complaining out loud. Allyssa loved running between the towering trees and over the moss-covered flooring. It was so different from Emperor's City which was where the royal family spent at least one season each year. Here in the forest, she understood why her mother had insisted they establish Lakeside as their primary residence.

"You seem rather distracted," Darmik commented, slowing his pace to run alongside her. He wasn't even winded, whereas she felt as if her lungs were on fire

even though it was freezing out. The sun hadn't crested the mountains yet, and a dull gray blanketed the land. "Anything you want to tell me?" Darmik asked between breaths.

She shook her head, unable to answer. Darmik started running faster. Was he upset over something she'd done? Did he suspect she had snuck out of the castle? Did he want her to confide in him about Prince Odar?

A dull clanging sound echoed through the forest. Since her father didn't flinch, he must know where the sounds were coming from. Darmik slowed his pace, allowing Allyssa to catch sight of the Fren soldiers sparring with one another up ahead.

Now that she was paying closer attention to her surroundings, Allyssa realized her father had taken her slightly off their usual trail. "Do they do this every day?" she asked, glancing at Darmik as they jogged closer to the men. He nodded. There had to be a good fifty soldiers out there, practicing sword work with one another.

"Good," one of the men yelled. "Let's try that exercise again, only faster."

She recognized the voice as Jarvik's. Why was the squire leading these men? Perhaps their captain had stayed behind in Fren.

Allyssa and Darmik slowed to a stop. The princess bent over, resting her hands on her thighs, breathing heavily as she watched Jarvik. The squire started running through the drill with another soldier. When they turned, she realized it was the prince. Prince Odar swung his sword, clashing it against Jarvik's. With a flick of his wrist, the squire disarmed the prince. Jarvik placed his hand on the prince's shoulder, speaking to him. The prince nodded.

"One would think the prince of a large kingdom would be a better swordsman," Allyssa whispered so only her father could hear. Their squad of soldiers stood about fifteen feet behind them.

"I agree. It's unusual for a squire to lead the exercises," Darmik commented. "At least Prince Odar is learning now and taking an interest in his army. That's a good sign."

"I'm surprised you approve of him as a son-in-law."

Darmik's eyes sliced over to hers. "Why do you say that?"

"Father," Allyssa said, pointing at the prince. "He's… he's … ." She wanted to say a daft cow, but she knew her father wouldn't approve of such language. "I just expected you to choose someone more like Marek."

Darmik folded his arms. "Honestly, I'd prefer if you married someone with a little more experience in commanding an army rather than a court. However, an alliance between our kingdoms is beneficial right now. I've done extensive research on Odar. All my reports indicate he is intelligent—even if we don't see it."

She was about to argue when her father put his hand on her arm and said, "You, of all people, should understand that people can show the world one side of them, and keep another side hidden. I say we give him time and become better acquainted with him." Darmik started jogging again. "Let's go," he called over his shoulder.

She ran after him as he led the way around the open area where the soldiers were practicing. All of them appeared to be good fighters—lethal and proficient with their moves. It was rather impressive to watch.

Allyssa tried not to look back at Prince Odar or

Jarvik, but she felt them watching her as she ran past. Did they know it was her? Did they recognize Darmik? Or did they assume they were simply a squad of Emperion soldiers out for a run?

She found herself able to sprint a little faster than before. Maybe the short break she'd taken had been enough to rest her lungs and muscles, allowing additional energy, or maybe it was the fact that she had an audience.

# Chapter Nine

That night, Allyssa considered not sneaking out of the castle. She was exhausted from not sleeping last night and then running ten miles in the morning. However, the idea of not seeing Grevik was enough to change her mind. Besides, she'd only be able to do this a little while longer, and then Grevik would be a City Guard and she would be married.

As she traveled along the dirt path that led from the castle to the servants' exit in the wall, she considered—not for the first time—asking Marek to accompany her on her nightly escapades. But he would never condone such activity, let alone be a part of it. Neco would have his son's head for allowing her to chase criminals.

The sentries manning the gate let her pass, thinking she was a worker. She exited the castle grounds and entered the city. Heading down the street, she had an eerie sensation that she was being followed. Glancing back, she didn't see anyone behind her. It was late at night, but there were still a few people out roaming the streets. Pulling her plain, black cloak tighter, she went to the apartment building where Grevik lived. Climbing the ladder, she shoved the window open and crawled into his dark bedroom.

He was on his cot sleeping. *Barmy.* Picking up one of his boots lying on the ground, she chucked it at him. "Wake up."

"Stop assaulting me," he moaned. "I'm awake." He sat up, fully dressed, and pulled on his boots.

"I was thinking we could head over to the river district tonight," Allyssa said, leaning against the window ledge.

"Sure," he said, standing and stretching.

"I can't believe you were sleeping," she chided him.

"I seem to remember a certain night not that long ago where I sat in a tavern all night long and you never showed up. Now, why was that?"

"Shut up," she mumbled, knowing she'd fallen asleep that night.

He chuckled and climbed out of the window. When he was out of sight, Allyssa crept out of his room and down the hallway. She placed a bag of coins in the pocket of his mother's cloak, which was hanging on the wall, just as she always did every time she visited Grevik's apartment. She hurried and went back into his room, climbing down the ladder after him.

On their way to the wealthy river district, they passed a group of soldiers on patrol. "What's going on?" Allyssa asked. The soldiers of the army were stationed in the barracks on the castle grounds. They only came into the city when the royal family did. Otherwise, designated City Guards were responsible for maintaining law and order here.

Grevik shrugged. "Not sure. There are rumors though."

"There are always rumors."

"Some say Russek spies have been spotted in Emperion. Others say Russek is mounting its army, preparing to go through Fia to enter Emperion."

Allyssa wondered how accurate these rumors were. If Russek truly was ready to invade, her marriage to Prince Odar needed to take place as soon as possible so they could merge Emperion's army with Fren's.

"Want to tell me why we're in this district tonight?" Grevik asked, interrupting her thoughts.

She wanted to come here to investigate, not catch criminals. "I've seen maps showing that this river travels straight through Krosek to the Great Ocean."

"It's not something I studied in school." He glanced sidelong at her, waiting for an explanation.

The river ran past the eastern portion of Lakeside. The homes along the water were the wealthiest homes in the city. Grevik and Allyssa rarely came here since there was practically no crime. However, she wanted to see the river for herself. Reaching the end of the street, they came to a small park bordering the water. Silently, the two friends walked through the park. Allyssa stood at the edge of the bank, watching the water rush by. In the books she'd read, the river originated in the north, somewhere in the mountains in Romek, which bordered Fia.

Allyssa jumped and spun around, certain that someone was standing behind her. No one was there. "Let's go," she whispered.

"Are you kidding? We just got here," Grevik complained.

"I think we're being followed," she hissed. She took his arm and pulled him back through the park. Allyssa's skin prickled, yet she didn't see anyone hiding in the shadows.

They hurried from the wealthy district and went

toward the center of town where they usually concentrated their efforts. However, no matter how fast they walked, she still felt someone following them. "First tavern you see," she said, "duck inside."

Grevik seized her arm, and they went down a narrow street. Since no one was around, they started running until they reached the next street, where they encountered a dozen or so people. Slowing so they wouldn't attract unwanted attention, they entered the closest tavern.

It was packed, every table taken. The smell of ale and stale bread wafted through the air. Allyssa could barely breathe from so many bodies packed so closely together. The sounds and smells made her head swim. She kept glancing to the door, watching to see if anyone entered after them. No one did.

Grevik briefly spoke with a barmaid and then turned to Allyssa. "There's another exit we can use in the back."

She nodded and followed him through the throngs of people. They went down a dimly lit hallway and came to a door that was bolted shut. Grevik reached back and took her hand. He opened the door and fresh, cool air greeted them as they stepped onto the dark street.

When they came to the corner, Grevik peered around the edge of the building. "I don't see anything suspicious," he said. "What now?"

Exhaustion consumed her, and she wanted nothing more than to go to sleep. "Let's just go home."

Grevik's apartment was on the way to the castle, so they continued walking together. She still had an eerie sensation that someone was watching her. She asked Grevik if he noticed anything amiss, but he didn't.

"Let me walk you home," he offered.

"That's okay. I'll be fine."

"I know you don't want your parents to meet me for whatever reason, but at least let me walk you to your building."

She had told him she lived in a small place on the western side of the city in an average neighborhood. He had even walked her there a few times, where he would bid her farewell. As soon as he was out of sight, she would sneak away and return to the castle. However, if she did that tonight, she would have to backtrack a solid mile in order to go home, and that was something she didn't want to do, not with the distinct feeling she was being followed. If her father and Marek had drilled one thing into her head, it was to trust her instincts.

"If you don't mind, I'll just go home with you. I'll only stay until I'm certain it's safe."

"Are you sure?" he asked, yawning. "I don't mind walking you home."

"But then who would walk you home?" she countered.

He chuckled. "And that's why I love you."

A few minutes later, she climbed through Grevik's window and into his bedroom. It was small—just a cot and a chest of drawers.

"Since you're such a pansy," Grevik teased, "you can have my bed. I'll take the ground."

Too exhausted to argue, she yanked off her boots and lay on top of his blankets, not wanting to get too comfortable and fall asleep. She just needed to rest for a few minutes.

"Wake up," a female voice gently said.

Allyssa peeled her eyelids open. She wasn't in her

bedchamber. *Blimey.* She jumped out of bed, nearly stepping on Grevik.

"What's wrong?" he asked, sitting up and rubbing his eyes. "My mum can walk you home and explain to your parents what happened. I'm sure they'll understand."

What was Allyssa going to do? The sun was cresting over the rise, which meant it was nearly breakfast time. How would she sneak onto the castle grounds and reach her bedchamber now? Even if she went in through the servants' entrance, she couldn't go to the laundry room and climb back up the chute to her room. There would be too many people working at this hour. She'd *never* made this mistake before.

Standing there, she rubbed her temples. There had to be a way out of this. A horrible thought occurred to her—what if someone already noticed she wasn't in her bedchamber? What would they do? Guards were posted outside her room at all times. If Mayra or Madelin discovered her missing, an alarm would be raised. Everyone would assume she'd been kidnapped.

"Is everything all right, dear?" Grevik's mother asked.

"Yes," Allyssa assured her.

"Would you like me to take you home?" she asked.

"No, that won't be necessary."

"You better be on your way if you want to make it to school on time," she said.

After putting on her cloak and pulling the hood up, Allyssa descended the ladder and jumped onto the street, Grevik right behind her. "I don't need your help," she told him.

He didn't respond. Instead, he stayed by her side. The streets were starting to become crowded with people heading to work. She walked as fast as she could, her stomach queasy with fear. She was going to be in so much trouble.

"You're not headed toward your home, and you're not going in the direction of any school I know of. So tell me, Lilly, where are you running off to, and why do you look like you're going to be sick?" Grevik demanded, his voice deep.

"I don't know what to do," she finally admitted, trying not to cry.

"I know," he said plainly. "Let me help."

Her parents were going to be furious, Marek would lose his position as the head of her personal guard, and she'd never be able to step foot out of the castle again. They walked in silence for several moments, a plan beginning to form in her mind.

"Why are we headed toward the castle?" Grevik asked when they were a block away from it.

"I … work there," Allyssa answered, pulling Grevik into an alcove of a building. Not a lie, but not exactly the truth either. "I need you to go to the servants' entrance located on the east side of the castle wall. Tell the guards you have an urgent message for Mayra." She hesitated, removing the plain silver ring she wore. On the inside, her full name and the royal family's crest were inscribed. It was made in case she ever needed to prove her identity, and very few people even knew of its existence. Wrapping the ring in a handkerchief, she handed it to Grevik. "Say you have a gift for her. Once she comes out to the gate, show her this, and bring her here."

His eyes narrowed, but he didn't question her further. He took the handkerchief with the ring and left.

Allyssa slumped against the door in the alcove, hoping Mayra recognized the ring and came. It was early

enough that there was a chance Allyssa could make it back into her room with Mayra's help. She started pacing, trying to think of the best way for Mayra to sneak her in.

What was taking Grevik so long? What if Mayra didn't bother to read the inscription in the ring? What if she thought Grevik had kidnapped her? What if Mayra called the soldiers to arrest him?

She slouched against the door again, sweating beyond belief. It had been foolish of her to fall asleep like she did. She deserved to be caught for her own stupidity. She heard the faint sound of footsteps running toward her. Sticking her head out of the alcove, she saw Grevik with Mayra and Marek quickly approaching. She stayed where she was so they wouldn't cause a scene. Fear hit her like a ton of stones. What if Marek told her parents what happened? She'd have to find a way to convince him to keep his mouth shut.

Mayra burst into the alcove, wrapping Allyssa in a hug. "Are you okay? I was so worried when this guy showed me your ring."

"I'm fine. Why did you bring your brother?"

"In case you needed him," Mayra answered.

"No one knows who I am out here," Allyssa whispered to her friend. "I want to keep it that way."

Marek yanked Allyssa out of his sister's grip. "What's going on?" he demanded. He had on plain brown pants and a nondescript tunic, blending in with the city folk. "Did he kidnap you?" He pointed to Grevik. "Or is there something going on between the two of you?" He raised his eyebrows, waiting for an explanation that she had no intention of giving him right now.

"I'd really like to know what's going on," Grevik quietly said, his hands resting on his hips.

"Now is not the time," she said, pulling free from Marek. "I need to sneak inside before anyone realizes I'm gone."

Marek started to say, "Your Hi—"

But Allyssa quickly cut him off. "No one knows I'm out here." She looked pointedly at him. "And I want to keep it that way."

"Who's this?" Mayra nodded toward Grevik.

"This is my friend, Grevik. I've known him for years."

"Years?" Marek practically screamed, his eyes getting huge and his face turning red.

"Someone please tell me what's going on," Grevik pleaded.

"Years?" Marek repeated, taking a step closer to Allyssa.

"I will explain everything to everyone later," Allyssa said, exasperated. "But right now, I need to get inside the castle."

"Give me a moment to think," Marek said, running his hands through his hair.

Allyssa made sure her hood was low over her face, trying to conceal as much of it as possible.

"I have an idea," Marek finally said. "Let's go."

The four of them stepped out of the alcove and onto the busy street.

"We don't need you," Marek said to Grevik. "You can go."

Grevik glanced to Allyssa for confirmation. "He's right," she said. "They can sneak me in safely."

He wrapped her in a hug. Mayra went rigid while Marek unsheathed his dagger.

"I don't have much time," Allyssa said, gently pushing away from him.

He nodded. "I understand, but tonight, I want an explanation."

"Of course."

Marek took hold of her elbow while Mayra stood on the other side of her. Together, the three of them approached a small entrance in the wall used solely by the soldiers living on the castle grounds.

The guard on duty immediately recognized Marek.

"I'm sorry this is a bit untoward," Marek said, speaking quietly to the guard as if they shared a secret, "but my sister had an emergency. Surely you don't mind if I escort her and the princess's lady-in-waiting into the castle this way, do you?"

The guard hesitated. "Only soldiers are permitted to enter here."

"I know," Marek responded. "But my father, Neco, was sure you'd understand and grant his daughter entrance."

"Yes, of course," the guard said, opening the gate and allowing them in. "I won't mention this to anyone. Enjoy your day, sir."

Keeping her focus on the ground, Allyssa forced herself to walk at a normal pace as she passed the guard and stepped foot onto the grounds within the wall. Relief filled her—one major hurdle down. Now all she had to do was make it to her bedchamber.

"How did you leave your room without your guards knowing?" Marek quietly asked as they passed the barracks and neared the castle.

Allyssa didn't want to tell him because he'd probably seal up the chute to prevent her from sneaking out again. However, she needed to get back into her bedchamber unseen, and that was the only way in besides the guarded doors. Sighing, she quickly told him how she'd been getting in and out.

Marek put his hand on the door latch and paused. "The laundry room will be too crowded at this hour."

"I have an idea," Mayra said. "Follow me."

Marek pushed open the door, and the three of them entered the castle. Mayra led them down a dimly lit corridor. They passed by the kitchen, which was already filled with servants preparing trays of food and cooks tending to the ovens. A few sentries were up ahead so Allyssa ducked her head, staying behind Mayra, hoping they didn't notice her. When the sentries recognized Marek, they didn't even question them.

"In here," Mayra said, opening the door to the wine cellar. "Wait here while I go and find a laundry basket for Allyssa to hide in. Then we'll smuggle her into the laundry room and cause a distraction so she can locate the right chute and climb back up."

"Why the wine cellar?" Allyssa asked.

Mayra chuckled. "No one respectable drinks this early in the morning, so there's no reason for any of the servants to be in here. I'll be back in five minutes." She hurried from the room.

Marek started pacing back and forth in the small space. Each of the walls was lined floor to ceiling with bottles of wine, and the place smelled of sweet wood. Marek turned to Allyssa, about to say something, when the door flew open and Jarvik entered.

The squire froze with his hand still on the handle. "What's going on?" he demanded, glancing back into the hallway and then stepping inside the wine cellar and closing the door behind him. "Why is the princess dressed like that, and why are the two of you in here alone?"

## Cage of Deceit

This was bad. Allyssa couldn't believe Jarvik, of all people, found her here. "It's none of your business," she replied. "But since you're going to run to Prince Odar to report my every move, you should know that I was outside running drills with Marek. Now tell me what you're doing here in the castle's wine cellar?"

Most likely, he hadn't been following her because he seemed too stunned when he first walked in. She tilted her head to the side, waiting for his response.

"Prince Odar asked me to select a bottle for tonight. He wants to ask you to supper. Again." His eyes scanned her body. "You don't look as if you've been running drills. You're not tired and sweaty." He cocked his head to the side. "You're dressed like a commoner, you have dirt smeared on your face, and your hair is a mess. I think you have some explaining to do."

How could he have the audacity to speak to her in such a manner? She was about to yell at him when Marek stepped in front of her and faced Jarvik. "I'm going to have to ask you to leave, squire."

Jarvik laughed. "So every time I ruffle the princess's feathers, you're going to ask me to leave? Is that it?" He took a step toward Marek, the two men now only inches apart.

"I'm not asking," Marek said. "I'm telling you to get out of here." His hand gripped the hilt of his sword so hard his knuckles turned white.

Allyssa had never heard Marek speak so forcefully before.

"It's not wise for you to order me around," Jarvik said in a deadly calm voice. "I'll leave when I'm ready to leave, not when some whelp tells me to."

"Stop," Allyssa demanded. She moved around Marek

and stood between him and Jarvik, forcing the two men to each take a step back, away from one another.

The squire's eyes narrowed as he looked from Allyssa to Marek and back again. "What are the two of you hiding?" he asked.

The door opened halfway and Mayra slid inside the room, carrying a large laundry basket. When she peered up and saw Jarvik, she froze.

"I want to speak with the princess, alone," Jarvik said, staring at Allyssa with cold eyes filled with contempt. Mayra nodded and left. Jarvik turned to Marek, waiting for him to leave.

Marek shook his head. "I'm her personal guard. She is never alone, especially with a squire."

Jarvik's face reddened and his hands clenched into fists. "I think I understand what's going on here," he said, his voice laced with anger. "The two of you," he pointed to Allyssa and Marek, "are having an affair."

"What?" Allyssa demanded, her temper rising. She'd had enough from this arrogant prick. "How dare you accuse me of such a thing? Why are you so determined to tie me to a lover?" She stood in front of him, pointing her finger at his chest, her hand shaking with rage.

He raised his eyebrows. "I'm simply looking at the overwhelming evidence."

She reached up to wrap her fingers around his neck, but he latched onto her wrists with surprising force. The tip of Marek's sword flew to Jarvik's exposed side, resting there.

"I hate you," Allyssa spit. "You're cruel, uncaring, and don't know what you're talking about."

"Trust me, the feeling is quite mutual. You're a pampered snob who is used to getting her way."

"Take your hands off the princess," Marek demanded. "Now."

The squire released her. "I'll inform the prince of what I saw," he sneered. "I doubt he'll want anything to do with you." He glanced down at the sword, and Marek lowered it. And with that, Jarvik stormed out of the room.

Allyssa stood there, steaming with fury. Marek sheathed his sword, and Mayra came back in with the laundry basket.

"I can't believe he thinks I'm having an affair," Allyssa said, rubbing her face. "I've never wanted to physically hurt anyone as much as I want to kill Jarvik. He's insufferable." She clenched her hands into fists. "I'm going to win the prince over just to irritate the squire. Mayra—go to Prince Odar's room at once and personally invite him, and only him, to dine with me this evening. Try to arrive before Jarvik does."

"Yes, Your Highness." She hurried from the room. Luckily, Mayra knew the stairwells the servants used and Jarvik did not.

"I can't wait to see the look of ire on Jarvik's face when the prince and I become friends."

"I'd like to remind you," Marek said, "that if you hope to still be alive and well in order to wreak havoc on Jarvik's life, then you need make it back into your bedchamber before anyone discovers you're missing."

Of course, Marek was right. In Allyssa's outrage over the squire, she'd forgotten she needed to slip back into her rooms unnoticed. She climbed into the basket. "I hope you can carry this by yourself to the laundry room." Curling into a ball, she made sure her cape covered her body. If anyone peeked in, they would only see plain fabric.

"Hopefully I put you under the right laundry chute and can create a distraction."

"I agree, seeing as how your job and my freedom are at stake," she said, her voice muffled by the fabric.

He lifted the basket, grunting as he did so. "Here we go," Marek whispered. "No more talking. You'll know when it's time to climb out and into the chute."

As he walked, the basket jostled from one side to the other, her head banging against the wicker. The muffled sounds of people talking could be heard as he made his way to the laundry room. He set the basket down with a soft thump, and Allyssa had to stifle a grunt from the impact.

"Can I have your attention please," Marek announced. "I have been sent to escort everyone outside for a random check. Please exit immediately."

"Sir, what are you checking?" a girl asked.

"I am making sure everyone is wearing the proper uniform and that everyone has reported for duty. Hurry now, I haven't got all day."

Allyssa heard several people pass by the basket on their way out of the laundry room.

"All clear," Marek said, and then the door closed.

Now was her chance. She stood and untangled herself from the basket. Wasting no time, she flipped the basket upside down and climbed on top. Reaching up, she grabbed ahold of the end of the laundry chute and hoisted her body inside. Once her boots connected with the side, she shimmied her way up the dark tube until she reached the small, wooden door.

Opening it up an inch, she peered inside her room. It was empty. Throwing the door open, she tumbled onto the floor of her bedchamber, thankful to have made it.

# Chapter Ten

The wind tossed Allyssa's hair as she sat low on her horse, racing across the field behind the castle, trying to catch up to Rema. The first one to reach the forest would be deemed the winner. Although Allyssa wasn't particularly crazy about horses—she much preferred sparring—she loved riding with her mother. It was one of the few opportunities they had to spend time together without the members of court watching.

Rema glanced back over shoulder, smiling at her daughter. Allyssa grinned and nudged her horse faster, hoping to at least tie. She didn't want to be flat-out beaten. Again. Her mother leaned forward in her saddle and her horse took off. Allyssa had no hope of catching her. When Rema reached the forest, she slowed, waiting for her.

"It's infuriating that you win every time," Allyssa said.

"Your father says the same thing," her mother replied. "Come, I want to show you something."

Allyssa guided her horse after her mother's. They wound their way between the trees, the soldiers accompanying them keeping a respectable distance. When they reached a small clearing, Allyssa immediately recognized where they were—it was the spot where

Prince Odar had been practicing with his soldiers. "Why did you bring me here?" she asked.

Rema dismounted, waiting for her daughter to do the same. Reluctantly, Allyssa swung a leg over and slid off her horse.

"I want to talk to you." Rema glanced up at their guards, making sure they were far enough away so they wouldn't overhear.

Allyssa had been afraid something like this was coming. Her mother probably wanted to convince her to marry Prince Odar. Rolling her shoulders back, she prepared for whatever her mother had to say.

"Don't look at me like that," Rema chided her.

"What?" Allyssa asked.

"Like you have to be here and whatever I say, you are going to tolerate, but not actually listen to."

Oh. Well, that had been exactly what she was planning on doing.

"I was your age once," Rema mused. "I wasn't raised in this lifestyle. I became empress when I was eighteen—two years older than you." Rema sat on a nearby boulder. "Did you know I was originally engaged to another man? Against my will? Twice as a matter of fact."

Allyssa didn't know that. She sat next to her mother on the boulder, waiting for her to continue.

Rema's eyes darkened with thoughts from the past as she explained how she'd been engaged to her best friend when a cruel prince forced her into an agreement with him. "I never want you to be in either one of those positions," she continued. "I never want to make you do something against your will." She patted her daughter's leg. "So, I need to know what you want."

"What I want?" Allyssa asked, confused. No one

ever asked her what she *wanted*. "Do you want me to be honest or give you the correct answer?"

"I want honesty," Rema said. "I need to know what *my daughter* wants, not what the princess or the heir to the kingdom wants."

"I'm not certain," Allyssa answered. "I've never allowed myself to dream about what I want because I'm on a path where I don't have choices."

"That's not true," Rema said. "You have plenty of choices. Some of them might not be the ones you want, but you will always have decisions to make." She wrapped an arm around Allyssa's shoulders. "I need to know if you want this life."

"Of course I do." How could she not want her life? She was lucky to have two loving parents and to be in a position of privilege.

"You misunderstand me. I need to know if you're willing to lead this kingdom, to keep it safe, and to make the hard choices for the betterment of the people you rule over. I'm not going to force you to do something you don't want to, so I need to know where your heart and loyalties lie."

Was her mother serious? Allyssa studied Rema's face, seeing only love and not an ounce of disappointment or judgment. Taking a deep breath, she answered, "Sometimes, I want to break out of this cage," she admitted. "But I love Emperion, and I will do what is best for the people who live here."

"Are you certain?"

If Allyssa didn't do it, who would? She was the only heir and therefore, the only one capable of helping to stop a war. "Yes, Mother. I am."

She sighed. "I'm glad to hear that."

"What's going on that you're not telling me?"

Rema clasped Allyssa's hands, squeezing them tightly. "Fia and Landania sent messages begging to join Emperion. There are stories of such horror and unimaginable atrocities at the hand of the Russek king and his soldiers." Tears filled Rema's eyes. "Honey, we are facing a real threat of war. I've been in battle before, and it's not something I care to see again—especially where your safety is concerned."

"What do you need from me?" Allyssa asked, desperate to help in any way she could.

"We need this alliance with Fren. If you marry Prince Odar, Telmena will support our acquisition of Fia, Landania, and Kricok. Then we can organize all our armies to fight Russek."

Allyssa had known it would come down to this. "I understand." She would do what had to be done for her people. By marrying the prince, she would save thousands of lives.

"I know Odar might not be what you imagined, but just because both of you are going into this for political reasons, doesn't mean you can't have a real marriage, eventually."

"At least we know everyone at court likes him," Allyssa said, trying to sound upbeat and positive.

Rema chuckled. "Yes, besides being easy on the eyes, he seems rather nice." Her mother paused and took a deep breath before continuing, "I'm sorry to put you in this position. When I had you, this was my one fear." A tear slid down Rema's face.

Allyssa had been so consumed with how this affected her, she never once stopped to think how her parents were handling the situation. Seeing her mother's tears

made her chest tighten. "It's fine," Allyssa assured her. "It will all work out." She wrapped her arms around Rema, hugging her. "I do have one question."

Rema laughed. "Just one?" She kissed the top of her daughter's head and released her.

"Why is Russek invading the nearby kingdoms? Do they seek power?" She'd only met Russek's king once, and he had seemed like a pleasant sort of man at the time.

Rema shook her head. "Your father and I have been discussing this very issue," she said. "We have theories, but that's it. We honestly aren't sure."

One of the guards approached. "Your Majesty," he said, bowing. "We need to head back to the castle. You have a meeting with the Legion."

She nodded, and he returned to the other guards.

"Mother, since I'm to marry Prince Odar, I should become better acquainted with him."

"I agree," Rema said, standing and going to her horse.

"I invited him to join us for dinner in the Royal Chambers."

"That's an excellent idea," Rema said. "Race you back to the castle."

Allyssa jumped to her feet.

"Loser arranges tonight's dinner with the steward," Rema called over her shoulder as she mounted.

*Blimey*, Allyssa thought as she struggled to quickly mount. She didn't enjoy planning these events, even on a small scale. Rema laughed as she nudged her horse and took off.

# Chapter Eleven

After Allyssa rode her horse back to the stables, and lost the bet to her mother by a long shot, she dismounted and handed the reins of her horse to a stable-hand. As she headed toward the alley doors where her guards stood waiting for her, Neco slid out of a stall and stepped in front of her.

"I'd like a word with you, Your Highness," he said, his voice cold and without its usual friendliness. The only time he spoke to her with that tone was when she was in trouble—which meant Marek must have told him she'd snuck out of the castle.

"I need to change," Allyssa said, trying to step around him.

"Excellent," he said. "I'll escort you to the Royal Chambers and we can talk along the way."

Her guards fell back, allowing Neco—who outranked them—to lead her from the stables to the castle.

Holding her head high, she tried not to be intimidated by the man standing beside her. He was like an uncle—if she'd had one—and she'd grown up with Neco's children. There was no need to fear him. However, if he knew she'd snuck out, he'd make sure she never did it again. And, chances were, if Neco knew, then her

parents did too. *Blimey.* She was in a heap of trouble.

So far, he hadn't uttered a single word to her as they walked through the castle, which meant he wanted to make her sweat. She knew all his tricks. When they reached the second floor, Neco finally said, "Marek came to speak to me."

"Is that so?" she replied, trying not to say too much since she wasn't certain what Marek had told him.

Neco gently, but firmly, took hold of her arm, pulling her next to one of the windows. He gave a hand signal to the guards, telling them to block the hallway on each side of them so no one could pass by and overhear their conversation. Once the guards were in position, they turned their backs, giving them privacy.

Her heart thundered in her chest and her hands became sweaty.

"Is there anything you would like to tell me?" Neco asked, releasing her arm but standing too close for comfort.

"Not particularly."

He stood there, staring at her, trying to intimidate her. She bit her tongue, refusing to tell him about her nightly escapades.

Neco sighed. "You have to understand, your safety is Marek's number-one priority." Allyssa nodded. "My son told me he has some concerns, although he didn't specifically say what they are."

Relief filled her. Neco didn't know anything that had happened this morning.

"When Marek came to speak with me, he was upset. I've never, and I repeat, *never*, seen him like that before." Neco folded his arms, his eyes boring into hers. "I'm not sure what you did, but I want to make sure it doesn't happen again. You can't put yourself in jeopardy. You are the only heir left."

His words stung. *The only heir left.* Her twin brother, Savenek, had died shortly after they were born. Now the entire line depended upon her since she was the sole remaining heir.

"I know," she replied, her voice weak.

He placed his hands upon her shoulders. "Allyssa," he said, using her name instead of her title, "I know you're under a lot of pressure right now. We all are. But that is no excuse to endanger yourself."

"I understand your concern," she said. "However, I haven't done anything reckless." Every precaution had been taken to ensure her identity remained a secret.

Neco raised his eyebrows. "Even though Marek didn't tell me exactly what you did, I've been around long enough to suspect what happened, or should I say, what has been happening."

His hands fell from her shoulders and she turned to stare outside the window, not really seeing anything on the other side of the leaded glass. Neco knew she'd been sneaking out. Rubbing her tired face, she tried to figure out what to do so her parents wouldn't find out.

"I need your word this ... behavior will stop," he said, leaning against the window ledge.

Allyssa didn't say anything. She supposed she could agree. After all, Grevik would be a City Guard shortly and she wouldn't be sneaking out any more. But the thought of not going into the city, of never seeing Grevik again, made her chest tighten and it became hard to breathe.

"You've always been so stubborn," Neco muttered. "Tell you what, how about if you just promise to have Marek with you?"

She hadn't expected him to say that. He was offering a compromise, and she had to take it.

"Not that I'm saying it's okay for you to do something stupid and dangerous," Neco clarified. "But if you decide to suspend all common sense, at least have my son with you."

"Very well," Allyssa said. "Should I choose to do something foolish, I'll be sure to include Marek."

"Promise me," Neco insisted.

She hesitated. If she gave him her word, she wouldn't be able to break that promise.

"Or I will tell the emperor everything."

He was serious, and she couldn't let her father find out what she'd been doing. Turning away from the window, she faced Neco again. "On my honor, I promise."

"Thank you."

Glancing over Neco's shoulder, she saw someone down the corridor, on the other side of where her guards stood blocking the hallway. Watching her and Neco speak was Jarvik. Why did he have to be everywhere she was? Was he spying on her for the prince? Or was she simply that unlucky to keep running into him?

Neco released the guards and they surrounded her once again, opening up the corridor. When Jarvik neared, he gave a curt nod, not uttering a single word as he passed by.

THE PRINCE, ACCOMPANIED BY HIS MOST DUTIFUL squire, entered the sitting room in the Royal Chambers. It took every ounce of self-control Allyssa had not to scream at Jarvik and demand he leave at once. When

Mayra had invited the prince, she specifically said it was a private dinner party for Prince Odar.

Rema and Darmik welcomed them before sitting next to one another on the sofa. Allyssa hurried and sat on the chair near the fireplace, forcing the prince and squire to share the other sofa. Her father looked at her and raised his eyebrows, questioning her behavior. She merely smiled as if she were happy to be with such lovely company.

"We're so pleased you could join us this evening," Rema said.

"Thank you for the invitation," Prince Odar replied. "I look forward to getting to know you and your family better."

Allyssa folded her hands on her lap.

"We appreciate you traveling so far to speak with us," Darmik said. "Especially considering how dangerous traveling is right now."

"It was necessary," the prince said, leaning back on the sofa. "This alliance is beneficial for both our kingdoms." He quickly glanced at Jarvik, who sat there staring at something on the side table. "If we hadn't received your invitation," Prince Odar continued, "I don't know what we would have done to stop Russek. So with all due respect, it is I who should be thanking you." He gave that dazzling smile of his.

Allyssa wanted to know what lay under his beautiful exterior. What sort of man was he? What did he enjoy doing in his spare time? "Prince Odar," Allyssa said, and all eyes turned to her. "I would love to know about your country. We hear so little about Fren."

The prince's eyes darted to his squire before returning to her. "Our kingdom is more like your northern lands.

We don't have any deserts like you do in your southern region." He paused and peered at Jarvik again. "Um … our coastal areas have great steep cliffs, most of the kingdom has excellent farmland, and the northern portion of the Biztanek Forest is teaming with oak trees, which we use for making furniture and homes."

Fren was known for keeping to themselves—they didn't import or export with any other kingdom except Telmena.

A tray of tea was brought in, and the servant handed Allyssa a cup. "Tell me about your parents, about court, and about your interests," she said. She took a sip of tea and waited for him to continue.

"My parents are kind but strict," he said, setting his cup down on the low table in front of him. "Our court is similar to yours—we have those vying for political positions, others seeking an advantageous marriage, and lots of gossips. As far as my interests go … I enjoy hunting and reading. However, I spend a lot of my time working, so there is very little time for such luxuries."

Taking another sip, Allyssa decided to question him on their marriage. Perhaps she could learn what to expect from him once the contract was finalized.

"How do you feel about us aligning ourselves in order to fight Russek?" Out of the corner of her eye, she saw her father cross his legs. He always did that when he wanted her to back off.

Prince Odar tugged his collar, and he swallowed hard. "As I said before, it's advantageous for both kingdoms."

"Yes, but how do you feel *personally* about the two of us marrying?"

The squire knocked over a statue that was sitting on the side table, and all attention turned to him. "Sorry," he murmured.

Darmik cleared his throat. "Jarvik, why don't you tell us a little bit about yourself?" he said, changing the subject to something more neutral.

"There is nothing to tell. I am a squire for the prince."

*Who knows how to fight exceptionally well,* Allyssa thought. Usually, squires oversaw the prince's lords-in-waiting, acted as a valet, accompanied the prince to various activities, and carried confidential messages. There was definitely more to Jarvik than he was letting on.

"Pardon the interruption," Neco said as he hurried into the room. "I must speak with Your Majesties immediately."

Rema and Darmik excused themselves and left the room with Neco.

Allyssa looked to the squire, who gave no indication he planned to say anything else now that her parents were gone. "Jarvik, how do you feel about Fren and Emperion's union? Do you, like Prince Odar, believe it to be advantageous?" She was pretty sure the squire despised her, but how did he feel about the marriage?

His eyes focused on her as he said, "Fren is a proud country, and there isn't anything I wouldn't do to protect it." He spoke with such conviction that Allyssa admired his passion. Yet, he hadn't answered her question.

"Does your loyalty lie with Fren or the prince?" she asked, leaning forward. Prince Odar obviously trusted the squire, but she wasn't sure he should. Perhaps Jarvik had his own agenda.

The squire's eyes narrowed. "They are one in the same."

"No," she said, shaking her head. "They most certainly

are not." Allyssa knew the difference. She knew who served her crown versus who served her as a person.

He rested his arms on his legs as he studied her. "What about you?" he quietly asked. "Where does your loyalty lie?"

Jarvik was a shrewd and cunning man. Allyssa wasn't sure if she should admire or fear him. "Like you," she responded, "I love my kingdom and will do anything to secure peace so that my people may prosper."

"So you'll align yourself with Prince Odar just to prevent war?" Jarvik asked. "Even though you obviously don't care for him?"

"Yes," she snapped. "I'll do whatever I have to for Emperion." He was about to respond when she cut him off. "I'm sure the prince's feelings for me are similar to my own for him. Friendship and love will come in time."

"You honestly aren't taken with him?" he asked, pointing to the prince.

She jumped to her feet, unable to sit still any longer. "That is none of your business. It is between the prince and me. Now back off."

Jarvik's eyes widened. "You have quite the temper."

She glanced at the prince, but he kept his head down, giving no indication that he intended to join in the conversation. Was he seriously going to sit there and allow his squire to speak to her in such a way? "I suggest you leave me alone," she said. *Before I wallop you,* she thought to herself.

"I'm simply trying to ascertain your disposition. The king and queen don't want someone volatile marrying their son and leading their army into war. They need a levelheaded girl by their son's side."

Putting her hands on her hips, she asked, "Are you in

their confidence? Did they send you here for this reason?" Perhaps the king and queen knew Prince Odar would do his duty, so they sent the squire to make sure this match was truly in the best interest of their son and kingdom. Even though she didn't like Jarvik, she admired his sovereigns for being so practical.

"The reason I am here is none of your concern," he said, standing before her.

"If it involves my kingdom, it is my concern. I am here tonight to try and become better acquainted with Prince Odar. I need to see if he is capable of ruling beside me since he will be coming to *my* kingdom. I did not intend to have you here interrogating me."

Jarvik's face went flaming red. "You'll make a horrible empress. You're too emotional and temperamental. I am going to my king and queen and recommending they find another solution. I'd rather Fren go to war than have Prince Odar marry you," he spat, shaking with rage.

It felt as if he'd slapped her face. She was too stunned by his outburst and hurtful words to respond. Didn't he just say he'd do anything for his kingdom? Yet, there he was, ready to single-handedly throw away this alliance simply because he didn't like her. She couldn't allow the squire to ruin everything her parents had worked so hard to build.

She opened her mouth to try and salvage the alliance when Prince Odar dragged Jarvik away from her. "As entertaining as it is to watch the two of you argue," the prince said, "this isn't helping. The both of you need to calm down." He released the squire.

Allyssa huffed and took a seat while Jarvik adjusted his tunic.

"That's better," Prince Odar said. "I don't know why

the two of you seem to hate one another so much, but I can't allow this animosity to continue. I understand you have objections to the marriage," he said looking at Jarvik, "but you need to give it another chance. For the sake of your kingdom."

Jarvik nodded, not looking at either of them.

Prince Odar continued, "I'd like to spend some time alone with Allyssa so I can become better acquainted with her. I think you should do the same. Then, if you still feel this marriage wouldn't benefit our kingdom, we'll leave and figure something else out."

"Fine," Jarvik snapped. "But I'm done for the night. Let's go." He threw open the door and left.

"I'm sorry for my friend's behavior," Prince Odar said. "I don't know what's gotten into him. I've known him since we were boys, and he's not usually like this. Please apologize to your parents for our early departure." He took her hand, quickly kissed it, and left.

Just as the door shut behind him, Rema and Darmik returned with Neco. She thought they would scold her for scaring the prince away, but as soon as she saw them both wearing their crowns, she knew something was wrong.

Her mother came to her. "I need to know for certain that you are ready and want to become a leader." Her eyes were glassy as if she were on the verge of crying.

"I am," Allyssa answered without hesitating. While roaming the streets at night certainly helped make a positive difference by putting criminals in jail, being a leader and ruling Emperion would be far more effective. By stepping into the position she was born to do, Allyssa would be able to help shape the future of the kingdom. The thought both excited and scared her.

"Then I want you to come with us."

"Are you sure?" Darmik asked Rema. "You've always insisted we shield her from this sort of thing."

"I know," she replied, delicately wiping her eyes with the corner of her handkerchief. "But if she's going to be married and one day rule Emperion, it's time she sees firsthand the evil that lives in others."

Darmik's mouth pulled tight. "Very well."

Allyssa had no idea what was going on or what she was about to witness. Her skin pricked with fear—whatever she was about to be privy to would not be pleasant. Rolling her shoulders back and standing tall, she steeled her resolve, preparing for what was to come.

Neco led the royal family to the Throne Room. When they arrived, dozens of advisors, all the dukes, and the entire Legion of Emperion were already there, along with a few nosy courtiers. Whatever was going on had to be of vast importance if all the politicians and lawmakers were gathered. Allyssa followed her parents down the aisle to the dais, where she took her seat at her mother's side. Directly in front of her sat Prince Odar, Jarvik, and several Fren soldiers.

Before taking his seat, Darmik briefly spoke to Neco, and then he came before his daughter. "Remember, you represent this kingdom. This is not about you, or your emotions. Think of Emperion, think of your people, and stay strong."

She nodded, and he sat on Rema's other side. Even though dozens of people were present, no one spoke. The doors opened, and three men staggered in. One had blood covering the side of his face, which was caked with mud. Another's nose was crooked and purple. The last man limped, holding his arm close to his chest. All

of their plain, nondescript clothing was torn and dirty. Whatever they had been through, it was bad. When they reached the bottom of the dais, the three men dropped to one knee.

"Your Majesties," Neco announced, "may I present three of my best scouts, First Division."

Rema nodded, and the three men stood.

"Your Majesties," the one in the middle said. "We are all that is left of our squad."

Allyssa's stomach twisted. A squad consisted of two dozen men.

"We were sent to Russek to spy," the man continued. "Our mission was to determine Russek's military strongholds and to uncover their plans for invading their neighboring kingdoms. When we first reached the border between Russek and Fia, we found it lined with thousands of soldiers. Some of them appeared to be as young as ten; others looked to be in their sixties." He took a shaky breath, his eyes glossing over with tears. "Behind the soldiers, there were spikes stuck into the ground. On top of each spike was a severed head. There had to be over a thousand of them."

Allyssa gripped the arms on her chair, her knuckles turning white.

"Rumors are that the heads belonged to the people in Melenia who fought or opposed the invading Russek soldiers. The heads are meant to serve as a warning to Landania and Fia of what will happen if they fight against Russek."

"Were you able to get past the soldiers?" Darmik asked.

"We were, Your Majesty," the man's voice shook. "Russek is preparing to attack the kingdoms to the north of us for the sole purpose of marching straight into Emperion to claim this land as their own. They have tens of thousands of soldiers ready and willing to fight and die to achieve this goal."

Fear coursed through Allyssa. Why did Russek want Emperion? How could they be so vicious as to kill thousands of innocent people simply to conquer more land? Had King Drenton no heart? No soul?

"What happened to you and your men?" Rema asked.

"We were ambushed by Russek soldiers," he answered. "They came out of nowhere. The three of us barely escaped. Everyone else … ." He shook his head.

Another one of the scouts spoke. "The Russek soldiers are animals," he said. "They don't fight honorably. When they ambushed us, their goal was to maim as many of us as they could, then drag us closer to a fire where we could be tortured. Over a hundred Russek soldiers took our men, slicing off body parts, burning hands and feet in the fire, and doing whatever they felt inflicted the most pain imaginable without killing. All the while, they made the Emperion men still alive watch." He started shaking. "Eventually, they all died. Mutilated."

Allyssa closed her eyes, wanting to block out the images of her people suffering at the hands of Russek soldiers. This crime could not go unpunished. What these scouts saw was not to be tolerated.

"Thank you for your sacrifice for this kingdom," Darmik said, his voice grim. "Let's continue this conversation in private. Unfortunately, I need to know more specific details."

Allyssa stood and went to the men. Her parents were watching her, but they made no attempt to interfere. She wanted to console the scouts.

"I'm sorry for your loss," she said, placing her hands atop each man's head, willing them to feel her sorrow and compassion. "What you've seen is tragic. No one should witness the deaths of friends and comrades in such a barbaric and gruesome way. I promise that this attack against Emperion will not go unpunished. Come to my private dining room so that I may feed you. We can talk there. While we eat, I'll have word sent to your families, letting them know you've returned safely home and will be joining them in a few hours." She glanced back at her parents. They both nodded their approval.

"Follow me," Allyssa said, heading down the aisle. The three men, her parents, Prince Odar, and Jarvik all followed her.

ALLYSSA SAT ON THE EDGE OF HER BED, EXHAUSTED. It was already well past midnight. After feeding the three scouts, Darmik and Neco had asked them hundreds of questions about their mission. She felt bad the men had to relive losing their friends' lives. Even Jarvik was relentless, demanding to know the minute details about their mutual enemy. On more than one occasion, Prince Odar offered to escort the princess to her bedchamber, looking as if he might be ill and wanted an excuse to leave. Allyssa insisted on staying, though. She owed it to these soldiers and herself—especially since she would one day rule this kingdom. She couldn't turn a blind eye when such atrocities were going on.

Finally, it had been Rema who insisted everyone stop questioning the scouts so they could go home, see their families, and clean up. They were to return tomorrow afternoon for further debriefing.

Allyssa rubbed her face and flopped back on her soft bed. She was supposed to meet Grevik an hour ago—she owed him an explanation. However, she had promised Neco that Marek would accompany her if she left the castle. *Blimey.* She quickly changed into the plain pants and tunic that she usually wore when she snuck out. After she braided her hair, she grabbed her black cloak. Exiting her room, she startled her guards.

"I wish to go to the training room." They nodded and led her through the vacant, dark hallways, not once questioning her intentions at this late hour.

Upon entering the training room, one of the guards asked, "Shall we light the torches?"

"No," she answered. "I need to speak with Marek. Please wake him and bring him here."

One of the guards nodded and hurried away. The remaining men took their positions near the door. She walked over to a window and stared outside into the dead of night. The moon wasn't visible, so the sky was filled with thousands of stars that seemed so close she could touch them.

"Do I even want to know why you've summoned me here at this forsaken hour?" Marek asked, coming into the room. His hair stood up in every direction, but at least he was dressed and not in his nightclothes.

She waved him over to the window, away from the door and listening ears. "I promised your father I'd let you do your job and protect me."

Marek snorted, folding his arms and leaning against the window.

"I'm serious."

"Listen," he said, "I don't know what you've been

doing or why, but you can't be endangering your life by leaving the castle unprotected."

"I know."

"I just … I can't even believe you did that." He started pacing. "And then Jarvik caught us together, and now he thinks we're having an affair. Do you have any idea how that makes me look?"

She was about to defend herself when he continued, "Then you pull that stunt tonight in the Throne Room and set the entire castle talking about how compassionate you are, how wonderful you are, and what a great leader you're becoming." He ran his hands through his disheveled hair and stopped pacing. He turned to face her. "You're maddening. Do you know that?"

She started laughing. "Are you done?"

He threw his hands into the air. "Have you heard a word I've said?"

"Yes," she answered. "But I asked you here because I need a favor."

He shook his head. "No way. I'm not helping you sneak out."

"If you don't go with me, I'll leave on my own."

He pointed at her. "You're going to be the death of me."

"Stop," she chided him. "I simply need you to escort me out of the castle so I can meet my friend."

"The one from today?" She nodded. "No," he answered.

"I owe him an explanation."

"Write him a letter. I'll deliver it."

"I'm going out. Are you coming?" She started walking out of the training room.

"Fine," he called after her, "but this is the only time I'm doing this. Do you understand?"

She spun around and smiled. "Thank you."

He told her to wait there while he got some provisions, which she assumed meant several knives, swords, and daggers. She reached down and felt her own weapons strapped to her thighs under her clothing. This was going to be an interesting night.

# Chapter Twelve

"This isn't going to work," Allyssa insisted. When Marek had said he needed provisions, she assumed he meant weapons, not more guards. "I was able to slip in and out of the castle unnoticed because I was alone," she said.

"We're not trying to leave the castle unnoticed," Marek retorted.

He might not be, but she certainly was. "We can't go traipsing around the city in a large group. We'll attract too much attention," she said, trying to make him at least understand her reasoning.

"I'm not letting the crown princess leave the castle without the proper protection, especially at a time of war," he answered simply. "Besides, they're all generically dressed and we're not going to walk together—we'll spread out when we enter the city."

"For the record," she muttered, "I think this is a bad idea."

"It is a bad idea," he agreed. "You shouldn't be leaving the castle at all, especially at night and unannounced."

"You know what I mean." She shouldered past him and exited the castle.

"So where to, *Lilly?*" Marek asked, following close

behind.

"We're going to my friend's apartment building near the center of town."

As they made their way along the city streets, her guards walked tall and stiff. Even though they were dressed as commoners, anyone looking at them would know they weren't.

"I can tell where every single guard is," she groaned. "Can they back off a little more?"

"No," Marek answered. "They are to keep you in sight at all times."

They finally reached Grevik's building. When she went to climb the ladder to the window of his room as she'd done so many times before, Marek grabbed her arm, pulling her away from the ladder.

"I don't think so," he said.

"Let go," she demanded.

Marek ordered one of her guards to climb up and knock on the window for her.

She couldn't believe they were all standing out in the open like this. "This is ridiculous," she complained. "We are going to attract attention."

"So what if we do?" Marek asked. "No one can do anything to us."

"I don't want word to reach my father that I'm out in the city."

Marek shrugged.

Allyssa leaned against the building, trying to blend in with the shadows. Something moved down the street and she squinted, trying to see if someone was there. The street appeared empty. Above, her guard spoke with Grevik. A minute later, her friend stood before her.

"What's going on?" he asked, focused only on her

and ignoring the half dozen men standing nearby.

"I owe you an explanation," she said, still leaning against the building. She had planned to have this conversation alone in his room.

He scratched his head. "I thought we were friends."

"We are."

"Then why do I get the feeling I'm not going to like what you have to say? That you've been keeping things from me all these years? Friends don't lie to one another." He leaned against the building next to her, waiting for her to speak.

The words started tumbling out. She told him about the time when she was only twelve years old and had snuck out of her house looking for freedom, but instead, found a dear friend. About how important their friendship had been through the years. About how she lived for their time together roaming the city, searching for criminals. And then she told him she wasn't really *Lilly*, but Allyssa, the crown princess.

His face went whiter than snow. "I knew you were hiding something from me," he whispered, his voice shaking. "I just didn't know it was this. I thought maybe you were a lady-in-waiting or someone of importance. Never did I imagine you were the actual princess." He cursed and ran his hands through his hair. "I even saw the princess speak once, and she looked nothing like you." He pushed away from the wall. "I don't even know what to say or how to act. Am I supposed to bow? Am I even allowed to talk to you?"

"It doesn't change anything," she said. "I'm still me."

"With a crown," he bitterly replied.

Allyssa hoped he would understand and forgive her for lying.

"Why all the guards tonight?" Grevik asked. Marek stood there quietly, having listened to the entire conversation.

"Now that the head of my personal guard knows I've been sneaking out of the castle at night, I can't slip by him anymore. I asked him to come with me so I could speak to you."

"I need some time to think about everything you've told me." He scanned her guards. "And I can't talk to you with people watching us."

She told him she understood, but she really didn't. The one thing she valued most about his friendship was his honesty—the fact that he liked her for her. If this lie—the lie that allowed them to become friends in the first place—ruined their friendship, she'd never forgive herself.

"When you're ready to talk," Marek said, stepping a little closer, "come to the castle. Ask for me. I'll make sure you're admitted and gain access to the princess."

That surprised Allyssa. Commoners weren't granted entrance very often.

Grevik scratched the back of his neck. "We'll see," he said to Marek. Facing Allyssa again, he muttered, "I guess I can't hug you anymore. So, good-bye." He turned and left without glancing back.

She was about to call out after him when Marek stopped her. "Give him time," he whispered. "He just found out his best friend has been lying to him."

"Maybe if I explained it again," she said, "he'll understand."

Marek shook his head. "I'm sorry."

Allyssa watched her friend climb back into his room. Her eyes swelled with tears. Grevik had to understand

why she lied. He just had to.

"We need to go," Marek gently said. She nodded. They started walking away when four men stepped into the street ahead of them. They fanned out, blocking the road. Marek's hand went to his sword, and then he relaxed.

Three of the men bore army uniforms with the colors of Fren. The fourth man was dressed in solid black. When he looked up, Allyssa saw that it was Jarvik.

*Blimey—could this day get any worse?*

"It seems you, Princess, are keeping a great many secrets," the squire said, crossing his arms.

"Stand aside and let me pass," she demanded.

"Not until you tell me why you're visiting another man—and a commoner no less. I guess your guard isn't the one you're having an affair with." He leaned toward her, hatred in his eyes. "This must be why Prince Odar hasn't been able to woo you."

"You disgust me," she said, her voice not nearly as strong as she'd intended. "You're boorish and judgmental. I want you to leave me alone."

"Come on," Marek said, taking her arm. "He'd never understand what you're doing anyway."

"You're right," she said. "And I don't want to stoop to his level." Holding her head high, she stepped around the squire.

Jarvik's head suddenly snapped to the side, and he squinted at something down the street. His hand went to the hilt of his sword, and he unsheathed it. "Take her away from here," he ordered Marek. "We have company."

Allyssa turned around and saw a single man standing in the middle of the street about twenty feet away, his arms casually at his sides. The man wore a long, black cape and hood, concealing his identity. Fear pricked up her spine—the same sensation she'd had over the past couple of days when she felt as if someone was watching her.

"Let's go," Marek whispered, tugging her arm.

Allyssa started to turn away when the man yelled, "Wait." She froze, somehow knowing he was speaking to her.

He pointed his black-gloved finger at Allyssa. "I want a word with the girl," he said, his voice deep and rough. "The rest of you can leave."

"Come on," Marek urged, yanking her arm. "Let the others deal with him."

Why did this man want to speak with her? Had he been following her in hopes of having the chance to catch her alone? She needed to know what was going on, so she stayed rooted in place.

To her surprise, Jarvik spoke. "You're not speaking to her now, or ever."

The man chuckled, the sound throaty and menacing. "As you wish." He stepped forward, unsheathing two twin blades. Before she realized what he was going to do, he threw the knives at two of her guards, hitting each one directly in the head with the hilt. Both men collapsed to the ground, unconscious.

The rest of her guards rushed toward the man. Jarvik ordered the Fren soldiers to hold their position. Marek was still clutching onto her arm. The man had all three of her guards on the ground in no time at all. Jarvik yelled at Marek to take her away from there. Allyssa knew she shouldn't turn and run because then the man could overpower her from behind. She removed her daggers and stood her ground.

Marek cursed when he realized she wouldn't

cooperate. He bent down to pick her up.

"Don't touch me," she said. "That's a direct order." He hesitated. "If you don't listen, I'll have you dismissed."

The man ran forward, directly toward her.

Jarvik yelled at her for not listening while Marek stood in front of her, attempting to shield her from harm. When the man was only five feet away, Jarvik's men surrounded him, but the man was able to render them all unconscious in less than thirty seconds. The only ones left were Allyssa, Jarvik, and Marek.

"Like I said before," the man sneered, not even winded, "I want to speak to the girl alone."

"Who are you?" Jarvik demanded.

"If you don't allow me to speak with her, I'll kill the two of you, and then I'll have her all alone, unprotected. The choice is yours."

Allyssa knew Marek would rather die than leave her side, so she stepped toward the man, still clutching her daggers. Marek went to grab her, but she quickly swerved out of his reach and moved closer to the man.

"Don't go any nearer," Jarvik said. "He's an assassin."

Allyssa stood still. If the man meant to kill her, he would have done it by now.

"I want to speak with you privately," he quietly said so only she could hear. His face remained hidden under his hood.

"This is all I can offer you."

He reached for her arm, so she twisted and smacked his wrist with her dagger. "Keep your hands off me," she said. "You can speak softly and no one will hear. Now hurry up, you have one minute."

"What is your name?" he demanded.

Her heart thudded in her chest, and relief filled her.

He didn't know who she was. Still, she needed to proceed with caution. "What's your name?" she countered, unsure where her bravado came from.

A few of the guards on the ground started to moan as they came back to consciousness.

"Do you work in the castle?" he asked. She nodded. "I have a proposition for you. Meet me in three days' time. Come to the tavern at the Wooden Inn. Alone." He turned and strode away without waiting for her response.

Marek was immediately at her side. "I don't know if I should hug you because you're alive, or kill you for not listening. You're infuriating."

"I'm glad I'm not the only one who wants to kill her," Jarvik said. "Seems there's a long list. I'll get in line."

Allyssa ignored them and replayed the encounter with the assassin in her mind. He wanted to meet her alone in three days. She rubbed her tired face and realized her arms were shaking.

Marek went over to the men on the ground, helping them to their feet.

Jarvik stepped closer to her. "What did the assassin want?"

"We're in the middle of a public street in the city. Is that really what you think we should be discussing right now? Especially when you have men lying on the ground?"

He glanced around. "You're right." He bent down, checking the pulse of one of his men.

Allyssa was too stunned to respond. Did Jarvik just say she was right?

## Cage of Deceit

SITTING IN THE ALCOVE, ALLYSSA KEPT THE CURTAINS drawn shut, hoping no one would find her. She'd even instructed her guards to stay out of sight so they wouldn't announce her presence in the library. Reading through a book on wooden jewelry, she found one paragraph that mentioned an old peasant tradition where a wooden ring was given from a man to the woman he wished to court. If she fancied the giver, she would wear the ring on her finger. It was an ancient tradition from centuries ago, before the reigning kingdoms of today even existed.

"I thought I'd find you here," Jarvik said, slipping between the curtains and taking a seat across from Allyssa.

"I'm busy and wish to be left alone," she said, not bothering to look up.

"What are you reading?" he asked, tilting his head to the side so he could see the title better.

"I'm supposed to be reading books my tutor assigns me," she said, trying to avoid answering his question.

"And your tutor assigned you books on wooden jewelry and the rivers of the continent?"

Why did he have to be so observant? It was highly annoying. She slammed the book shut.

Early this morning when they returned to the castle, Jarvik had taken his men and her guards to the barracks—not the infirmary—while Marek escorted her to her bedchamber. It had been early enough that no one was about to question what they were doing. Marek asked her not to say anything about the encounter with the assassin until he had time to think on the matter. She agreed and hadn't seen Marek since.

"What can I help you with?" Allyssa asked as sweetly as possible since being rude didn't make Jarvik go away.

"Here's the deal," the squire said. "I won't report last night's incident to Prince Odar or your father on one condition."

She groaned. Everyone in this castle wanted something.

Jarvik leaned forward on his elbows. "Have you ever seen the man from last night before?"

The question caught her by surprise. "No, of course not."

He nodded. "What did he say to you?"

"Not much," she admitted. "He asked me to meet him in three days' time at the Wooden Inn. He said he has a proposition for me."

"Have you spoken to Marek about this?"

"Not yet. What are you getting at?" Did he know something about the assassin?

"You plan on going to meet him, don't you?" Jarvik asked.

"I'd like to find out what he wants." However, she didn't think Marek would let her leave the safety of the castle ever again, especially to meet an assassin.

"Why have you been sneaking out of the castle at night?" he asked, sounding genuinely curious.

She shook her head, unable to explain something so personal to someone she despised.

"I don't understand you," he admitted, leaning back on the cushion, studying her. "I hear such different accounts about you that I find you utterly puzzling."

He'd been asking around about her? *Bloke*. She felt silly and naïve for knowing nothing about the prince and squire when they'd clearly been digging up information about her. Trying to keep her features calm and collected, she asked, "What have you heard?"

"Everyone seems to love you," he said, shaking his head as if the thought were absurd. "They say you're beautiful, kind, and will make a great ruler."

She chuckled. "What are the contradictions?"

He leaned forward on the table again, his eyes intense. "Whenever you open your mouth around me, you're nasty and rude. I must conclude that you have one personality for the court, and another side you keep hidden. I wonder who the real Allyssa is?"

Her face paled. She had the desire to hide behind one of the books on the table, shielding herself from him. He'd been more observant than she'd realized.

"And then there's that little stunt you pulled," he continued, not taking his eyes off her. "You certainly acted like a true princess in the Throne Room with those soldiers. Even *I* was impressed."

Suddenly eager for this conversation to be over, she went to stand.

"Wait," he said, reaching out and snatching her hand. The gesture caught her off guard, and she froze. "Like I said before, I won't say anything about what happened last night so long as you let me accompany you when you meet the assassin."

"He told me to come alone," she said.

"I'll remain unseen, I promise."

She stared at their joined hands. He held tight, waiting for her answer. "Very well," she said, having no doubt that if she didn't agree, the squire would march straight to her father and tattle on her. Then she'd have no hope of meeting with the assassin. "You can come."

He released her hand. "Oh, and one more thing," he said as he stood. "Prince Odar requests your presence this afternoon."

"Of course."

He quickly bowed and exited the alcove, leaving Allyssa standing there feeling like a fool.

# Chapter Thirteen

Allyssa wanted to kick something. Her mother had insisted she and Prince Odar spend their time together in a highly visible place. So here they sat on a blanket at the base of the water fountain in the middle of the smaller courtyard. She felt as if she were on display for the entire court to see—which was precisely what her mother had intended. It was awkward and awful all rolled up together.

"We finally have some time to ourselves," Prince Odar said.

They weren't by any means alone. Her guards stood not far away, along with Jarvik and a handful of Fren soldiers. Whenever she examined the windows overlooking the courtyard, she always saw someone watching.

"Yes," she said, forcing herself to smile. "At last we have an opportunity to become better acquainted."

"The empress informed me that a grand ball is being held in our honor at the end of the week."

This was the first she'd heard anything about a dance. "I'm looking forward to it," she replied. A servant approached and set a tray of food down on the blanket, curtsied, and left. Allyssa took a pear even though she

wasn't hungry.

The prince nibbled on a piece of bread. "If we've finalized the marriage contract by then, we can announce our engagement that evening."

She was staring at a rose bush a few feet in front of her, lost in thought. *Engagement.*

Prince Odar took his pointer finger and lifted Allyssa's chin, forcing her to look at him. "What are you thinking about?" he asked.

She glanced over at the guards and Jarvik watching her every move. "Why is your squire always with you?" she asked.

"Most people never notice Jarvik when I'm around," he said. His hand dropped away from her face, and he answered, "He's my best friend and closest confidant. Since I'm in a foreign country and I'm not sure who I can trust, I asked him to accompany me."

"Will he move to Emperion with you?"

"I'm not sure. I'd like to have him here, but I don't want to ask him to leave his family—it wouldn't be fair."

*Family?* She never considered the possibility of Jarvik being married. He wasn't particularly handsome, and he was derogatory. "He doesn't seem the sort of person who would have children."

Prince Odar laughed. "I understand why you say that, but he is actually quite good with kids. However, the family members I am referring to are his parents."

She took a bite of her pear.

"What necklace do you have on?" Prince Odar asked.

She was wearing the wooden ring strung onto a golden chain around her neck, concealed by her dress. Her face flushed. She dared not pull it out for fear he'd laugh. It was not something a princess should be wearing.

"It's nothing," she said, putting her hand to her neck, ensuring the ring stayed safely tucked under her dress. She didn't know why she wore it. Perhaps it was because it had been carved by hand and had a special meaning. Most men lavished her with expensive gifts. However, this one came from the heart.

Wanting to change the subject, she said, "I'd like for you to tell me more about yourself." She twirled the pear between her hands.

Leaning back on his elbows and stretching his legs out, he said, "I grew up at court with Jarvik. Our parents are close."

That sounded familiar. Maybe she and the prince weren't as different as she thought.

"I was engaged, once," he admitted, surprising her. "I was young, and I thought I was in love." Staring up at the sky, he continued, "It turned out she only wanted to marry me for my wealth and position. Luckily, my parents discovered the girl's true motives and prevented the marriage. I was angry at the time." He rolled onto his side, staring at her. "What about you?" he asked. "Have you ever been in love?"

"No," she admitted, tossing the pear back onto the tray. An uncomfortable silence stretched between them.

"I'm not much of an army man, much to my father's disappointment," Prince Odar said, filling the quiet. "I can wield a sword, but not very well. Jarvik is the real sword master. I am, however, a superb dancer." He continued talking about himself, about growing up in Fren's court, the subjects he studied, the books he'd read, and what he enjoyed doing in his free time. Allyssa finally felt as if she had an idea of who Prince Odar was.

When he finished talking about himself, he asked

her all sorts of questions about her life. He wanted to know who to avoid at court, why she enjoyed running with her father early in the morning—which he found highly amusing—and what her favorite desserts were. She laughed, telling him her choice of cake and pastries were not important, but he insisted the information was vital.

Before she knew it, hours had flown by. The sun was setting and the sky darkened. Prince Odar sat up beside her. "Thank you for today," he said. "I enjoyed becoming better acquainted with you." He leaned toward her, too close for comfort. Reaching his right hand out, he cupped her cheek. He was so close she felt his breath caress her face.

He inched forward. Was he going to kiss her? She'd never been kissed before and had no desire to be kissed right now, especially in such a public place with so many people watching them. The prince tilted his head and closed his eyes. She stiffened and slid her hand onto his chest, gently stopping his advance. "I'm sorry," she whispered. "I like you, I really do, but I'm not ready."

His eyes widened with surprise. "That's a first," he replied. "Don't worry. I understand. We can take this slow."

"Thank you."

He slid his hand down her neck, along her arm, and to her hand, pulling her to her feet. Two servants rushed forward to gather the blanket, along with their discarded plates and drinks.

"Let me have the honor of escorting you into the castle," he said, offering her his arm.

She took it and they strolled inside, passing several courtiers smiling at them. Clearly, the court liked the idea of her marrying a prince from a large and wealthy kingdom. They would have to officially announce the engagement soon to make sure her people maintained hope when war loomed on the horizon.

ALLYSSA RETURNED TO THE CASTLE TIRED, BUT gratified, from having spent most of the day working at a local shelter feeding those in need. It was something she did with her mother a couple of times each season.

Entering her bedchamber, she found Mayra waiting for her.

Her lady-in-waiting jumped to her feet. "There is something I need to discuss with you," she said.

"What is it?" Allyssa asked, sitting on the sofa and pulling Mayra down next to her.

"I've been discreetly asking around about Prince Odar and Jarvik, just like you instructed me to."

Since Mayra was so good with other languages and spying, Allyssa had asked her to see if she could uncover anything of importance about the men from Fren.

"Did you know the prince didn't bring any servants with him?" Mayra asked. "Not even one."

"Are you certain?" Allyssa thought back to the day he arrived in such grandeur.

"Yes. Every single person here from Fren, with the exception of Jarvik and the prince, are high-ranking officers and soldiers from the prince's personal army."

"What about the elaborate entourage we saw? All the lords-in-waiting?" Allyssa asked.

"Soldiers dressed as servants," Mayra answered.

"Why?" Had the prince feared something foul would

happen when he reached the Emperion court? Or was there a darker, more sinister reason behind the sham?

"I'm not sure," Mayra replied. "What I'm hearing from our castle workers is that the roads are dangerous near the Russek border. Perhaps the Frens expected to encounter trouble on the way here."

That made sense. But why maintain the ruse? Possibly for the way home? "What about the prince and squire? Did you learn anything about them?"

"No," Mayra admitted. "No one will speak about either man. If there was a servant with them, I could probably coax or bribe the servant into speaking, but these soldiers are extremely loyal and therefore, closedmouthed."

"Keep investigating," Allyssa instructed her friend. "I'd like to see what else you can uncover." She had an eerie feeling she was missing something vital.

Allyssa entered the training room and found her father sparring with Jarvik. The sight of their wooden practice swords swinging toward one another was so unexpected, she froze, watching them.

When her father saw her, he stopped sparring and pointed his sword at her legs. "Pants?"

"I want to practice my front and side kicks," she answered.

"If you need to kick, chances are you'll be wearing a gown. We've been over this—I want you practicing in a dress so you'll be able to defend yourself if necessary." His shirt was soaked through with sweat, his hair disheveled. She wondered how long he'd been sparring.

"Yes, Father," was all she said.

Darmik wiped his forehead with his shirt sleeve. "I have a few things to attend to," he said. "Here." He handed her his wooden sword. "I've worn Jarvik down, perhaps you can take him." He kissed her forehead and mumbled, "He lifts his chin ever so slightly before he strikes."

After Darmik left the room, she peered over at the squire, and he smirked. *Bastard.* Well, she'd wanted an opportunity to hit him, and now she had it.

"I don't usually fight girls," he said, standing with his feet shoulder-width apart, the sword loosely clasped in his right hand.

"Fren doesn't employ women in its army?" she asked. That didn't seem fair. If a girl wanted to fight, she should be able to.

"I'd never heard of such a thing until I came here. Women should be home tending to the house, not defending their kingdom. That's a man's job."

*Bloody two-bit snake pits.* She swung, and he easily deflected her blow.

"For a squire, you sure know how to use your sword," she mused, going on the offensive. "I assumed all you'd know how to do is manage the prince's affairs and see to his needs." She wanted to upset him enough to throw him off balance.

He didn't respond. His mouth drew tight in concentration. Jarvik sidestepped her attack and began one of his own, putting her on the defensive.

"So how'd you learn swordplay?" she asked, trying to sound as if sparring with him was easy and she wasn't even exerting herself. "By watching your fearless prince practice with his army?"

His eyes flashed with anger. It was all she needed to

have the advantage. He didn't even see her roundhouse kick coming. She struck his sword arm, but he maintained a strong hold on his weapon. Having the element of surprise, she went into full-blown attack mode. Just when she thought he'd go down, he spun and caught her by surprise, sweeping her legs out from under her. Hitting the ground hard, she forced herself to roll and jump to her feet, swinging at the squire again, this time with more force than necessary.

"Your technique is exceptional," Jarvik said, surprising her. "If you speed up your attack, you'll have the advantage."

She was moving as fast as she could. Even though she didn't want to admit it, Jarvik was rather good, too. He was better than Marek and possibly on par with her father. No wonder Darmik had been so sweaty.

"What other weapons are you familiar with?" Jarvik asked.

She lowered her sword, breathing heavily. "Daggers, bow and arrow, that's about it."

"Let's take a break," he said, not even sounding winded. "What weapons do you plan to take when you meet with the assassin?"

She practically laughed. It didn't matter what she had with her. The assassin was obviously a skilled fighter since he'd managed to render all her guards unconscious in less than ten seconds.

"Not here," she replied, glancing at the soldiers near the doors.

"We should talk before we go," he whispered.

"I know." They needed to have some sort of plan in place. "Meet me in the library tonight," she said, putting her practice sword away.

"Only if you can manage to be civil and not bite my head off."

She rolled her eyes, unable to promise him anything.

AT DINNER THAT EVENING, ALLYSSA HAD BEEN SEATED next to Prince Odar. She supposed it was her mother's way of making it clear to everyone present that the two of them were officially courting. As soon as the marriage contract was finalized, they could announce their engagement and start planning the wedding.

"You're awfully quiet tonight," the prince whispered so only she could hear. Jarvik sat on his other side, Darmik beside her.

"I didn't realize I was being unsocial," she replied.

"I'd like to take you riding. You do ride, don't you?"

"Of course," she said.

"Are you available tomorrow?"

Besides being present in the Throne Room for the people's petitions and on the balcony during the weekly address to the city, she didn't have anything else scheduled. "I believe I can make time for you," she answered. "Your squire can make the necessary arrangements with Marek, the head of my guard."

The prince gave a slow nod. "Speaking of my squire, I have a few questions for you."

She coughed, choking on a piece of food. Her father looked at her, and she waved him off. She was fine, just caught off guard by the subject matter. "What would you like to discuss?" She hoped it didn't have anything to do with the assassin.

"The two of you ... well, how shall I put it? You two

seem to dislike each other," the prince said pleasantly.

Allyssa glanced sidelong at Jarvik. He wasn't looking her way, but she wouldn't put it past him to be listening even though he seemed engaged in conversation with the man to his right. Setting her fork down, she gave the prince her full attention. "And this concerns you since we plan to marry?"

The corners of his lips lifted into a slow smile. "It does present some difficulties."

"I understand," she said. "You want him to move here with you, but not if there's going to be animosity between him and me."

"Exactly." The prince picked up his goblet and took a long drink.

"Would it help if I made an effort to become better acquainted with him?" After all, she still needed the squire's approval for the marriage to go through.

"You're a good person," Prince Odar quietly said. "I had feared that someone so young and beautiful, who had grown up in the luxuries of the Emperion court, couldn't be a wise and just ruler. Now that I've met you, I can see my fears were unfounded." He focused on his plate, eating his food without looking her way.

"I have a question for you," she said. Glancing around, she made sure no one was paying them any heed. "Why Emperion? You already have a strong alliance with Telmena. Why not join forces with them and attack Russek?"

"We need Emperion's army," he answered. "It is the strongest and most capable on the continent."

She opened her mouth to ask another question when he said, "I think we've talked enough about politics for one night. We can discuss such matters later, but not now." He lifted his glass of wine, taking another drink.

"Of course," she said. There was something the prince wasn't telling her—something he was hiding. Otherwise, he wouldn't change the subject every time she brought up their alliance or the upcoming war with Russek. Allyssa was determined to find out what it was.

# Chapter Fourteen

Allyssa sent a message to the squire, instructing him to meet her on the castle rooftop instead of the library as planned. There were several questions she needed answered before they started working together. As of now, she'd feel safer sneaking out alone rather than entrusting her life to him.

Her father and Neco were so wrapped up sending spies to the front lines to obtain information about Russek that she'd barely seen either of them lately. Her mother was trying to finish contract negotiations with Prince Odar while managing to find the time to call up all the military reserves Emperion had.

Leaning on the stone railing, Allyssa gazed out over the city. Thousands of sparkling lights glittered below from windows, the breeze gently rustled her hair, and the moon cast a soft glow over the rooftop. Her guards were stationed near the door, far enough away to give her the illusion of being alone, and certainly far enough away not to overhear a word she spoke.

Jarvik's soft footsteps approached behind her. "Why does this not surprise me?" he mused, coming to stand next to her.

"What?" she asked, glancing back and signaling for

her guards to hold their position.

"You seeking solace out here."

"How do you know that's what I'm doing?" He didn't know anything about her, so how had he guessed this was one of her favorite places to come when she needed comfort?

He leaned against the stone railing, gazing out at the city. "Trust me, I know."

They stood in silence for several minutes, neither one of them attempting to speak. Finally getting up enough courage to ask him what she needed to, she took a deep breath and said, "Why are you here?"

His eyes sliced over to hers. "You asked me to come up here."

"No," she responded. "Why are you here with the prince?"

He shrugged. "He brought all his closest advisors."

"But is that the only reason?" she asked. "Simply to give your opinion as to whether Prince Odar should marry me or not?"

Jarvik rubbed his face. "Yes," he finally said, turning to face her.

"But why you?"

"The king and queen are eager for this alliance. However, they have some serious concerns. The prince believes it solves all of Fren's problems. I'm here for a second opinion. May I speak plainly?"

She nodded—didn't he always?

"The king and queen of Fren don't want Prince Odar to do anything stupid—like marry you without certain guarantees in place in the marriage contract. I am here to ensure Fren's best interests are followed."

"So you're here to decide if this alliance is truly the

best course of action for Fren?"

"Yes."

His honesty was refreshing.

"It's not like Fren is without options," he continued. "They have a strong army, the prince has several suitors, and so the question becomes what is the best move in the long run?"

"What I don't understand is why our kingdoms can't work together. Why must we have a marriage treaty in place?"

"If only it were that simple," he muttered. "The emperor before your parents focused solely on war. Even though your parents have restructured your army and made no move against your neighboring kingdoms, few people trust Emperion. Therefore, your word isn't good enough. Only a marriage treaty will suffice in order for our courts and armies to be on board. I've studied all the great battles of the mainland. The only way we can join together, and have Telmena's approval, is with this contract."

"Why are you being so open and honest with me?" she asked.

"I don't know." He turned and gazed out over the city again. "I guess because time is running out, and I must decide Fren's next move."

"I've tried talking to Prince Odar about politics and treaties, but he's evasive. It's almost as if he's hiding something from me. I find it rather bothersome."

Jarvik cocked his head to the side, looking at her. "Really? Why?"

"If I'm to rule with him and he isn't honest with me, or he doesn't passionately care about his subjects, or want to strategize by my side, how can we ever be partners?"

Jarvik smiled. "You're going to be the empress. I think you'll outrank him and be the one in charge." He sounded almost envious.

"That's not how I see it," she responded. "I am seeking an equal partner. I want an open, honest relationship like my parents have. That's why I keep pressing him for answers."

"Perhaps he's not answering you because he's still determining your worth."

His comment stung. "Well," she replied, her voice hard, "perhaps he should have done that before we entered into marriage negotiations. You know, the two of you are infuriating. If my parents had any idea you still weren't sure about this alliance and the prince might back out, they'd ... they'd ... I don't know, but it wouldn't be pleasant."

Jarvik started laughing.

"What?" she demanded, putting her hands on her hips.

"Did I offend you?" he asked, trying, but failing, to stop laughing.

"Yes," she said, folding her arms. "You know what, I have other things to do besides argue with you." She turned and started to walk away.

He grabbed her arm, stopping her. Out of the corner of her eye, she saw two of her guards unsheathe their swords. Allyssa put her free hand up, signaling for them to stand down.

"I'm sorry," Jarvik said. "I didn't mean to upset you. You can't honestly tell me you aren't still weighing the prince's worth. If you wanted to back out, you know your parents would support you."

Allyssa didn't particularly like the squire and she

wanted to be out in the city, not standing there looking at it. She missed Grevik and hoped he wasn't still mad at her. The meeting with the assassin was to take place tomorrow night and fighting with the prince's lackey wasn't getting her anywhere. She kicked the stone wall, frustrated.

"I said I'm sorry," Jarvik reiterated.

"I heard you the first time." She tried pulling away. "Let go."

He released her. She turned and headed for the door.

"Wait," he said, jogging to catch up to her. "I know how to sneak you out of the castle," he said softly enough so only she could hear.

She stopped. "I'm listening."

"Come with me to my rooms. I'll explain everything there."

*To his rooms?* That was highly inappropriate. However, if he had a way to slip past her guards, it might be worth it. If anyone questioned her, she would say she was visiting the prince.

Allyssa agreed, and the squire led her to the east wing of the castle. When they reached the rooms dedicated to the people from Fren, Allyssa ordered her guards to wait outside the doors in the hallway. Thankfully, Marek wasn't on duty. She was certain he wouldn't have let her go in unaccompanied.

Inside, the sitting room was warm and toasty. Next to the hearth, Prince Odar sat on a chair, reading a book with his feet propped on a stool. The top portion of his shirt was untied and hung loose around his neck, exposing his chest.

When the prince saw her, he jumped to his feet. Jarvik led him to the corner where they spoke in hushed whispers. Allyssa awkwardly stood there, glancing around the large room. There were six doors off the sitting room, each leading to a separate bedchamber. She could hear people talking on the other side of the doors. She found it strange that no one was in the sitting room with the prince. Perhaps he valued his privacy like she did, and he made the guards stay out of sight.

Several trunks were shoved against the walls. One stood open. It was filled with weapons—shining swords, a few bows, and some quivers. She supposed the Fren soldiers needed to be heavily armed in order to protect their prince on the journey to Emperion.

Prince Odar came over to her. "Princess Allyssa," he said, a smile on his lips, his bright blue eyes gazing at her. "My squire tells me the two of you have something planned." He gave her the opportunity to speak, which she didn't. She had no idea how much Jarvik had told him. "I must admit I'm a little jealous. Alas, he is my best friend, and you should become better acquainted." He gently took her hand and kissed it. "I'm turning in for the evening. Goodnight." And with that, he went to one of the doors and slipped inside his bedchamber.

Jarvik was looking at the ground, his face hard, not revealing any emotions. He waited a minute before going to the doors on the right side of the sitting room, knocking on each one and briefly speaking with the men inside. When done, he rummaged through one of the trunks, pulling out some plain clothes. "I assume you want to scout out the site with me for your meeting tomorrow?"

"Of course."

"You can change into these," he said, handing them to her. "Then we'll leave the castle, pretending we're going

into town for a drink. Six of my men are accompanying us. I've instructed them to stay close by while on the castle grounds in order to hide your identity. Once we've entered the city streets, they will fall back into position."

She nodded, impressed with his plan. He escorted her to one of the empty rooms and told her she could change in there. Once alone, she laughed. He had no clue. How in the world was she supposed to take her dress off? She couldn't reach the ties at the back. After awkwardly twisting her arms one way and her torso another, she gave up. Poking her head into the sitting room, she saw Jarvik there with six men all dressed in nondescript clothing.

"Excuse me," she said, and Jarvik rushed over. "I require some assistance." She opened the door, and he came inside.

"With what?" he asked.

She needed Mayra, but she knew the squire would never agree. She couldn't sneak out of the castle with Jarvik if her guards or her ladies-in-waiting knew what she was doing. Sighing, she said, "I can't remove my dress."

"Why not?" he asked, confused.

Turning her back to him, she said, "Can you... uh, untie it, please?"

Jarvik didn't respond. She knew he'd traveled with only men, and there wasn't a woman here to help her. Peering over her shoulder, she saw him standing there, rapidly blinking.

"Never mind," she stated. "This plan isn't going to work." She went to leave when he stopped her.

"I can assist you," he said carefully. "You just need me to loosen the ties, correct?"

She nodded. It wasn't like he had to actually help her out of the dress. She could do that on her own. It was just the ties Mayra had cinched and knotted together that Allyssa couldn't undo.

He came closer, fumbling with her strings. "These things are really knotted together," he muttered. After a couple of minutes, she felt the dress loosen. "Done," he said, stepping quickly away and leaving the room. She didn't even have a chance to thank him.

After pulling off the outfit, she quickly changed into the clothing he'd given her. The pants were a little big so she rolled them at the waist. She had a dagger already strapped to her thigh so she kept that on, but she really wanted more weapons since they were going into the city.

Exiting the bedchamber, she found Jarvik and six men waiting for her in the sitting room. She was about to ask for a knife when the squire handed her two, instructing her to attach them with the straps sewn into the material of her pants. She thanked him and slid them into the hidden folds like he said. She'd have to have some of these pockets sewn into her own clothes—they were quite handy.

"I informed your guards that you are having a cup of tea with the prince and playing a card game. They are to send word to your ladies-in-waiting you won't be back to your rooms until quite late."

"Thank you," she said, surprised by his prudent planning.

"You still need to do something with your hair," he said.

Allyssa removed the pins, and her hair cascaded down around her shoulders. Jarvik's cheeks reddened and he quickly squatted to retie his boots, keeping his eyes cast downward. She combed her hair back with her fingers and hastily braided it. Then she wrapped the

braid around her head and used a pin to secure it in place. One of the soldiers offered her his hat. She put it on, concealing her hair completely.

Jarvik stood and went to the servants' entrance at the back of the sitting room. He explained that it led to the lower level near the kitchen where they could easily slip outside. In order for this plan to work, Allyssa had to pretend to be a man joking and carrying on as they walked together in a group. Rounding her shoulders, she steeled her resolve, ready to play the part of a Fren soldier.

THEY MADE INTO THE CITY WITHOUT INCIDENT. TRUE to Jarvik's word, the Fren soldiers melted into the shadows, doing a much better job at remaining unseen than her own guards had done the other night. Allyssa walked alongside the squire as if they were friends. Which they weren't.

"Do you know where the inn is?" he asked.

"Yes, it's just a few blocks up ahead."

"Is there anything I need to know about this inn? Any particular reason the assassin would have chosen it?"

"I don't know," she answered. "I've only passed by; I've never gone in."

"It doesn't have any sort of reputation?"

"Not that I'm aware of." She and Grevik tended to avoid inns, instead focusing on taverns and ale houses to locate criminals.

They walked in silence for several minutes.

"How do you feel about the prince now that you've spent some time with him?"

She shrugged, surprised he was attempting to

converse with her on something other than the task at hand. "He's not as arrogant as I originally thought. Honestly, he isn't the man I'd choose to marry, but then again, this isn't about me. This is about doing what's best for Emperion."

"Most women swoon over him."

"He is handsome," she admitted. "I'm sure we can grow to love one another in time."

"Ideally, what sort of man do you wish to marry?"

*Blimey.* Why was he asking the tough questions right now? "I always imagined marrying someone who loves this kingdom as much as I do, someone who is willing to fight alongside me to protect our people. I want a husband who knows his mind, is passionate, and who makes me a better ruler. I don't know if that makes any sense," Allyssa said, "but that's what I want." She desired a strong and loving marriage like her parents had. Not only did they love one another, but they complimented each other when it came to ruling the kingdom.

Jarvik didn't respond. They walked in silence. She wondered if he'd heard her—if he'd even been listening—if she'd said too much. Maybe he'd just asked to make conversation. He probably didn't really want to know. After all, they hated each other, didn't they?

"Is that the Wooden Inn over there?" he asked.

"It is. Are we going to head inside and sit in the tavern in order to scout it out? Or do you want to walk around outside?"

His eyes darted around the street, observing the nearby buildings and the few people lingering nearby. "Three of my men will remain outside on patrol," he whispered near her ear, making her jump. "The other three will go inside with us to check the place out." He

wrapped his arm around her shoulders. "You can't attract unwanted attention, so we need to appear friendly with one another. For the time being, let's act like we enjoy each other's company."

"Very well," she replied. "But you do understand that means you'll have to be cordial to me, my dear Jarvik." She smiled sweetly at him.

He shook his head. "I'm always nice. It's you I'm worried about."

They entered the inn and made their way to the tavern inside. The place was busy, but there were still tables available. Sitting down off to the side near the wall so their backs were protected, they ordered two bowls of stew and two cups of ale.

Allyssa leaned back and propped her legs up on a nearby chair. The squire raised his eyebrows, but he didn't say anything. Bloody hell, she loved the freedom of the city, of not having to act like a princess. It was fantastic. The three Fren soldiers came inside and headed to the bar, blending in with the patrons.

A serving wench brought their food. Jarvik picked up his spoon and started eating, Allyssa intently watching him. "What?" he mumbled between bites.

"Nothing," she replied, putting her legs down on the ground. "I'm just trying to get a read on you."

"Well, don't. We're not here for pleasantries."

She snorted. Didn't he say that they needed to pretend they liked one another? He probably meant that as long as they appeared friendly toward one another, they didn't actually need to be cordial. "Forgive me, how could I have been mistaken?" she sarcastically drawled. After taking a few bites of her own stew, she wiped her mouth and leaned forward. "Did you notice the man in the corner, east end, brown cloak, hood on? He's not the man we're looking for, but he's definitely up to no good."

"Why do you say that?" Jarvik asked, putting his spoon down.

"The guy's alone, but he keeps looking around and fidgeting with the handle of his mug. He's nervous." She wished Grevik was here. He'd be over there talking to the man by now, attacking trouble head on without hesitation. When she and Jarvik were done here, she'd have to take the long way home and pay her friend a visit.

"Will you focus?" Jarvik said, recapturing her attention.

"I am." After all, the squire was the one oblivious to the fact that there was a criminal sitting twenty feet from them. Jarvik was so wrapped up in scouting out the place for her meeting tomorrow with the assassin that he was missing what was going on right in front of him.

Picking the spoon back up, the squire said, "The upper rooms are going to be a problem." He nodded to the second floor, which overlooked the tavern. There were approximately sixteen rooms up there. "I can see why he picked this location." He took a bite of his stew.

The man in the corner stood and headed to another table, where he sat down and spoke with the two men sitting there. From under his cape, he removed a small, black bag the size of his palm. He slid it across the table to the men, who in turn handed over several coins. Then he stood and headed to the exit. She recalled hearing about a supply cart that had been robbed a couple weeks ago. Among the items stolen were jewelry and expensive, rare spices.

"Let's go," Allyssa said, standing and putting a few coppers on the table to pay for their food and drinks.

"I'm not ready," Jarvik responded. "I have a few more things I want to see."

They had already checked the place out—there was nothing else to do. Shaking her head, Allyssa headed after the thief, not wanting to lose him. Jarvik cursed before joining her.

"What are you doing?" he hissed. She just smiled at him. They were in her domain, and this was what she lived for.

Outside in the brisk air, she saw the man head down a nearby alley. Allyssa ran to catch up with him. Jarvik and a couple of his men were close behind her. When she reached the corner of the building, she peered around the edge. The man was about fifteen feet away. Taking a big breath, she unsheathed her daggers.

The squire grabbed her wrists. "What are you doing?" he demanded.

"That man is a thief," she replied. "I'm going to capture him. Then I'll deliver him to someone so he can be properly arrested."

"I can't let you do that," he said. "It's too dangerous."

Allyssa chuckled. "What do you think I do every night when I come out here?"

Jarvik's eyebrows pulled together. "You've been going after criminals?" he asked in disbelief.

She didn't have time to stand there arguing with him. The thief was getting too far away. Slipping out of Jarvik's grasp, she headed after the man, rolling her shoulders and loosening up so she could fight. Allyssa whistled, garnering his attention.

The thief spun around to face her. "Who are you?" he demanded, pulling out a knife.

"Who am I?" she asked, feigning shock. The man

stepped back, away from her. "I'm here to retrieve what you stole."

He turned and started running away. Allyssa aimed her dagger and threw. As planned, the hilt hit him on his back and he stumbled, turning around to face her again. Stalking toward him, she asked, "Where are you going?" The man's knife shook in his hand. *Good, that means he's nervous.* "I told you I'm here to collect the goods you stole."

He reached up with his free hand and unlatched his cape, throwing it to the ground. "Come on," he taunted her. "You seem a bit small and scrawny. You sure you want to fight me?"

"I'd enjoy nothing more," she replied, sheathing her remaining dagger. The thief's stance was all wrong. She'd be able to take him down in less than a minute without any weapons.

Sparing a quick glance over her shoulder, she saw Jarvik and two of his men at the end of the street, making no attempt to help or stop her. Focusing on the thief again, she smiled up at him. Rushing to her, he punched toward her face. She ducked.

"Oops," Allyssa said. "You missed."

He swung again, aiming for her side. She twisted. "Missed again. I thought you said something about fighting me. I'm not sure what you call this, but clearly, we're not fighting. It's more like dancing if you ask me."

"Harlot," he growled, the word echoing between the buildings in the alley.

"That is not a very nice word to use," she said. "Now you've made me mad." Clutching her hand into a fist, she drew her arm back and punched the thief in the stomach. He grunted and leaned forward. Allyssa swung her knee up, hitting him again. He tried reaching for her. *Fool.* She grabbed his arm, twisted around, placed her back to his front, and flipped him over her shoulder. He landed on the ground with a loud *umph.*

"Now that, *thief,* is how it's done." She stepped on his wrist, pinning his arm to the ground.

Jarvik came forward. "You have a death wish."

"And yet, you just watched."

"I was curious to see you in action."

"What did you think?" she asked.

"You're actually pretty good."

She smiled. That was the nicest thing he'd ever said to her. "After we take the thief to my contact at the City Guard, can we swing by and see my friend Grevik?"

"I'm not even going to acknowledge that with an answer," Jarvik declared.

"Why not?"

"That's where the assassin found you last time. I hardly think going to the place that started this fiasco is what you should be doing right now."

"I'd like to visit my friend."

"I know," he said. "If you wait until after the assassin is dealt with, I'll personally take you to see him."

# Chapter Fifteen

Standing at the archery range, Allyssa watched Prince Odar raise his bow, aim the arrow at the target, and release the bowstring. The arrow sailed through the air and struck the target in the center ring.

"Nice shot," she said. It wasn't dead center, but still in the middle.

"I'd like to see you shoot," he said. "I've heard you're rather good."

Strolling forward, she grabbed an arrow from the quiver, nocked it, aimed, and released the bowstring. Her arrow landed with a *thunk* dead center.

"You're not good," he mused. "You're exceptional. I've never seen a woman shoot before."

Putting the bow down, she faced the prince. "You can't be serious."

"In Fren, women don't take up such hobbies."

She shook her head. How was that possible? "Women don't go hunting or protect their land?"

He smiled, his blue eyes sparkling. "That's what men are for." He gave a look that implied she was the crazy one, not him.

"I'm not sure I care to see your kingdom," she said half serious, half joking.

"I'm not sure Fren is ready for you," he countered.

Dark clouds gathered overhead. A storm was coming. "Shall we go inside?" Allyssa asked. She really wanted to walk around the flower field, but it looked like it would begin pouring at any moment.

"Would you do me the honor of showing me around the castle?"

There wasn't much to see, but she agreed, and they went inside.

"Where's your squire?" she asked. Prince Odar was rarely seen without Jarvik hovering close by.

"He had a few things to tend to." The prince offered her his arm, and she took it. "Why do you care where my squire is?"

She shrugged. "I wanted to know if we were alone."

Her answer seemed to appease him. As they meandered down the hallway, they saw the torches and candles being lit since the corridors were so dark from the storm.

"You're quiet today," Prince Odar said.

"Sorry," she answered. "I have a lot on my mind." She hoped to take a nap this afternoon so she'd be well rested for tonight. The fact that she was meeting an assassin made her stomach ache.

"What room is this?" he asked, stopping before two open doors. Inside, dozens of portraits hung on the walls. "The paintings are beautiful," he murmured. "The detail is exquisite."

They walked around the perimeter of the room, gazing at the various rulers who'd held the throne in Emperion over the past five hundred years. "Why isn't your picture here among these rulers?"

Stopping before a painting of Allyssa's parents, she

said, "When I become empress, then my picture will go here, next to my mother's."

Prince Odar took a step closer to the portraits, examining them. "I've been taught that your parents overthrew the previous rulers. Is that true?"

"To an extent," she replied. "The previous ruler, Emperor Hamen, wasn't the true heir—my mother was. After his death, my mother took the throne and sent his wife Eliza and their daughter into exile."

"Really?" he asked, stepping to the side to look at Hamen and Eliza's portrait. "What was their daughter's name?"

"Jana."

The prince turned to face her. "Did your mother kill Hamen?"

"No," Allyssa answered. "One of her companions did."

"What about Eliza and Jana?"

"My mother couldn't sign the execution warrant, so she banished them. Eliza and Jana were supposed to be living in a secluded house that was guarded by soldiers at all times. However, a few years ago, they escaped and are believed to have fled the kingdom. If they are still alive, Eliza would have to be around sixty years old. Her daughter, Jana, would be in her early thirties, a little younger than my father. Jana is my father's half-sister—they both have the same father, Hamen."

"But the line is entailed through your mother?"

"Yes," she said. "Why all the questions?"

"I want to know if Emperion has any weaknesses we're unaware of," he said. "Aren't you at all concerned where Eliza and Jana are? What plots they could be concocting?"

Allyssa shrugged. She hadn't given them much

thought. "My mother never seemed worried. Jana was supposedly very sick, and it was believed she'd die at an early age."

"Your kingdom has a rich history, that's for sure." Prince Odar chuckled. "What else haven't I seen in this castle?"

Allyssa decided to take him to one of her favorite places. Entering the solarium, she watched the rain fall, pattering against the glass above her. She strolled between the low bushes and roses that lined the pathway to the water fountain. Closing her eyes, she tilted her head back and listened to the sound of water all around her. Two hands gently rested on her shoulders, making her jump. She opened her eyes. Prince Odar was standing right behind her.

Her future husband.

"Allyssa," he whispered. He'd never called her by her name. It felt too intimate. She turned to face him. "I want to kiss you," he whispered.

She took a step away from him. Weren't they taking things slow? Getting to know one another? Prince Odar's face hardened with a look of determination as he put his hands on her shoulders once again, stepping toward her so they were only inches apart.

"Why?" she asked. Was it because he was curious to see if there was something between them? Did he actually desire a kiss from her? She couldn't decipher his intentions.

"Because I want to," he said, smiling.

Movement caught her attention. She looked past the prince and saw Jarvik entering the solarium with several Fren soldiers. He stopped a few feet behind the prince.

"Your squire—" she started to say, but the prince cut

her off.

"Why are you always talking about him? Why can't you just focus on me?" Prince Odar asked.

"What's going on?" Jarvik interrupted, saving her from answering.

The prince startled and dropped his hands, abruptly taking a step back, away from her. "Nothing," he answered. "The princess and I were just talking." He turned to face his squire, his head shaking ever so slightly in disappointment.

"Prince Odar," Jarvik said, "I need to speak with you alone for a moment."

"If you'll excuse me," Allyssa said. She went to the other end of the solarium in order to give the prince and Jarvik privacy. Gazing outside at the falling rain, there was nothing she wanted more than to run out there, letting the water pound on her head. Instead, she was stuck inside the castle, forced to entertain the prince.

"I'm sorry for the interruption," Jarvik said, coming to stand next to her, staring outside at the storm with her.

"It was actually well timed," she mumbled, not really intending for him to hear. They stood in silence for several minutes. Lightning flashed across the sky and a moment later, thunder boomed. For the first time ever, she was glad Jarvik stood beside her. There was something about his steady stoicism that made her feel safe and not so lonely.

"I hope it lets up before tonight," he said, folding his arms.

"It'll be easier to conceal our movements with the storm."

"As it will be for the assassin, too."

She hadn't told Jarvik yet, but after she met with

the assassin, she planned to see Grevik. This time, she wouldn't ask. She would just go to her friend. Her chest ached from not seeing or talking to him. She had to make sure he understood why she lied. Their friendship couldn't be over—not after all these years.

"Did you need something?" she asked, curious as to why he was still there.

"I just had to tell the prince something," he said.

Scanning the solarium, she didn't see Prince Odar anywhere.

"He left. He is needed elsewhere," Jarvik said.

Closing her eyes, she listened to the pattering rain.

"Are you all right?" he whispered, his voice sending a shiver through her body.

"I'm fine," she lied, forcing a smile. "If you'll excuse me, I need to prepare for a meeting this afternoon." It was the first time she felt the need to flee not because Jarvik had upset her, but because his presence was preferable to the prince's.

Approaching her bedchamber, she heard Marek arguing with Madelin and Mayra inside. It was nothing new for the brother and sister to fight; however, it was unusual for Madelin to be involved. Allyssa went in, closing the door behind her. "What's going on?" she asked, hoping it had nothing to do with her.

All three of them stopped talking at once. Madelin's eyes were bright red, Marek wouldn't look at Allyssa, and Mayra's hands were fisted on her hips.

"Someone had better tell me," Allyssa said.

Mayra cleared her throat. "My brother put in a

request to join the army. He wants to go to the frontlines to fight when we go to war."

The unexpected news made Allyssa feel as if she'd stumbled head-first into a cold lake. "What?" she screeched. "Are you crazy?" He would be killed.

"I'd like a moment to speak with the princess alone," Marek said, his voice hoarse.

"Try talking some sense into him," Mayra said as she stormed out of the room. Madelin meekly followed Mayra, crying as she walked past Marek.

Once the door closed, Marek held up his hands. "Before you start yelling at me," he said, "at least hear what I have to say."

"Very well," she said, folding her hands together and waiting for him to continue.

"We're going to war," he said. "We are starting to organize the army and move soldiers into position to fight Russek. You're doing your part by marrying Prince Odar of Fren. I want to do my part, too. I can't stay in this castle while everyone I know is fighting for our kingdom. I'm a trained soldier. You need me fighting for you." He ran his hands through his hair. "There. I've said my part."

"I need you here, guarding me. You're the *head* of my personal guard. There is no one I trust more than you." Protecting her might not be the most exciting job, but it was a position of value and respect.

"There are others who are qualified. You'll have no trouble filling my spot." He went over to the window, leaning on the ledge, looking outside at the pouring rain. "Protecting you is an honor, but I want to be where the action is."

A lot of men his age probably felt the same way. Her parents had managed to keep Emperion out of any major

scuffles for the past twelve years. He'd never seen or experienced war before. The battles she'd studied and the wars Darmik had told her about were all vicious, bloody, and brutal. How could she possibly allow Marek to fight on the frontlines? How could Neco or her parents be okay with this?

"What did your father say when you told him?" she asked, taking a seat on the chair near the hearth. The fire roared nice and high, warming her room.

"He was furious and said my position is here." Marek turned around to face her. "But you outrank him. You have the power to let me go."

"Marek . . . ." She didn't want to let him go. It was selfish of her, but she felt like being selfish with her dear friend.

"You don't understand. Your father and my father are going."

The room swayed before her. "What do you mean, they're going?" she demanded, her heart thundering in her chest.

"To the frontlines to fight."

She thought she was going to vomit. Her father couldn't lead the army into battle—what if he died? Leaning forward, she rested her head on her hands.

"Your Highness, are you okay?" Marek asked, kneeling before her.

"Yes," she answered. "I just need a moment."

"I'll get my sister."

She grabbed his arm. "Wait," she said. "I understand why you want to go." He needed to protect his father, and so did she.

Their eyes locked, and they stayed that way for a minute. "You're not going to try and talk me out of it?"

he whispered.

"I want to. But no, I'm not."

"Will you sign my orders?"

She nodded.

"Thank you." He left to find Mayra.

She sat there, staring into the fire. The sound of men marching pounded in her head. War was coming. Those she loved would die. She had to protect her family and her people.

ALLYSSA WAS ALMOST TO THE MEETING ROOM WHEN she heard angry voices around the corner. Slowing her pace, she gave the signal for her guards to fall back and remain silent. She stopped at the corner and leaned against the stone wall, listening to Jarvik and Prince Odar arguing with one another. Allyssa knew she shouldn't stand there eavesdropping, but she couldn't make herself move.

"I forbid it," Jarvik said, his voice low and angry.

"Why? What's changed?"

"We shouldn't be having this conversation here."

"No one's around."

Jarvik sighed. "Stick with the plan ... but back off."

Prince Odar chuckled. "Why can't I have a little fun? It's not as if you like her. So why do you care?"

There was a thud as if someone had been thrown against a wall. "That is none of your concern," Jarvik said, his voice low and dangerous. "Remember, this is a business deal, nothing more."

"I thought it was more about getting revenge for what Shelene did than business," Prince Odar replied.

"Besides, I think things have changed."

"This situation is already dangerous and complicated enough. I don't need you adding to the fray."

"Fine," he said. "Anything else?"

"No," Jarvik snapped.

"For the record," the prince said, "I think you should tell her. I know you've become distrustful, but I think this one is worthy. Don't ruin it by being deceitful."

Allyssa heard footsteps approaching so she hurried down the hall away from the men.

# Chapter Sixteen

Inside the meeting room, large maps hung on the walls. One was covered with red marks, showing where enemy soldiers had been spotted. Another indicated where the Emperion base camps were hidden. The evidence of imminent war sent a chill through Allyssa as she took her seat next to her mother, waiting for the meeting to start.

"There's been a change in plans," Darmik said, standing. "We've just received a letter from Russek."

The room went silent. Every single duke and all the members of the Legion sat staring at the empress and emperor. Rema lifted a piece of paper, handing it to Darmik.

He cleared his throat and read:

# Cage of Deceit

Empress Rema and Emperor Darmik,

I won't waste time with pleasantries. As you know, I desire your kingdom, and Emperion will be mine. Out of kindness, as you have shown in the past, I will give you an option. If the two of you step down from the throne, along with your daughter, I will allow you to leave the kingdom and live in exile on Greenwood Island.

However, if you should mistakenly feel you can actually win against my mighty army and remain in power, I will have no choice but to forcibly remove your entire family, which will result in your untimely deaths.

I expect your answer within a fortnight. If you don't agree to leave, we will march into your kingdom, destroy your farms and villages, and murder every Emperion we come into contact with.

King Drenton of Russek

The room remained silent. Allyssa went over the letter in her head. It was rather oddly worded, especially the part about showing kindness in the past and being offered exile instead of being slaughtered outright.

Darmik paced back and forth behind Rema and Allyssa, the letter still clutched in his hand. "I want all the dukes to return to their residences. Prepare your land for war. Protect the children and elderly. All able-bodied men must be ready to fight."

The five dukes nodded and left the room.

"We will continue to finalize the marriage treaty between Princess Allyssa and Prince Odar. I believe our armies united will be enough to stop Russek."

"As for the members of the Legion, do any of you object to us going to war to protect our land?" Rema asked.

"I, for one," said an elderly man, "am honored to serve in the Legion. If we need to go to war to protect our kingdom, so be it."

A chorus of, "Here, here," rippled around the room.

"Thank you for your trust and support," Rema said as she stood. She began walking around the table. "You all should know, I have a contingency plan in place."

The door flew opened and Audek, Madelin's father and one of her parents' closest friends, entered the room. "Your Majesty," he said.

"Thank you for coming, Audek. As I was saying, the emperor and I have taken precautions should Emperion ever be threatened. I want each and every one of you to know that no matter what happens, the royal line will be preserved. That is all I can say on the matter right now."

She went and stood next to Darmik, the two of them holding hands. "We will meet tomorrow to continue to

strategically plan our attacks, but for now, the meeting is over."

Rema firmly placed her hand on her daughter's shoulder, keeping her in place while all the Legion members left the room. Once everyone was gone, Audek shut the door.

Audek rarely came to court. He lived on the outskirts of town in a modest home with his wife, Vesha. He was one of her parents' most trusted friends since he came from Greenwood Island and was instrumental in restoring Rema to the throne. Allyssa always enjoyed his company because he liked to make jokes and play pranks—he wasn't stuffy like most of the nobles she knew. Madelin had a dash of her father's wit about her.

"Allyssa," Rema said, sitting once again next to her daughter, "there is something we must tell you."

Darmik came and sat on the edge of the table on the other side of his daughter.

"Should I, uh, be here for this?" Audek asked.

Rema reached out for his hand. "My dear friend, thank you for your loyalty over the years." She smiled, and his face reddened. "I need you to go and see Trell. He is the only one besides Mako who knows where Nathenek is. Find Nathenek and tell him that we're entering stage one."

Audek knelt on the ground. "Yes, Your Majesty." He stood and left the room, winking at Rema before he closed the door behind him.

"What is going on?" Allyssa asked. "Who is Nathenek and what is stage one?"

Her parents exchanged worried glances. "Honey, you must know that we love you very much," Rema said. "We never meant to be deceitful, but sometimes, as a ruler, you have to do things that are in the best interest of the kingdom."

Darmik reached out and placed his hand on Allyssa's shoulder. "We never wanted to lie to you," he said. "But we had to do what was best."

"When I took the throne," Rema said, "I promised to always preserve the royal line no matter what. My own mother sacrificed herself so that I could live and carry on the line. Sometimes, we have to make such sacrifices. It is part of being a ruler."

Allyssa had no idea what her parents were getting at, but she was suddenly scared.

The door opened, and Neco slipped into the room. "Sorry to interrupt, but I have some vital information that can't wait." He tugged his right ear and tilted his head.

Darmik jumped up and ran out of the room after Neco.

"We'll continue this conversation later," Rema said to her daughter as she stood and kissed Allyssa on her forehead. Then she, too, hurried from the room.

Allyssa sat there stunned, having no idea what her parents were about to reveal. She wanted to yell at them to come back and force them to tell her. Throwing her hands up in the air, she cursed.

"Given the threat from Russek, your father should increase security around the castle. We shouldn't be able to enter and exit so easily," Jarvik said as he and Allyssa walked along the street, heading deeper into the city. The rain had stopped, but everything was still wet, the streets littered with puddles.

She'd been thinking the same thing, but she hadn't wanted to say anything to her father until after she met with the assassin tonight.

"Just so we're absolutely clear, you're not to follow or fight with any criminals this evening. Understood?"

This was the tenth time Jarvik had said something on the matter. She wasn't sure what bothered her more—him ordering her around, or constantly saying the same thing so many bloody times as if she were incompetent. "I said I'd behave and I will."

"I already have six soldiers at the inn," he continued. "An additional two are ahead of us and two more are behind."

"You don't plan on hovering over me at the inn, do you?"

"No," he said, "but I will be close by. Don't look at me. Just pretend like I'm not there—that you don't even know me."

"The assassin could already be watching us." She scanned the buildings around them, wondering if there were any threats lurking in the shadows.

"Figure out what he wants and leave. I'll have him followed."

She stopped walking and folded her arms, waiting for Jarvik to realize she wasn't next to him.

He swung around to face her. "Why'd you stop?"

"Is everything okay with you?" she asked. She recalled his argument with Prince Odar earlier today, wishing he'd tell her about it. But he would never confide in her, especially since they weren't friends.

"Yes, why?" he asked, his eyebrows pulling together as if he was trying to solve some mystery.

"You haven't stopped talking since we left the castle,

and it's exhausting."

He shook his head. "I'm the exhausting one? I'm worried because if anything happens to you, it'll be my head on the line." He started walking again. "You're the exhausting one, not me."

She jogged to catch up to him. "Nothing is going to happen."

"You're about to meet a man you know nothing about except for the fact that he took down your guards and mine as if it were nothing. So yes, I'm very concerned."

"If I wanted a lecture, I would've brought Marek with me."

"There's a reason he's always lecturing you," Jarvik replied. "You're reckless, impossible, and infuriating."

The inn was just ahead. The last thing the two of them should be doing was arguing. "Make yourself scarce," she said, not wanting to be seen with the squire in case the assassin was watching.

He slowed his pace, allowing her to walk a few feet in front of him. The assassin hadn't specified a time to meet, he'd just said for her to come here alone tonight. Shoving open the wooden door, she entered the inn and headed straight to the tavern on the bottom floor of the establishment. Most of the tables were taken, and the bar was packed. She made her way through the patrons, searching for the assassin.

As she passed by a table where three burly men sat, one reached out, grabbing her around the waist. Before she even thought about what to do, her dagger was out and at the man's throat. "Release me," she demanded, not even blinking.

He let go, putting his hands up in surrender. "Apologies," he muttered. "Didn't mean no harm."

She slid her dagger back in place and continued searching the tavern. A serving wench carrying a tray filled with mugs of ale approached Allyssa. "I was told to give this to a girl wearing a long cape and hood." She held out a piece of paper.

Allyssa took it and read: *Room 205*.

*Blimey*. He wanted to meet in a private room, so there wouldn't be any witnesses. She stood there, trying to figure out the best course of action. The smart thing would be to turn around and leave—go home and tell her father what had happened. He could investigate further if he felt the need.

However, if she didn't meet with the assassin, then he'd find someone else who worked at the castle and proposition them. If he was sent to kill the royal family, she needed to know about it so she could protect her parents. Given the threat from Russek, she had to consider that the assassin might have been sent by King Drenton. Therefore, she really had little choice—she had to meet with him.

Out of the corner of her eye, she saw Jarvik enter and take a seat at a table in the back corner. Shoving the paper into her pocket, she casually strolled through the tavern, moving closer to the stairs. She had to be quick before the squire or one of his guards realized what she was about to do and stopped her. Nearing the steps, she bolted up them two at a time to the second floor. Room 205 was located at the end of the hallway.

Allyssa was about to knock on the door when it creaked open a few inches and she was yanked inside.

# Chapter Seventeen

Darkness surrounded Allyssa, and she couldn't see a thing. Fumbling for her knife, it wasn't there. She reached down for the one in her boot, but it was gone as well.

*Blasted.*

Someone banged on the wooden door to the room. "Open up!" a man shouted. She couldn't tell if it was Jarvik or not.

Fingers curled over her mouth, and she felt a body behind her. "Do exactly as I say," a man whispered in her ear.

She nodded.

"Get rid of whoever is out there. Now."

The assassin led her forward in the dark. The door opened a few inches, and Allyssa saw a man standing there. Behind him, she glimpsed Jarvik on the stairs, his face white and panic stricken.

"Can I help you?" she asked. The assassin squeezed her arms, and she had to stifle a yelp. She knew if she screamed, Jarvik would storm in there and rescue her.

"I'm looking for a barmaid," the man said, swaying on his feet as if drunk. His eyes however, were keen and alert. He had to be one of Jarvik's guards. "Long, blonde

hair, fine body, if you know what I mean."

"I'm sorry, I haven't seen her."

"My apologies," he slurred. He moved to the next door and banged on it.

The assassin closed the door and released her. There was a scuffling sound and a candle was lit, casting a soft glow over part of the room. The man stood in the corner, hidden in shadows. He wore a cape concealing his face and obscuring his body.

Allyssa shivered. "What do you want?" she asked.

"I've seen you entering and leaving the castle. I assume you work there?"

Thankfully, he hadn't figured out who she was yet. "Yes," she answered.

"I have a proposition for you," he said, speaking with an accent that indicated he wasn't from Emperion. He had a slight drawl, like the northerners did.

"What makes you think I'm interested?" she asked.

His head tilted to the side. "I know you've been coming and going from the castle. Don't you think it's safe to assume I've been watching you? Both you and your *friend*, Grevik."

She reached for her weapon that wasn't there.

The assassin *tsked*, shaking his head. "You can't harm me—not when your friend's life hangs in the balance."

If he harmed Grevik, she'd kill him.

"Sit," he ordered, pointing to the sagging bed cot.

"What do you want from me?" she asked as she took a seat.

"Information."

"What kind?" Allyssa tried to look scared—which wasn't hard since she was terrified.

He took one step toward her. The carefully planned,

threatening movement sent a chill down her spine, making her lean away from him.

"I need to know when the royal family will be out of the castle."

"So you can kill them?"

"That is not your concern."

"I don't have access to their daily schedules."

"You seem resourceful. I've watched you fight with thieves. I saw you a few moments ago threaten that patron downstairs. I have no doubt you'll be able to acquire the information."

She almost laughed. It was absurd. He was here to assassinate her. Only, he didn't know it. She sat there, violently shaking, unable to make herself stop. *Blimey.* She needed to gain control of herself before he saw through her disguise and realized who she was.

"Very well," she said. "Once I provide the information, will you release Grevik unharmed?" she asked, trying to determine if the assassin actually had him or not.

"I will release your friend," he said. "Meet me back here tomorrow night."

She noticed he never said *unharmed*. Her heart pounded, and a rushing sound filled her ears. Grevik couldn't be hurt—he just couldn't. "It may take me longer than a day to find out when the royal family will be out of the castle."

"Meet me back here tomorrow night, or your friend dies."

"Fine," she snapped, jumping to her feet and exiting the room. The low-life assassin had no idea who he was dealing with. If Grevik was harmed in any way, she would be sure the assassin paid dearly for his crimes.

# Cage of Deceit

She exited the tavern, knowing the assassin was somehow watching her. Searching the rooftops, she didn't see anything amiss. Pulling her cloak tight around her body, she hurried along the street.

Up ahead, a man stood near the entrance to the alley. It had to be Jarvik. Shaking her head infinitesimally, she indicated for him to stay away from her. Passing by as if she didn't know him, she went straight toward the castle to the army's private entrance, where she waited for Jarvik and his men to catch up. *Blimey.* What was she going to do? The assassin had Grevik.

"You're shaking," Jarvik said by way of greeting.

"I want to go inside. Now."

His men were suddenly there. As a group, they were granted entrance at the gate. The soldiers swayed on their feet, singing and hanging on to one another as if they were drunk. Allyssa tried to play along, but it was difficult with Grevik's life dependent upon her.

They went up the servants' stairwell and into the prince's chambers. Prince Odar wasn't in the sitting room. Jarvik ordered the soldiers to go to their bedchambers, and they all obliged. Going over to the fireplace, the squire threw a few more logs onto the fire, warming up the room. Allyssa sat on the ground next to the hearth, staring at the flames, trying to figure out what to do.

Jarvik sat next to her. "Tell me everything," he gently said.

She hesitated, remembering the conversation she'd overheard between the squire and the prince. However, Allyssa needed help in order to save her friend, and she had no doubt Jarvik was more than qualified to concoct a way to undermine the assassin. She quickly explained the note the serving wench had given her, what happened when she went in the room, and everything the assassin said.

"I think we should tell your father what's going on."

She'd been wondering the same thing, too. However, her father's priority would be protecting Rema and Allyssa, not saving Grevik's life. "Before we say anything, I'd like to figure out who sent the assassin." That would give her time to rescue Grevik.

"Can't we assume it was the king of Russek?" Jarvik asked.

She had been considering that option while walking back to the castle. "I don't think it is." Wrapping her arms around her legs, she rested her head on her knees. "King Drenton wants war. There's no way he'd send a lone assassin here now. He would've sent one before he mobilized his soldiers." The fire crackled in the hearth.

"You know, you're not at all what I thought you'd be," Jarvik said, leaning back on his hands and stretching out his legs. The glow from the fire radiated off the squire's face, softening his features.

"I should be getting back to my bedchamber," Allyssa said, jumping to her feet. "I need to figure out how to help Grevik." Her friend was in mortal danger while she was safe inside a castle, talking to a man she thought she hated.

Jarvik's eyebrows drew together. "Please don't yell at me for asking, because I'm honestly curious, what is your relationship with Grevik?" He stood next to her, waiting for an answer.

She debated telling him. After all, last time, he'd accused her of having an affair. Looking into his eyes,

her chest tightened—she didn't see hatred or loathing there. "He's my best friend," she admitted. "We've been friends for years. He's a commoner who only learned my identity a few days ago, and I fear he won't forgive me for lying to him."

"Are there any romantic feelings between you two?"

"No. We've been meeting at night, tracking down criminals together. It's a long story." Her eyes filled with tears. "I have to save him."

Jarvik rubbed his face. "Grevik knows you're the crown princess?" She nodded. "Do you think he'll keep that information to himself? Even if being tortured?"

Tears slid down her face. Grevik was a good fighter, but he was no match for the assassin. If her friend was being tortured because of her, she'd never forgive herself for dragging him into this mess. "He knows to keep my identity a secret," she said, "but I can't be absolutely certain he'll be able to." She wiped the tears from her cheeks.

"A couple of my men are taking rooms at the inn. If the assassin is keeping Grevik there, we'll find him."

"I have a feeling the inn was just a meeting place."

"I also have several men stationed outside watching the exits. When the assassin leaves, my men will follow him. We will find your friend."

"I'm supposed to meet the assassin again tomorrow night. What am I going to do?"

Jarvik put his hand on her lower back, leading her to the door. "Go to sleep. I'll come up with a plan. I promise."

"Thank you." She squeezed his hand, letting him know how much she appreciated his help.

She left Prince Odar's rooms, pulling her cloak tightly around her body so no one would see her clothing underneath. As the royal guards escorted Allyssa to her bedchamber, she felt strangely comforted that she was working with Jarvik to save her friend.

WALKING TO THE MEETING ROOM, ALLYSSA WAS suddenly overwhelmed with panic. Changing directions, she ran to the library and hid in the alcove, closing the curtains so no one could see her. Her heart beat erratically in her chest.

Mayra slid inside after her. "Marek wants to know what's going on," she said.

"I can't breathe," Allyssa uttered.

"I'll fetch a healer." She turned to leave.

"Please don't." Allyssa grabbed her necklace, holding the wooden ring tightly. "I just need a moment."

"Are you upset because of the marriage?" her friend asked, taking a seat.

Leaning against the table, Allyssa took several deep breaths. "I'm about to sign a marriage contract to a man I barely know, and ... and ... Jarvik ... he ... I ... ."

"What are you saying?" Mayra asked. "If you hate Jarvik so much, you can have him reassigned. You mustn't worry about that."

"That's the problem," Allyssa whispered. "I've grown rather fond of the squire."

Mayra's eyes widened in shock, and she bit her bottom lip. "You like him?"

"Only as a friend," Allyssa confided.

"Then what's the problem?"

She sighed. "I'm not as strong as I thought I was."

"I'm not sure I'm following you. Are we still talking

about the squire?"

"I need to be stronger to do this."

"That's not true. You're incredibly confident and capable of ruling a kingdom."

"I'm not," Allyssa insisted. "I don't know if I can lead the kingdom, marry Odar, and protect my people. Right now, I can't even help my friend Grevik, who is in trouble. I wish I was stronger."

"I don't think I've ever seen you so emotional," Mayra commented. "Maybe you're just overwhelmed by everything. We're all under a tremendous amount of stress with the impending war."

"I have this awful feeling everything rests on my shoulders—that I am responsible for the fate of Emperion."

Mayra hugged her friend. "I'm glad my fate is in your hands," she whispered, "because you're the strongest person I know."

Someone cleared his throat on the other side of the curtains. "Your Highness," Marek said. "We need to go to the meeting. Everyone is waiting for you."

Mayra released her. "You can do this," she said. "I'll be close by if you need me."

"Thank you."

Allyssa glided into the room. Only two members from the Legion were present at the table, her parents sitting across from them. There was one empty chair at the end of the square table, so Allyssa quickly took her seat. Directly across from her sat Prince Odar and his squire. Jarvik's eyes met hers for a brief second, and she quickly looked away. What was he doing there? Why did her breath catch just by looking at him? He wasn't even that handsome. Sure, he was interesting with his black hair, brown eyes, and freckles covering his nose. *Blimey.* He was staring right at her with that bloody expression of his that she couldn't decipher.

"Let's begin," Darmik said. "Jarvik will receive a copy of the executed contract to deliver to the king and queen of Fren. Two members of the Legion will also retain a copy."

The princess stared at the stack of papers on the table. There had to be over a hundred pages. She knew there were a lot of details to work out regarding their armies, but a hundred pages seemed a bit much.

"Empress Rema, the Legion, and Jarvik have already read the contract. Therefore, we will go quickly through it. I'll highlight a few points, and Princess Allyssa and Prince Odar will sign each and every page."

Allyssa sat there, pretending to be calm and serene when inside she was a nervous, screaming wreck. As soon as the contract was signed, the marriage could take place.

Darmik began reading. The first page addressed the issue of how Allyssa would ascend to the Emperion throne at the age of thirty, becoming the empress, and Rema and Darmik would step down. However, if Rema and Darmik died before Allyssa turned thirty, Allyssa would ascend to the throne at that time. Whenever she took the throne, so would Odar.

The next section of the contract discussed the fact that Odar and Allyssa would also be the crown heirs of Fren. Upon the death of the king and queen, they would take the throne, and Prince Odar would choose a regent to rule in his place.

It had been decided that the marriage ceremony would take place in two days. Afterwards, Fren and Emperion's armies would join forces, officially declaring war on Russek. Emperion would seize control over the three kingdoms to the north, unifying all their armies.

Lastly, the contract touched on the logistics of bringing Fren and Emperion together when separated by another kingdom. Luckily, Rema had plenty of advice on this matter since Emperion ruled over Greenwood Island, a journey two weeks by boat.

Allyssa turned to the last page and found the spot for her final signature. It was next to the place for Prince Odar's signature and above a spot for a witness to sign. By signing this page, the terms were officially agreed upon and all that was left to take place was the marriage ceremony in two days. Allyssa's hand shook as she picked up the quill, placing the tip of it to the line she was supposed to sign on.

"Honey," Rema gently said, garnering her daughter's attention. "You don't have to do anything you don't want to." She smiled reassuringly at Allyssa. "The choice is yours."

"We need this," Allyssa said. "It's what's best for Emperion. It is my choice, and I choose to help."

She signed the contract and set the quill down.

Looking up, she found Jarvik staring at her, his eyes cold and obstinate. She sat up a little straighter. She was the princess of Emperion, she loved her kingdom, and she would yield to no one.

Darmik reached for the signed contract and handed it to Prince Odar. Jarvik rested his hand upon the prince's arm, indicating for him to withhold his signature until the squire was done reviewing it.

"Do you mind if I sign as the official witness?" Jarvik asked her parents.

"By all means," Rema said. "We would be honored."

Jarvik nodded and signed the contract. When he was done, he pushed it toward Prince Odar, who took the quill and signed.

# Chapter Eighteen

Allyssa entered the stables and noticed the squire in one of the stalls, saddling Prince Odar's mare. Glancing around, she didn't see the prince anywhere.

"I need to talk to you," Jarvik said, peering over his shoulder. "It's important."

"I'm going riding with the prince."

"I know." He exited the stall. "This will only take a minute of your time." He wiped his hands on his pants. "Why did you decide to sign the contract?"

She hadn't expected him to ask her that. "For the same reason Prince Odar did—for the good of my kingdom."

"So you understand that rulers have to make decisions and do things that are in the best interest of their kingdom?" He sat down on the bench outside the stall, patting the spot next to him.

"Of course. What are you trying to tell me?" she asked, sitting down next to him.

"You don't really know Prince Odar."

"I realize that. He knows nothing of me either."

"You need to understand that some things have happened to him in the past to make him extra cautious." He picked up the horse brush lying on the bench and started fidgeting with it. "He wants to tell you the truth, but he's not sure how. When he finally gains the confidence to do so, please listen to him and try to understand why he did what he did." Jarvik was staring at the brush while he talked, not looking at her.

"You're scaring me," she said.

"You told me you hoped your friend Grevik understood why you lied to him and that he forgave you." He peeked up at her.

"What has Prince Odar done?" Allyssa demanded, afraid she'd just signed the marriage contract and was about to tie herself to a man who had done something horrendous.

"He'll tell you when he's ready." He set the brush down and rubbed his hands on his pants again. "Did you know the prince was previously engaged?" Jarvik asked.

"Yes. He said the girl was only after his title."

The squire nodded. "She wanted to unite her kingdom with Fren's."

Much like Allyssa was doing, only she didn't pretend to love the prince. "Who was the girl?"

"King Drenton of Russek recently married a woman," Jarvik began. Allyssa had heard rumors the king remarried, but she didn't know any details beyond that. "The story goes that a beautiful woman showed up at the Russek court with her elderly mother and her gorgeous daughter. The king was quite taken with the woman, and they married a short time later. Her daughter was officially crowned Princess Shelene. The princess visited our court, seeking to marry Prince Odar and align our two kingdoms."

Allyssa recalled overhearing Prince Odar and Jarvik talking that day in the corridor. The prince had

mentioned the name Shelene. Rage started to boil inside of her. "What are you saying?" she asked. "That Princess Shelene was only using Prince Odar to gain access to Fren's army?"

"Yes." Jarvik swallowed and peered at her. "When he discovered the plot to seize control of our army in order to invade Emperion, he broke off the engagement." The squire reached out and took hold of Allyssa's hand between his two strong, calloused ones.

The prince must have been hurt from Shelene's betrayal. Did he only come to Emperion with the intention to marry Allyssa to get back at Russek? She opened her mouth to ask when Jarvik squeezed her hand.

"There's more." His eyes looked imploringly at her. "Please listen to all I have to say before you become upset."

She nodded, hoping to keep her temper reined in.

"Because of Prince Odar's lack of judgment when it came to Princess Shelene, the king and queen of Fren won't condone a marriage treaty between Fren and Emperion unless they meet you. They want to make sure your intentions are noble and your word good." He leaned slightly away from Allyssa, as if waiting for her to explode.

"We signed the marriage contract today," she said. "Prince Odar and I are supposed to marry in *two days*."

"Yes, that's why I'm telling you the marriage can't take place yet. You must travel to Fren to meet the king and queen."

Utter shock rolled through her. "My parents are going to kill Prince Odar." She tried to stand, but the squire kept hold of her. "Our armies can't join forces until we're married," she said furiously.

"It'll take your soldiers several weeks to reach

Russek's borders. There's time to travel to Fren. You can even marry there if need be."

Balling her free hand into a fist, she asked, "Why didn't Prince Odar say anything sooner?"

"I'm not sure," Jarvik mumbled. "Perhaps he was still trying to determine your worth."

"Oh, so now I'm worthy?" she shouted.

Jarvik stared at her, his eyes intense. "Yes," he whispered. "I'm sorry I didn't tell you sooner."

Her parents were going to be furious. Russek was ready to slaughter her family, and she was doing all she could to keep her kingdom safe. Prince Odar should have disclosed this information before now.

"Allyssa," the squire said, still holding her hand. "When we came here, we were sure you were just like all the other courtiers we'd met. I never realized you'd be—"

"Ready for our ride?" Prince Odar asked, approaching them, his eyes on Jarvik and Allyssa's latched hands.

Yanking her fingers out of Jarvik's grip, she abruptly stood. "Yes."

The prince held a small basket, which he took to his horse and slid inside the saddlebag.

Turning to face the squire, Allyssa said, "I suggest you speak to my father immediately. When I return, I'll discuss the matter with him."

"Follow me," Allyssa said to the prince as they rode into the woods. The leaves on the trees softly rustled in the light breeze. She breathed in the warm air, reveling in the freedom of being outside the castle. A handful of the prince's soldiers, along with her usual guards, rode

close behind them.

Allyssa steered her horse up a small rise between the towering trees. When she reached the river that ran down past the city, she followed it upstream for about a mile until she came to a small, rocky hill. Most of the boulders were covered with soft, green moss and various plants grew between the rocks where dirt had deposited.

Allyssa dismounted and handed her reins to one of the guards, Prince Odar doing the same.

"I thought we could rest here," she said.

One of the guards spread a blanket out on the ground while the rest set up a perimeter about fifteen feet away.

"Wow," Prince Odar exclaimed as he pulled out a small basket from his saddlebag. He sat on the blanket. "It's beautiful here."

"We need to talk," Allyssa said as she sat on the blanket next to him.

"I gathered that." Prince Odar set the basket between them. "What did my squire say to you?"

"He told me about how I have to go to Fren to seek the king and queen's approval before we can marry." She sat there, staring at the trees, wondering if Jarvik was speaking to her father at this very moment. "My parents are going to be livid the marriage can't take place as planned."

"Are you mad?" Odar asked, fidgeting with the handle on the basket.

She sighed. "I understand why your parents want to meet me before we wed. Jarvik explained what happened in the past with Princess Shelene, and I can see why they are cautious. I just wished you'd been honest with me from the start."

He didn't respond.

Allyssa peeked at him. "Did the princess ever say why Russek wanted to invade Emperion?"

Prince Odar scratched his head. "No. But after the marriage negotiations were severed, she started screaming that she would have her revenge—just like her mother." He lifted the basket on top of his lap. "Did Jarvik tell you why she wanted to marry me?"

"He said she wanted to gain control of Fren's army."

"Yes, and she planned on joining Fren's soldiers with Russek's in order to conquer Emperion."

"Which Russek is doing anyway," Allyssa said, "even without your soldiers."

"Maybe that's why Russek invaded Melenia—to gain more soldiers."

Allyssa feared they were overlooking something. After all these years, Russek wouldn't suddenly decide to wage war on Emperion for no reason.

"Enough about politics," Prince Odar said, opening the lid of the basket. "I have something for you."

It irritated her that every time she tried discussing their countries and things that mattered, he changed the subject. Did he not care? Did Jarvik handle these issues for him?

Odar withdrew a pastry. "This is for you."

It was her favorite—an apple tart flipped upside down, covered with gooey butter and sugar. "You remembered," she said, taking a bite. It was utterly delicious. "Thank you."

As they sat there, eating in comfortable silence, her thoughts drifted to Grevik. Where was he and what was he enduring right now at the hands of the assassin? When she returned to the castle, she needed to find Jarvik to see if he'd come up with a plan to save her friend yet. As soon

as Grevik was rescued, she could go to Fren to seek the king and queen's approval and then save Emperion.

"You seem overly distracted," Odar said, patting her leg.

"I'm sorry," she replied. "There's a lot on my mind." She smiled at him.

He finished eating his pastry, licking his fingers clean.

"Do you have any concerns about ruling the kingdom with me?" she asked. She questioned his ability to do so effectively. At least they had a few years until they became emperor and empress—unless something happened to her parents. She couldn't even think about that.

"I can easily navigate through the court," he said, smirking. "I've never had a problem charming courtiers." He flashed a half grin at her.

Allyssa had no doubt the ladies of her court would fawn all over him. She'd have to use that to her advantage.

"As far as politics are concerned," he said, his smile gone, "you'll have to guide me. It will take some time to get a feel for how things are done here in Emperion." He reached in the basket and withdrew another pastry, handing it to her.

"No, thank you," she said, and he put it away.

Mulling over his answer, she liked the fact that since he wasn't overly opinionated, it would be easy to mold him into the type of ruler she wanted him to be. However, when she was truly torn on an issue, he wouldn't be able to offer her steadfast advice. At least her mother and father would continue to guide and support her.

As she sat there next to Odar, she felt as if something was missing. Even though he was handsome, well mannered, and friendly, there wasn't a connection between them. With Grevik, she immediately knew she could tell him any and everything. They shared common goals and interests. The same was true with Madelin, Marek, and Mayra. They'd been friends since they were children, and she trusted them implicitly.

How was she going to marry Prince Odar and share a bed with him? As a child, she had always imagined falling in love and having an intense desire to be with that person. Right now, she didn't even want to travel to Fren with the prince. What would they talk about?

"Would you like to ride further upstream and see what we find?" Prince Odar asked.

"No, thank you. I need to return to the castle." She wanted to see how her father took the news of her not being able to marry Odar until she traveled to Fren to meet his parents.

She stood and mounted her horse. *Deep breaths.* Her relationship with the prince would work—it would just take some time for their friendship to develop. Right now, she had more important matters at hand than dealing with Odar, like facing her parents and saving Grevik.

Nearing the stables, Allyssa saw her father blocking the alley doors. She slowed her horse and dismounted, handing the reins to the stable-hand who came running out. Darmik didn't even glance her way—his focus was solely on the prince.

Odar swung his leg over and jumped off his horse. "Your Majesty," he said.

"We need to talk," Darmik said, his voice hard. "Come with me, now." He turned and stalked away.

# Cage of Deceit

"Thank you for the ride," Odar said softly to Allyssa before hurrying after the emperor.

Curious as to what would happen now that the marriage contract was signed but the ceremony couldn't take place until she went to Fren, she hastily followed them along the stone path leading to the castle.

Her father swung around to face her. "I'm going to speak privately with the prince," he said in a clipped tone. "Jarvik is waiting in the training room for you." He grabbed Odar by the arm and dragged him down the path.

# Chapter Nineteen

Allyssa entered the training room. She assumed Jarvik wanted to work with her to ensure she was prepared for her meeting with the assassin tonight.

"I hope you have a solid plan," she said.

Jarvik was sitting on the ground, stretching. "Have a nice ride?" he asked, a bit of hostility to his voice. He had on plain pants and a loose shirt. His hair was tousled, making him look handsome in a rugged sort of way. *Bloody hell.* Her face warmed. She couldn't afford to think of him that way. As he stood up, she couldn't help but think of how his beauty shone in a different way from Odar's. While the prince's was on the outside for all to see, the squire's was hidden deep inside of him.

"You're staring at me," Jarvik stated. "Is something wrong?"

Allyssa shook her head, tongue-tied for once.

"Since the assassin managed to capture your friend, I want to go over some basics with you to ensure you're not kidnapped as well."

"I know how to fight," she replied.

"Yes, but I'll feel better if we go over a few things."

She shrugged. "Okay."

"We'll focus on hand-to-hand combat first," he said,

placing his hands on his hips. "Most likely, the assassin will be armed and you won't, so you'll be at a disadvantage."

"How long have you been here?" Allyssa asked. Jarvik had a sheen of sweat covering his forehead.

"Not long," he answered. "I've just been punching the practice dummy over there."

"Why?"

His eyes flickered to hers and then away. "It helps me think." He rubbed his hands over his face. "Let's get to work."

"Very well," she said, pulling her hair back and quickly braiding it.

The setting sun shone through the windows, casting a soft light on Jarvik. "Let's pretend the assassin comes up behind you, like this," he said, putting his arm around her neck and placing his other hand on her hip. "What would you do?"

Allyssa automatically raised her hands to try and pry his arm off her neck.

"Focus," Jarvik said. "He'll be taller and stronger than you. You'll have to outsmart him."

Closing her eyes, she took a deep breath and thought over everything her father and Marek had taught her. She was unarmed and would have to fight her way out of this. Since Jarvik's left hand was on her left hip, she moved her body to the right and swung her left arm down to his groin. As soon as he released her, she spun around and rammed her knee into his stomach.

"Excellent," Jarvik said, his voice high pitched from the impact. She hadn't meant to hit him that hard. "Now if he comes at you head on," he said, "you'll need to do something different."

He wrapped his hands around her neck, gently

touching her with his calloused fingers. Their eyes locked, and Allyssa's breath caught. He was so close.

"In this case," she softly said, swallowing, "I'd raise my hands and do this." She lifted her arms between his and then swung outwards, knocking his hands away from her neck.

He immediately reached forward and grabbed her upper arms, holding them tightly.

She'd never felt self-conscious working with Marek, so why was she embarrassed with Jarvik? Why was she so acutely aware of where his hands were? She felt her face warm and prayed he didn't notice her reaction to him. She wasn't a harlot; she was the crown princess and needed to act like it.

"Now what are you going to do?" he asked, his eyes still on hers.

Holding her head high, she attempted to regain her confidence and composure. Reaching forward, Allyssa grabbed Jarvik's hips, holding him in place while she kneed him in the groin.

"Keep ramming your knee into him until he lets go," Jarvik said. "Then kick his head, if you can."

"I know how to properly kick."

"You need to hit him hard enough to knock him out, without him grabbing your leg or foot. It needs to be clean and quick."

"I can do that," she said.

"After you've disabled him, run as fast as you can. You have to assume he'll be after you again after thirty seconds or so."

"What if he has me locked in the room?" she asked.

"After we're done practicing here, I'll teach you how to pick a lock."

Allyssa laughed. "You are a man of many talents."
"You have no idea."

When Allyssa returned to the Royal Chambers, her father and Neco were speaking to Marek, along with a few members of her personal guard in the sitting room.

"What's going on?" she asked.

"Go to your bedchamber," Darmik ordered. "Marek will be with you shortly."

Her father must still be furious with Prince Odar. She opened her doors and found her ladies-in-waiting standing by the windows, looking outside. Allyssa rushed over to see what they were doing.

In the courtyard below, at least a hundred soldiers stood at attention. A chill ran down Allyssa's spine. Were these men preparing to leave to defend Emperion's border? Would Marek be joining them?

Mayra wrapped her arm around Allyssa. "Have you ever seen so many fine-looking young men?" she asked.

Madelin chuckled and moved away from the window. "You can admire the soldiers all you want," she said. "I've found my prince." She went into the dressing closet. "Do you care what you wear for dinner?" she asked Allyssa.

"No," Allyssa replied, wishing dinner was already over so she and Jarvik could be on their way to the inn.

"Why are you all sweaty?" Mayra asked, scrunching up her nose.

"I was sparring with Jarvik," she answered.

The doors flew open and Marek stepped inside, his face flushed and eyes alight. "Your Highness," he said, bowing. "I must speak with you alone."

She dismissed her ladies-in-waiting, and Marek came to stand before her. "I heard about Prince Odar not being able to wed you until you travel to Fren and receive the king and queen's approval."

"I assume our fathers are upset?"

"They're livid. They claim the prince deceived them."

She wondered if her father was having second thoughts about the union now. However, the contract was signed and she wasn't sure it could be broken.

Marek continued, "Prince Odar insists it had to be done to determine Emperion's true intentions."

That was what Jarvik had told her as well. "Does my father approve of me traveling to Fren with war on the horizon?"

"He says there are no other options and you must go. The emperor wants it done as soon as possible so the marriage ceremony can take place." Marek knelt on the ground in front of her. "My father doesn't want me to fight in the war. Your father specifically asked me to remain by your side during your journey to Fren. I'm to coordinate a security team with Jarvik for you and the prince."

Knowing how much fighting in the war meant to Marek, Allyssa said, "I won't make you stay if you don't want to." She reached for his hands, clasping them tightly. "If fighting is what you desire, especially alongside your father, I'll make it happen. The choice is yours."

Kneeling on the ground, he stared up at her. "You'd do that for me?"

"Yes, because I value your friendship."

He closed his eyes for a minute, his head bent down. When he reopened them, he said, "As much as I want to go, I know you need me. I will stay and guard you."

Marek withdrew his right hand from hers and placed his fist over his heart—the symbol of loyalty, friendship, and honor.

A sense of pride and pure relief filled her. She hadn't realized how much she wanted him at her side until she told him he could go. There was a knock on the door, and Jarvik came into her room. He froze when he saw Marek on his knees before Allyssa, their hands clasped together.

"I'm sorry," the squire stuttered. "I didn't mean to interrupt."

"You're not," Allyssa quickly replied. Releasing Marek's hand, she said, "Thank you for your loyalty. I'm glad you'll be staying. However, if you ever change your mind, please don't hesitate to tell me."

Marek stood. "Thank you, Your Highness."

"Besides," she smiled, "I'm sure Madelin would hate to see you go."

The corners of Marek's lips rose and his face reddened. "Yes," he said. "We're officially courting now."

"So I heard," Allyssa replied, unable to suppress a smile. Madelin had told her all the details yesterday when she was doing Allyssa's hair.

"If you'll excuse me, Your Highness. I have a few things to discuss with my father." Marek turned and left, leaving her alone with Jarvik.

"Is something the matter?" she asked, wondering why he'd come to her room. She still needed to bathe and change out of her sweaty clothing. Suddenly embarrassed by her appearance, she sat on one of the chairs, trying to act like a proper princess, even though she didn't look or feel like one.

Jarvik moved to the fireplace, his back to her, not uttering a single word. He stood there, still as a statue.

She wished he'd turn around so she could see his face. He hadn't changed either, although his shirt was now tucked in.

"Did you need something?" she asked.

He shook his head. "I wanted to talk to you—to tell you something. Although, now is not the time." Allyssa was about to insist he tell her anyway when he continued, "Are you ready for your meeting with the assassin tonight?"

She'd gone over everything in her head a hundred times. "Yes. I'll do what needs to be done to ensure my friend's safety."

He turned around to face her. "I'm worried about you coming to the prince's rooms so late at night again. It isn't proper."

So far none of her guards had said a word or questioned her behavior. However, she didn't want rumors to start either. "I'll use my laundry chute. You can meet me in the laundry room. We'll leave from there."

With the fire burning behind him, a soft glow surrounded Jarvik, making his face appear dark. "Very well," he murmured.

The wind howled outside. "You should know I've assigned some of my men to join your guard."

"Why would you do that?" Marek wouldn't appreciate Fren soldiers stepping into his domain.

"I want my men to start working with your soldiers since they'll be traveling together. They need to be familiar with one another."

"You seem well versed with managing an army and military strategies." More so than what a squire should. She wondered what position his father held at court.

"I grew up with the prince," he explained. "We've taken the same classes, learned how to fight under the

same instructors." She couldn't be sure with the heat of the fire, but Jarvik's ears appeared exceptionally red.

"You seem to excel."

"What do you mean?" he asked.

"Simply that you're able to take charge and see things through."

"What are you implying?"

"I haven't seen the same... commitment from the prince. I wonder how effective he is as a ruler." Perhaps the only reason the prince had a reputation for being a competent and fair leader was because Jarvik was at his side helping him.

"I think you'll be surprised once you get to know him," the squire said, turning back to face the fire. "Sometimes appearances can be deceiving. He isn't the court fop you think he is."

"I hope not," she replied. "Because I need a strong man by my side, not some pretty face."

# Chapter Twenty

Walking briskly along the street next to Jarvik, Allyssa huddled in her cloak, trying to stay warm against the frigid air. Even though it wasn't raining, the wind whipped between the buildings, making her eyes water and her nose run.

The squire hadn't spoken since they left the castle. His shoulders were stiffer than normal, and his eyes darted to every person they passed.

Allyssa shivered. If all went well, she would meet with the assassin, tell him her information, and he'd release Grevik. She had wanted to go and see his mother, to let her know she was trying to save her son. However, Jarvik wouldn't let her. After he verified Grevik was indeed missing, he'd sent one of his men to speak with Grevik's mother about his disappearance.

"Are you sure you want to do this?" Jarvik asked. "I can send my men in to apprehend the assassin. We can interrogate him until he reveals where your friend is."

"The last time we met the assassin, I seem to recall him rendering your men unconscious in less than a minute."

"We're better prepared this time," he said.

"I want to continue with our original plan," she

replied. The squire nodded, like he had expected her to say that. "Can I ask you something?"

"You can ask me anything," he said.

"Why are you helping me?" Their relationship had progressed from pure hatred, to a level of tolerance, and now to respect. However, Allyssa didn't know if Jarvik thought of her as a friend, ally, or colleague. She wasn't certain what she considered him—none of those felt quite right.

"I'm here because if I was in your situation, and my friend had been kidnapped, I'd want all the help I could get to save him."

His answer surprised her, and she couldn't help but admire his loyalty. As annoying as Jarvik could be sometimes, she was glad he was there with her. It was nice having someone to collaborate with, especially someone as sharp as Jarvik. *Blimey*. Did she actually think he was intelligent?

"In case I haven't told you," she said, "thank you for your help."

He stopped and turned to face her. "I must have heard you wrong. Did you just thank me?"

The wind thrashed against her cloak, tangling it around her legs. "Yes," she said. "I did."

He laughed, surprising her. The simple act transformed his face, making him look younger and ... *blasted*, he was alluring. She stiffened, suddenly unsure how to act around him.

His smile faded and he placed his arms on her shoulders, gazing into her face. "We should stop walking together, just as a precaution," he said, his voice gruff.

Nodding, she whispered, "Are your men in position?"

"Yes." She peered down at his fingers, waiting for

him to release her. "Be careful," he said. "Remember what we talked about—what questions to ask and how to act."

"I will." She bit her lip, needing to clear her head. An assassin who held her friend captive awaited her. All of her energy and focus needed to be on Grevik.

Jarvik hesitated and then let go of her shoulders.

Not knowing what else to say, Allyssa walked away and rounded the corner, the inn in sight. She slouched, trying to act like a commoner, and entered the inn. She'd played this part often enough that she shouldn't have been nervous. However, after working with Jarvik this afternoon and having him point out every little thing she did wrong, she was suddenly hyper aware of every movement she made. Allyssa suspected the assassin would be scrutinizing every detail, and under no circumstance could she reveal her true identity.

Once inside the tavern, she headed upstairs and knocked on the wooden door to room 205. It creaked open enough for her to slip inside the dark room. Her heart beat frantically, knowing the assassin was near and Grevik's life depended upon her.

The door clicked shut, and silence greeted her. Hands deftly slid over her body, removing her weapons. The assassin tugged a blanket off the oil lamp, illuminating the small room. They stood facing one another, both hidden under black cloaks.

The assassin folded his arms. "Well?" he demanded.

"I have information," she replied.

"And?"

Remembering what Jarvik told her, she said, "I won't tell you unless I know my friend is safe." Making demands was dangerous. With a flick of his wrist, he could kill her. Holding her breath, she waited for his response.

"If your information is of value, I'll take you to your friend. If it isn't, you can watch me slice his throat."

Jarvik had warned her this might happen. Taking a few deep breaths, she attempted to remain calm and not answer right away. She didn't want the assassin to know she'd do anything to save Grevik.

After counting to twenty like Jarvik had suggested, she said, "I overheard the empress talking to the princess. They are going to the local shelter to feed the poor."

"When?"

"In four days."

"Is the emperor going with them?"

"They didn't say if he was going."

The assassin nodded. "I deem your information worthy. I will allow you to see your friend."

Her shoulders relaxed. Now all that had to happen was for Jarvik and his men to follow the assassin as he took her to Grevik. Then they'd storm in, killing the assassin while she rescued her friend.

"Obviously, he isn't here. I'll need to take you to where I'm keeping him." He moved to the corner of the room. "You don't have a problem being blindfolded, do you?"

Allyssa had expected him to take her somewhere else, but she hadn't anticipated being blindfolded. When they left the building, patrons would notice such a thing. Which meant they weren't leaving out the front door.

"Of course I do," she said, trying to control her temper. "You're an assassin here to kill the royal family and you've kidnapped my friend." She needed to watch her language—make sure she didn't speak too formally. "I'll go with you, but there's no need to cover my eyes."

He laughed, the sound harsh and menacing. "I

haven't managed to stay alive so long by being stupid. If you want to see your friend, you'll go blindfolded. It's up to you."

*Blimey.* Her heart pounded in her chest. What should she do? She needed to know that Grevik was alive and well. Jarvik had told her he had men watching all the exits, so even if she went out the side, one of the Fren soldiers would notice and follow. Just because she wouldn't be able to see didn't mean Jarvik wouldn't.

"Very well," she said. "After I visit my friend, you'll release me?"

He nodded. "I'll bring you back to this inn."

If Marek were here, he'd be screaming at her not to go anywhere with an assassin. He'd say that this was a terrible idea and she shouldn't risk her life. Jarvik, on the other hand, had sparred with her and taught her how to pick a lock in order to prepare her for this. He understood that her friendship with Grevik wasn't something she could easily dismiss. Grevik was in this mess because of her, and she planned to make sure he was freed and returned safely to his mother. Allyssa remembered how devastated Grevik's mum had been when his father was murdered. She knew his mother would never be able to handle the death of her only child.

The assassin ripped off a strip of fabric from the blanket on the cot. He came up behind Allyssa, and she removed her hood. The assassin slid the fabric around her eyes and secured it at the back of her head.

"Let's go," he said as he wrapped his arm around her waist, making her jump.

The door was to her left. However, he led her in the opposite direction. There weren't any other exits in the room, nor were there any windows. She lifted her hands to remove the blindfold, and he pinned her arms down.

"Leave it alone," he ordered.

"Where are we going?" she demanded.

"If I wanted you to know, you wouldn't be blindfolded."

The sound of wood creaking echoed through the room. Was the assassin removing some floorboards? He shoved her down into something.

"You'll need to crawl," he said. "And keep your head down."

Reaching out, she felt wood right above her. The sound of clanking mugs and people talking was directly below her. She had to be in between the ceiling of the first level and the floor of the second level. This must be how the assassin was entering and exiting the inn without Jarvik's men knowing.

Pulling herself along in the cramped space, Allyssa felt a splinter dig into her palm.

"Stop," the assassin said. It sounded as if a wooden door creaked open, and then cool air brushed past her skin. "Turn around and lower your feet until you hit a ladder. Then climb down."

Allyssa did as he said, sliding outside the opened door on the side of the building, praying she didn't fall. She lowered her legs, fumbling for the first rung of the ladder. Her foot connected with it, and she started climbing down to the street.

When she reached solid ground, the assassin pulled her hood lower over her face, probably making sure no one on the street would see her blindfold. Linking his arm with hers, they started walking. It took some getting used to—being led along the streets, unable to see. She tried memorizing each turn, but he took so many that she couldn't keep track. At times, it seemed as if they walked around the same block multiple times to ensure she didn't have her bearings. To keep from losing her temper and screaming, she kept picturing Grevik's face. It was enough to keep her going.

After a good twenty minutes, they climbed a flight of stairs. A door clicked open, and the assassin led her a couple of paces forward. The door shut behind them, and her blindfold was quickly removed. In the middle of the small, dimly lit, empty room, Grevik sat tied to a chair.

Running over, she dropped to her knees before him. "Are you all right?"

He slowly lifted his head, looking at her. She gasped. Grevik's face was covered with bruises, his right eye was swollen shut, and his breathing was labored, indicating he had a damaged lung.

"What did you do to him?" she demanded, swinging around to face the assassin.

"I asked him a few questions," he said.

Rage and hatred consumed her—she wanted to kill the assassin for hurting her friend. However, she couldn't attack him until Jarvik and his men arrived—if they came at all. They were probably still back at the inn, having no idea she'd left with the assassin. Still, she decided to give them a few minutes before she tried to render the assassin unconscious long enough to free Grevik.

"I'm so sorry," she said to her friend.

"This isn't your fault."

Knowing he'd been interrogated, she wondered if the assassin knew her true identity. Perhaps this had been an elaborate plot to isolate her. She shivered and mouthed, "Does he know?"

Grevik muttered, "No."

If Jarvik and his men had followed her, they would

be in here by now. Help wasn't coming.

"Don't worry about me," Grevik said. "Take care of yourself."

She opened her mouth to argue, but Grevik silenced her with his stare. "Leave," he said. "Before this sadistic madman hurts you."

Tears formed in her eyes. She couldn't leave him there—she had to try to fight the assassin. Putting her hands on either side of Grevik's dear face, she whispered, "I'll find a way to rescue you. I promise." Allyssa stood and kissed the top of his head.

"This reminds me of that time we caught those snake dealers," Grevik said, his head hanging.

They never caught any snake dealers. It had to be some sort of clue. "Yes, it does," she said, forcing a laugh.

"Time to go," the assassin said. Holding the blindfold, he moved closer to her to put it on.

When he was directly behind her, she spun around and kneed him in the groin. At the same time, she swung her hand toward his head. The assassin caught her wrist midair, squeezing it tight.

"That was a very foolish thing to do," he chided her, not even winded from her hit.

Allyssa went to kick him again. He blocked her leg and backhanded her across the face hard enough to hurt, but not to leave a mark. The assassin whipped out a dagger and pointed it at Grevik.

"Please no," she said, shaking her head.

"Touch me again, and I'll kill him."

Grevik was struggling against his binds, trying to wiggle free, his eyes wide with horror.

"Stand still." The assassin once again came up behind her. He quickly tied the blindfold around her head, and then he grabbed her arm. He led her back down the stairs, and they began the trek through the city.

Now that she'd seen Grevik and the condition he was in, she knew the assassin would never let him go—especially if Grevik had seen the man's face while being tortured. Most likely, the assassin would kill her as well to ensure no one could tie him to the crime he planned to commit.

"Meet me tomorrow. Same time, same place," he said, close to her ear. "I want to know if the emperor will be going to the shelter with his wife and daughter."

Tomorrow was the ball. Getting out of the castle unnoticed would be infinitely more difficult. "I'm working," she said. "I'm not sure I'll be able to leave."

The assassin stilled. "Will you be attending the royal ball tomorrow evening?"

"How do you know about that?"

"It's not hard to figure out when deliveries are being made and people all over town are talking about it." He started walking again, keeping her at his side.

It would be the perfect time for him to gain entrance into the castle when all the guests arrived. She hated being blindfolded and not having any idea what was going on around her. They walked in silence for several moments.

"If the royal family is still alive in two days, you are to meet me at the inn with information about the emperor." He untied her blindfold.

Allyssa ripped the material off her face and found herself standing all alone in the alleyway next to the inn, the assassin nowhere in sight.

She glanced up at the building, looking for the ladder that led to the door she must have exited from, but she

didn't see anything. She shivered and went to the street in front of the inn, hoping Jarvik and his men saw her. Since the assassin could be watching, she kept walking, heading back to the castle alone, instead of waiting for the squire to show himself.

A couple of blocks away from the soldiers' entrance, Jarvik finally caught up to her. He wrapped her in a hug, holding tightly. "I thought we lost you," he stammered.

"I'm fine." His body was hard and solid against hers.

"What happened?" he demanded as he held her at arm's length, looking her over for any signs of injury. His eyes lingered on her swollen lip.

Her eyes darted to the rooftops of the nearby buildings. "Let's go inside first." She feared the assassin could be hidden anywhere watching them. "I have a lot to tell you." When they neared the soldiers' entrance, the Fren soldiers joined them and they were granted entrance.

Once inside the castle, Jarvik dismissed his men, trying to minimize attention. He continued on with Allyssa. Heading along the dark, empty corridor, the squire abruptly stopped next to one of the windows, the moonlight shining on his worried face.

"What happened?" he demanded.

She quickly told him as many of the details as she could remember. When she got to the part about her trying to take on the skilled assassin by herself, his eyes darkened and he put his hands on his hips, shaking his head.

When she finished, she said, "You may yell at me now."

He stood there staring at her a moment before asking, "You can't retrace your steps?"

"No." Wasn't he going to tell her how stupid it had

been to go with the assassin? To fight him when there was little hope of winning? To put her life in danger like that?

Jarvik ran his hands through his hair, letting out a sigh. "The ball will be tricky. With so many people attending, the assassin could easily slip in to try and kill the royal family."

Reaching up, she touched her lip. It was split, and there was some dried blood on it. Once Mayra applied some coloring to Allyssa's lips, no one would be able to tell she'd been hit.

"I can't believe the assassin struck you," Jarvik said, "and that I wasn't there to help you."

"I'm fine." She shrugged. It really was no big deal. She'd been in plenty of brawls to know this was minor.

He took a step closer to her, his chest almost touching hers. She started to lean away from him but he put his hand on her back, holding her in place.

"What are you doing?" she asked.

He lowered his face closer to hers. "I'm looking at your cut. I want to make sure the assassin didn't have his gloved hand laced with poison."

She hadn't even considered the possibility.

"It's not red or oozing," he declared. "You're fine."

His gaze moved from her lips to her eyes. For the first time in her life, she wanted to be kissed. He hastily took a step away from her.

Realizing what had almost happened, she said, "I should go to my bedchamber." Jarvik nodded as she stepped around him and practically ran down the hall to the laundry room.

# Chapter Twenty-one

"Shoulders back," Rema said. Allyssa couldn't believe her mother had given her this dress to wear. It was the gown Rema had worn to her coronation ball in Emperion almost twenty years ago. "This is a special occasion," Rema continued "You must look the part."

"The gown is stunning on you," Mayra said.

"Definitely something fit for the future empress," Madelin added.

The ivory-colored dress had a neckline that went straight across her chest and shoulders, leaving her neck and upper arms exposed. A diamond necklace rested above her bosom. Madelin had braided Allyssa's hair and twisted it up and around her jewel-encrusted crown.

"Where's Prince Odar?" Allyssa asked. She hadn't seen him all day and thought he'd be here by now, preparing for the announcement.

"I saw Jarvik on his way to get him," Mayra said.

Rema adjusted Allyssa's necklace. "Sweetheart," she whispered, gaining her daughter's attention. "Please focus. You're about to make an important announcement to the city."

Allyssa nodded. Her mother was right. She should be going over her speech, not worrying about where the prince was.

Darmik entered the small antechamber, his eyes settling on his daughter. "You look beautiful," he said, kissing her on the cheek. "Are you ready to announce your upcoming marriage to Emperion?"

"Speaking of which," Allyssa said, "since I'm traveling to Fren, when will the wedding take place?"

Rema rubbed her daughter's arm. "We are working out all the details with the prince. Once it's settled, we'll let you know."

Prince Odar and Jarvik entered, wearing handsome tunics embroidered with Fren's royal crest. Jarvik glanced briefly at Allyssa before going to Neco, who stood in the corner. The two of them began speaking in hushed whispers.

"Stop staring," Rema whispered. "You can't afford to be distracted by the prince's squire."

Allyssa felt her face heat up. She wanted to contradict her mother, but the look on Rema's face said the subject was closed for now.

"You and I will talk later, just the two of us," Rema whispered.

"Your Highness," Prince Odar said, taking Allyssa's hand and kissing the top of it.

She forced herself to focus on him. "Are you ready?"

"As ready as I'll ever be." He offered her his arm, and she took it.

Darmik cleared his throat and came before the royal couple. "We're going to make this brief," he said. "We must assume King Drenton of Russek has sent spies to our city to track our movements. He won't be happy to learn our kingdom is joining forces with Fren."

"Make sure the two of you don't look too serious,"

Rema said, smiling at them. "You need to show everyone that you are happy, in love, and strong. We must give them reassurance before this war."

"Let's go," Darmik said, joining hands with Rema. Together, they walked onto the balcony, and the crowd below roared. Allyssa hoped that when she became empress, the people loved her as much as they loved her mother—that her decisions, policies, and actions deserved such loyalty.

Odar patted Allyssa's hand that rested on his arm. "Have I told you how utterly astonishing you look?"

Thankfully, Mayra had applied some color to Allyssa's lips, concealing the cut the assassin had given her last night. Without meaning to, she glanced at Jarvik again. He was staring right at her, and she quickly looked away.

Rema began speaking to the crowd, telling them that she had a special announcement to make. "My lovely daughter, Princess Allyssa, your future empress, is engaged to Prince Odar of Fren. The marriage contract has been signed. After my daughter travels to Fren to meet with the king and queen, the ceremony will take place."

That was Allyssa's cue. Together, she and Prince Odar walked onto the balcony, and the crowd roared their approval. She smiled and waved, just as she'd been trained to do. Glancing sidelong at Prince Odar, he was doing the same thing, and the people of Emperion loved it.

Rema raised her hands, and the crowd went silent. Darmik briefly spoke of the upcoming war and Emperion's mighty strength. Then he started talking about Fren and their lethal army. While her father spoke,

Allyssa scanned the crowd, wondering if the assassin stood among them. Guards had checked everyone who entered the courtyard and weapons were confiscated. However, she was sure if the assassin wanted to be there fully armed, he'd find a way. Standing on the nearby rooftops were several archers intently watching the people below.

The cheering resumed and Odar gently led Allyssa forward, closer to the railing. It was her turn to speak. The people started cheering *Princess Allyssa* and *Prince Odar*, shouting their approval of the union. What if the assassin decided to murder the royal family right now? He wanted an opportunity to kill them, and here he had it. Odar reassuringly squeezed her hand.

Allyssa raised her hand, and everyone quieted down. "My dear people of Emperion," she bellowed. "Thank you for coming today." Fear coursed through her at the possibility of the assassin standing below, ready to throw a knife into her heart.

"I'm deeply honored and humbled to be marrying Princess Allyssa," Odar said, saving her from speaking. "Emperion is a beautiful kingdom with hard-working citizens and just rulers. I promise to serve you and to cherish this kingdom as my own."

The crowd shouted their approval. The guards ushered the royal family off the balcony and back into the antechamber.

"I messed up my speech," Allyssa moaned. She'd been so afraid of the assassin, it had paralyzed her.

"It's fine," Odar consoled her.

"It truly is," Rema said, hugging her daughter. "The people needed to see you, and they did."

Jarvik came before her. "I'll escort the prince and

princess back to their chambers," he said.

"Thank you," Rema replied as she left with Darmik and Neco.

Allyssa, surrounded by Odar, Jarvik, her ladies-in-waiting, and two sets of guards, made her way through the corridors.

Pulling free from the prince, she stopped walking. "Is something the matter?" Odar asked.

She glanced to Marek, trying to figure out an excuse to leave the prince and his men so she could be alone for a little bit. She couldn't claim training or riding—she wasn't dressed appropriately for either activity.

"Pardon the intrusion," Madelin said. "Don't forget you need to see the seamstress before the ball this evening."

Allyssa wanted to kiss her friend for her quick thinking. "Of course," she said. "Prince Odar, Jarvik, if you'll excuse me." Without waiting for either one of them to respond, she turned and strode away.

"I see you have some new guards," Madelin observed.

"Yes," Allyssa replied. "Apparently, the Fren and Emperion guards must learn to work with one another." She waved Marek closer, away from the other guards. "Where can I go to at least have the illusion of privacy?" she whispered.

The corners of his lips lifted. "Certainly a dress fitting would accomplish that."

She couldn't help but laugh. "Yes, well, I was thinking somewhere outside."

"I understand," he said. "However, you might want to consider that your entire guard, along with some of Prince Odar's men, heard you say you were going to a fitting. You might not want them to see you lying to your future husband. It won't instill faith."

Allyssa sighed.

"I'm sorry if I overstepped my place," Marek quickly said.

"No, I appreciate your candor, and you are correct."

When they reached the seamstress's room, they found it void of people. All the guards waited outside while Allyssa entered with her ladies-in-waiting. "I've never been in here before," Allyssa said. The seamstress always came to her.

"I guess we'll just sit in here for fifteen minutes or so," Madelin suggested.

There were several worktables, and fabric was strewn all over the place. The room was on the ground level, and there were half a dozen windows along one of the walls.

"With the ball tonight, you think there would be several people in here working," Mayra said.

Madelin laughed. "This is the seamstress for the royal family only," she informed them. "If she's not here, then she's most likely in the Royal Chambers. She's probably delivering the princess's dress as we speak."

Marek stepped inside the room. "Your Highness, Jarvik needs to speak privately with you. He said it's important."

"When?" Allyssa asked.

"He'll be here shortly."

Marek escorted Madelin and Mayra just outside the entrance. A moment later, Jarvik stealthily slipped inside the seamstress's room, using an interior door Allyssa hadn't noticed before now.

# Chapter Twenty-two

Jarvik waved her over to the corner of the room so that if anyone passed by the entrance or peered inside, they wouldn't be seen.

"Do you think it wise to be meeting like this?" Allyssa asked. "I feel as if we're doing something we shouldn't be doing."

"That's never stopped you before," he said. "But to answer your question, I don't want my soldiers that have been assigned to guard you to be aware of this conversation."

"What do you want to talk to me about?" Not that she minded him seeking her out; she was grateful for the opportunity to see him.

"Let me ask you a question," he said. "If you were in Grevik's position, and the assassin tortured you and threatened your family, could you keep a secret even under such strenuous circumstances?"

"If you're concerned about him revealing my true identity, don't be."

Jarvik leaned against the wall. "But if the roles were reversed, could you keep a secret that big?"

Why did he care? "Of course," she said. "I'd do anything to save my friend."

"What if the assassin threatened to kill your family?" he asked.

"I don't know."

He tilted his head back, gazing up at the ceiling. "I want you to know that I never meant to deceive you."

"I know," she said. "You were only following Prince Odar's orders."

He focused back on her face. "I need to tell you something, and you're probably going to be upset with me." His eyes flickered to the door and back to her. "But it's going to have to wait."

She nodded, wondering what he had to tell her.

"Right now, I'm concerned about the assassin."

She was too. The couple of hours she managed to sleep this morning had been plagued with visions of the man killing her parents.

"Since he told you to return in two days if the royal family was still alive, I have to assume he's going to attempt to assassinate you tonight at the ball."

"Do you think he'd be so bold?"

Jarvik ran his hands through his hair, messing it up. "I don't know, but we can't risk it."

"What are you suggesting?"

"We need to tell your father so he can notify the sentries on duty."

That was what she feared Jarvik would suggest. Telling her father meant she'd have to tell him everything. He was going to be livid; however, it was the right thing to do. She had to protect her parents. Her only fear was that she wouldn't be able to save Grevik. How could she trade one life for another?

"Allyssa?" Jarvik asked. He hesitantly placed his calloused hand on her bare shoulder, sending a jolt of

warmth through her. "If you want, I'll speak with the emperor now."

"Let me handle it," she said.

"What are you going to tell him?"

"The truth."

He removed his hand.

Allyssa turned to leave when she remembered something. "Grevik said it reminded him of that time we caught snake dealers." She couldn't believe she'd almost forgotten this important detail.

"You caught snake dealers?" Jarvik asked.

"No. That's the problem. We never caught illegal snake traders. Grevik said it for a reason, although I haven't figured out why."

"I agree," he said. "It has to be of importance. If I think of anything, I'll let you know."

She turned again to leave.

"Wait." She froze, not turning around to face him. "Allyssa," Jarvik whispered her name like a soft caress, the feeling in the room suddenly shifting.

She closed her eyes, knowing he stood a few feet behind her dressed in a handsome tunic with his hair a mess from him running his hands through it.

Fabric rustled, and the sound of his breathing neared. Neither of them spoke. Her bare skin warmed from the closeness of him. She wanted to turn around to face him, but knew she couldn't. Something light and soft like a feather caressed the base of her neck.

"Allyssa," he whispered in her ear. She shivered. His finger delicately traced a line from her shoulder down to her hand. "I'm afraid you're locked in this cage of deceit with me. When you break free, you're going to hate me."

"What are you talking about?"

"Just … be careful today in case the assassin is lurking somewhere."

"Of course," she said, her voice hoarse.

"Are you armed?" He must have moved further back because she was suddenly cold, and he no longer spoke by her ear.

"Yes."

"Good. Make sure you're armed at all times—even at the ball tonight. Don't eat anything unless it has gone through your food tasters twice."

"Why the sudden concern?" she asked, still not facing him. "I didn't think you liked me."

There had to be more going on than just his desire to protect Prince Odar. Did he have feelings for her?

"I don't know," he answered. "Let's just say you've grown on me."

Biting her swollen lip, she finally decided to turn around to face him. Only, Jarvik was gone, the interior door slightly ajar.

"Why did the squire want to speak to you?" Mayra asked as they walked down the hallway.

"Oh," Allyssa stuttered, not sure what to say. It would be wonderful to confide in her friends; however, admitting that she had any sort of attraction to Jarvik was dangerous. "He just wanted to go over some security measures."

Mayra glanced sideways at her. "Whatever you say."

"Let's head outside," Madelin suggested. "We've been to the seamstress. No one will find fault if we go to the courtyard."

"Are you all right?" Mayra asked. "You seem a little frazzled."

Allyssa stopped walking and turned to face her two ladies-in-waiting. "I'm sorry. I'm just distracted." She wished she could tell them about Grevik. Glancing at her guards a respectful distance away, she was acutely aware of them watching her every move. Before she faced her father, she needed some time alone to organize her thoughts.

"Is there anything we can do to help?" Madelin offered.

"Why don't the two of you prepare my dress for this evening? I want to stop by the library to grab a book. I'll be along shortly."

"You're always at the library," Madelin commented, rolling her eyes.

"She likes hiding in there," Mayra added, playfully jabbing Madelin in the ribs.

"If the two of you must know, I need a moment alone before I find my father to tell him something."

"What are you going to tell him?" Mayra asked.

"I will explain everything later." As Allyssa walked away, her guards trailing behind her, something tugged on her memory. Something about snakes, but she couldn't quite pinpoint the memory she was searching for.

A group of courtiers stood up ahead, talking to one another. Striding straight down the hallway, Allyssa maintained her position in the middle, expecting them to move out of her way. She hated to be so bold, so forward, but it was the way a princess was expected to act. Keeping her head held high as she passed them, they all bowed and offered words of congratulations. Allyssa thanked them as she strode past, not stopping.

When she reached the entrance to the library, she saw Jarvik and Odar sitting inside at a table with a pile of books between them. Several Fren soldiers sat at nearby tables, also combing through books. No one noticed her hovering in the doorway, so she backed up and proceeded down the hallway.

Turning the corner, she headed to the north tower, throwing the door open and entering. She climbed the hundreds of stairs, her legs burning from exertion. When she reached the top, she opened the door and went outside, the cool air caressing her skin. Allyssa smiled, reveling in the feeling of being up so high. The sun warmed her skin, and a sense of calming peace filled her.

The guards remained inside on the stairs. Marek pushed past them and came outside to join her.

"Am I to have no peace?" She sighed.

"There is no such thing with war looming on the horizon."

"I came here to be alone so I can think. I can't do that with you here."

He leaned against the waist-high stone wall. "I can't allow you to be out here alone."

They stood shoulder to shoulder in silence, overlooking the city.

"What's bothering you?" he asked.

The image of Grevik bruised and strapped to the chair while the assassin sauntered around him, threatening him, was seared into her mind. She had to tell her father about the assassin, but she feared it would result in her never seeing Grevik again.

"Is there something going on between you and Jarvik?" Marek asked, reaching out and clutching her hand. "I'm the head of your personal guard and one of your best

friends. You can tell me."

"I came out here to organize my thoughts before I go and speak with my father." She took a deep breath, holding tightly onto Marek's hand. "Grevik is being held captive by an assassin sent here to kill the royal family."

Marek rocked back on his heels. "The one we ran into that night?" She nodded. "You mean to tell me you left the castle without me—which you promised not to do—and went to meet him?"

"Yes."

His jaw clenched and he released her hand, punching the wall. "Is this why you're suddenly so close with Jarvik?"

"Yes, I took him with me."

"You trusted the squire from Fren, but not me?"

"I knew you'd never let me go. I had to find out what the assassin wanted."

Marek made an odd noise, shaking his head in disgust. "You're lucky to be alive."

"He doesn't know who I am." She proceeded to tell Marek about her two meetings with the assassin, along with seeing Grevik last night and his cryptic message.

"Snake dealers?" Marek questioned.

Leaning against the stone wall, looking out over the city, she replied, "Yes. We captured many criminals over the past couple of years, but snake dealers weren't among them."

There was some commotion on the stairs behind them. A Fren soldier emerged out of breath. "Your Highness," he said. "I was told to give this to you immediately." He held out a piece of paper.

Allyssa took it, and the Fren soldier left. Unfolding the paper, she read a hastily scribbled note:

> *Found a reference to snake traders.*
> *Emperion uses the term for traitors who are put into exile.*

She turned the note over. There wasn't anything else. Marek leaned over her shoulder and read it. His face paled.

"What is it?" she asked, her heart pounding in her chest.

"This term originated twenty years ago when your mother took the throne. My father said she couldn't sign the execution order for Empress Eliza or Princess Jana."

"Yes. Instead, she banished them to a remote place in Emperion."

"Do you remember anything else from your studies?"

The air rushed out of her and her head spun. "Eliza and Jana were taken away on a wooden cart under the guise that they were illegal snake traders—which was rampant at that time—so no one would know who they were." How had she forgotten that? "They lived in exile for several years until they suddenly disappeared. No one knows where they went or what happened to them."

"My father suspects they left Emperion completely. He thinks they sought protection from a neighboring kingdom."

Did her father's half-sister Jana really send an assassin to kill them? "Do you think she wants to reclaim the throne?" Allyssa asked.

"Possibly, but the timing is questionable. I think this is somehow tied to Russek."

Jarvik's words came back to her—the king of Russek recently married a widower who came to court with her elderly mother. Could King Drenton have married Jana? If so, was it Jana's daughter who went to Fren to woo

Prince Odar? She recalled Jarvik saying no one knew who Princess Shelene's father was.

"It doesn't make any sense," Allyssa said.

"It makes perfect sense. King Drenton of Russek sent your family that letter telling you to go into exile in order to avoid the upcoming war, just as your family had sent Eliza and Jana into exile all those years ago. Jana wants to reclaim the Emperion throne and is using Russek's might to do it."

"If so, then why send the assassin? Grevik's message indicates the assassin came from Eliza and Jana—not Russek."

"I don't know, but my gut tells me this is all tied together."

"I want you to go and tell Neco what we've uncovered. I'll go and tell my father everything—sneaking out of the castle, Grevik, the assassin—everything."

"Very well," Marek replied. "Anything else?

"I've been doing research on the main river that runs from the mountains in Romek down through Lakeside, straight through Krosek to the sea. Now, I don't have any proof, this is just a theory, but I believe Russek will use the river to move their soldiers into Emperion. It's the best way to travel with large amounts of people and supplies. It'll take them right into our country without us even knowing."

"I don't know," Marek responded. "I haven't heard any reports of boats being spotted or read anything about rivers being used in war before.

"Like I said, it's just an idea. Will you at least present my theory to your father?"

He nodded. "Have you decided what to do about Grevik?"

She'd been going over that in her mind and hadn't come up with anything yet. "I'll see if Jarvik has any ideas."

Marek elbowed her in the ribs. "Jarvik? Really?" He raised his eyebrows.

She rolled her eyes. "There's nothing going on between us."

"I didn't say that there was. Interesting your mind went there, though," he teased.

She punched his arm.

"That's not very princess-like, or lady-like for that matter," Marek stated.

"Perhaps I'm not in a princessy mood right now," she said. "Beware."

"With you, I always am." He turned and led the way down the stairs of the tower.

# Chapter Twenty-three

She sat in her father's office, waiting for him to say something—anything. She'd told him about the first time she snuck out of the castle all those years ago, her friendship with Grevik, his father's death, the two of them tracking down criminals, and then her encounter with the assassin. She finished with Marek's suspicion of Jana being behind the war and the assassination attempt.

Clutching her hands together on her lap, she maintained eye contact even though she wanted to run screaming from the office. Her father's face was blank, revealing nothing. He'd sat there the entire time she spoke, listening and not uttering a single word or asking any questions.

He finally leaned back on his chair, his gaze going to the window. His silence was making her sweat—she wished he'd talk to her.

The door flew open, and Neco stormed in. *Blimey.* Marek must have already told him what happened. Darmik held up his hand, indicating for Neco to wait. Neco stood there with his hand clutched on the door handle, his shoulders rising and falling from having run there. A moment later, Marek stumbled into the office, his face red from running after his father. Marek opened his mouth to speak, but one look from Neco had him snapping his jaw shut.

Darmik focused on his daughter as he slowly stood. "You've put our family in unnecessary danger," he said in a deadly calm voice that sent a chill through her body. The best course of action was to keep her mouth shut and allow her father to speak. "Come in and close the door," he ordered Neco and Marek. They did as he instructed, and the door clicked shut.

"How long have you known?" Darmik asked Neco.

"My son just told me now."

Darmik turned his gaze to Marek.

"I only recently found out," Marek answered.

"We don't have a lot of time before the ball," Darmik said, his voice still unreasonably calm. Now standing, he carefully placed his hands on his desk, leaning forward, towering over Allyssa as she sat on the chair. "I have a lot to discuss with your mother. She's going to be furious with you, as am I."

His words felt like a slap across the face.

"We must act quickly," Neco said. "Especially since we heard from Audek this morning."

"Yes," Darmik responded, folding his arms. "First, we need to put everyone on high alert for the ball tonight. Marek, go and tell the entire guard on duty that an assassin is attempting to try and gain entrance into the castle. All food to the royal family will go through six tasters, all doors and entry points will be secured at all times."

Marek bowed and left.

"Rema and I will leave directly after the ball for Emperor's City. Not only is our largest military base located there, but Audek has arranged for us to meet

Nathenek there with, well, with someone we need to meet up with." He shook his head and rubbed his temples. "Decoys will be put in our places here."

Neco nodded. "And the princess?" he asked.

Darmik's eyes fell on Allyssa again. Fury and disappointment shone on his face and she ducked her head, unable to meet his gaze.

"Everyone knows she's to travel to Fren next week. We can't change that without altering the agreement." He moved around the desk, standing next to his daughter. "Allyssa, you and Prince Odar will leave with Marek and an elite guard tomorrow night."

Shock rippled through her. If she left tomorrow night, then she couldn't meet the assassin. What would happen to Grevik?

"Is there a problem?" Darmik asked.

"I'm not going with you and Mother?"

He shook his head. "We must preserve the royal line. If anything happens to us, you will be Empress of Emperion." He put his hand on her shoulder. "You will leave without anyone knowing. I'll put decoys in your and Odar's places. Then, a week later, the decoys will make a big show of leaving, drawing the assassin out after them."

"What's going to happen to the decoys?" she asked.

He looked pointedly at her. "Their job."

She couldn't bear the thought of someone dying for her. It didn't seem fair—her life wasn't any more precious than anyone else's.

"These plans do not leave this room," Darmik continued.

"And what of my daughter?" Neco asked. "If Marek is traveling with the princess, what about Mayra?"

Darmik went back around his desk and sat down

again. "She needs to stay here with the decoys."

Neco gave a curt nod. "And where can I best serve you?" he asked.

"I need you with Rema and me."

"I'll start making the necessary arrangements." He bowed and left the room.

"Anything else?" Allyssa asked her father. She needed to speak with Jarvik as soon as possible about trying to save Grevik. Maybe there was something they could do tonight after the ball.

"When you arrive at Fren, charm the king and queen so you can receive their approval immediately. A simple ceremony will be held, and you will marry Prince Odar. As soon as it's done, Marek will send word. I've already made plans with Jarvik to coordinate Fren's soldiers joining with ours."

She wasn't going to be married here in Emperion? Her parents weren't even going to be there? Not knowing what to say, she stood and went to the door, feeling numb.

"Allyssa," Darmik said, stopping her. "Keep Marek with you at all times. Besides him, you can trust Jarvik. You'll be well protected. I promise."

"I'm sorry," she said, "for deceiving you."

"This isn't a punishment, by any means." He rubbed his face. "Your mother and I have withheld certain information from you in order to protect Emperion. We never meant to deceive you either. I'll forgive you, if you forgive us."

"What haven't you told me?" she asked. "Does it have to do with Audek and Nathenek?"

"Yes, it does. However, I have a lot to do to prepare for my departure tonight," he said. "And we need to have this conversation with your mother."

Allyssa nodded and left, wondering what her parents and Audek were hiding, and who Nathenek was.

"That's not the gown I designed with the seamstress," Allyssa said to her ladies-in-waiting.

"I know," Madelin replied. "Neco arrived while you were bathing and said your father insisted you wear this dress tonight."

Allyssa eyed the pale pink fabric. "I don't care for that particular color."

"Perhaps it will look better once it's on," Mayra suggested. "These long gloves came with it, too."

"Gloves?" She never wore gloves.

Madelin nodded. "We were told to make sure you wore them. Neco wants your hands covered at all times." Because of the assassination threat, he probably didn't want her skin exposed to poisons.

Once she was in the gown, it wasn't nearly as bad as she thought it would be. The dress was simple, yet elegant. There were several hidden pockets in the folds of the fabric from her waist down, concealing a handful of daggers. The top was form-fitting and covered by an intricate lace, leaving her neck and shoulders bare. Madelin had artfully twisted Allyssa's hair on top of her head, showcasing her delicate diamond crown.

"This is not the current style," Allyssa mused, turning in front of the mirror. "But I can easily move in it."

"It doesn't matter what the style is," Mayra said. "You're exquisite."

"Since you are the princess, you set the trends," Madelin added.

"We need to hurry down to the Great Hall before you arrive," Mayra said. "Is there anything else you need from us?"

Allyssa shook her head and her ladies-in-waiting left. She wished she could tell them she was leaving for Fren tomorrow night without them. They weren't to know until a decoy had been put in place and Allyssa left. Then her personal guard and ladies-in-waiting would be the only people notified of the situation in order to maintain the ruse.

Allyssa went to the sitting room to wait for her parents. She strolled around the room, thankful no gifts had been sent to her before the ball. Since she was officially engaged, it was no longer proper for men to send a token to her.

"You look stunning," Rema said as she glided into the room, wearing an elaborate green gown. Her blonde hair glowed and her blue eyes sparkled, making her look exquisitely regal. "Before your father joins us, there is something we must discuss." She grabbed Allyssa's hands, holding them tightly.

Allyssa prepared herself for her mother's scolding for sneaking out of the castle and putting herself in danger.

"I love you more than life itself," she began. "I want you to have a wonderful life filled with happiness."

Allyssa nodded, not sure what her mother was getting at.

"You are the crown princess, and you are engaged to and will marry Prince Odar. I've seen the way you look at Jarvik—and the way he looks at you. I want you to leave the squire alone. Put all thoughts of him out of your head. It can't possibly end well, and you'll only end up hurting yourself."

Biting her lip, Allyssa nodded, unable to believe her mother was talking to her about Jarvik. It was embarrassing. Besides, she wasn't even clear on how she felt about the squire.

"Promise me," Rema continued, "that you'll behave as the future empress would. You will put your kingdom and your subjects first. You have the power to protect Emperion by marrying Prince Odar. Don't jeopardize that."

"I promise." Allyssa knew how important this alliance was. There was no way she'd allow Russek to destroy Emperion and kill its citizens by chopping off their heads and skewering them on spikes. It was vulgar and disgusting.

"Here are the two most beautiful women in Emperion," Darmik said as he came into the room. After kissing Allyssa on the cheek, he wrapped his arms around Rema's waist and kissed her neck. "I love you," he mumbled against her skin.

"And I love you," Rema replied.

"I would like to remind the both of you to be extra vigilant tonight," Darmik said. "As soon as the ball is over, your mother and I are leaving."

"It's imperative that we reach Emperor's City as soon as possible," Rema added.

Allyssa wished her parents didn't have to leave her. However, she understood the necessity. "I love you both," she said. "I pray you have a speedy and safe journey."

Rema wrapped her arms around her daughter, squeezing tightly. "And I wish you the same."

Allyssa released her mother and Darmik hugged her, kissing the top of her head. "Please do what Jarvik and Marek ask of you. Be safe, be smart, and know I'll think of you each and every day we are apart."

"I love you, Father." Allyssa hated good-byes—they always made her want to cry.

"We're late," Darmik said, heading toward the door. "Let's go."

Rema squeezed Allyssa's hand. "I wish we didn't have to part ways," Rema said.

Allyssa nodded, a lump forming in her throat.

"You'll go to Fren. You'll charm the king and queen. You'll secure the troops we need to fight this war. I have full confidence in you." Rema kissed Allyssa's cheek. "Never doubt my love for you. Do you understand?"

"I do," Allyssa whispered. "Thank you, Mother. I love you, too."

"I want you to know that it will be okay. You have to trust in yourself. You can and you will be able to do this."

"I won't disappoint you." She headed to the door where her father stood waiting.

The three of them left the Royal Chambers as a family and headed to the Great Hall.

# Chapter Twenty-four

After a formal dinner in which Allyssa had been seated between her parents, unable to speak to Jarvik, she was thrilled to be heading to the adjacent room where the dancing would take place. As soon as the opportunity presented itself, she would seek the squire out to discuss Grevik.

"What's taking so long?" she asked as she stood next to Rema and Darmik, waiting to be announced.

"Security," her father answered. "We're being extra cautious."

Marek remained off to the side, looking mighty handsome in his formal Royal Guard uniform, his hair combed back, and a shining sword strapped to his waist.

"Since you're engaged," Darmik said, "Prince Odar will escort you inside once he joins us."

"Is he aware of the upcoming events?" she asked, trying to be vague since others were nearby.

Darmik leaned in close to Allyssa. "I told Jarvik everything so arrangements could be made. The squire seems to be well-equipped to handle these sorts of situations. I had a long conversation with him, and I trust he has your best interest at heart. He is working with Marek to secure two additional soldiers for the journey."

"So few men for such a long way?"

"You can't attract attention."

She couldn't believe she was set to leave tomorrow night with Grevik still captive. There had to be a way to save him before she left.

Movement caught her attention, and she glanced up in time to see the prince and squire strolling toward her. Her breath caught. Jarvik looked stunning dressed in what had to be Fren's high-ranking military uniform—dark blue fabric with the royal seal embroidered on the front of his tunic. The color set off his dark hair, suiting him well.

Prince Odar cleared his throat, forcing her attention from the squire to him. The prince took her gloved hand and kissed it. "You look beautiful," he said, seductively smiling under hooded eyes. He placed her hand on his arm, and they took their place beside her parents.

"You look handsome," she said, complimenting him. He wore a sapphire overcoat with ivory embroidery down the center. The color set off his piercing blue eyes, making him look every bit the pretty prince that he was.

A steward announced Princess Allyssa and Prince Odar, and they entered the Great Hall while the hundred or so guests inside bowed and curtsied to them. After the empress and emperor came in, the festive music began. Prince Odar swung Allyssa into his embrace for the first dance.

Jarvik stood off to the side among the Fren soldiers, who all wore their military uniforms with polished swords strapped to their waists. His eyes roamed around the room, observing every detail. Allyssa spotted Marek speaking with a group of guards, pointing to the doors, which were all closed. Four times the standard amount of

guards were stationed throughout the room. The guests didn't seem to notice, and if they did, they didn't show any indication something was amiss.

"Like my squire, you seem a bit off," the prince mused. "Is something the matter?" He twirled her around and brought her back to his chest, holding her tightly.

"I'm sorry for my distraction," she said. "I have a lot on my mind."

"Care to tell me? I am a good listener."

"I assumed Jarvik already apprised you of events."

His eyes darkened. "You are mistaken. He hasn't disclosed anything to me." He forced his smile to remain in place.

She glanced over to where the squire stood watching her, his arms folded across his chest. "There was a security issue earlier." She smiled up at Odar. "It must not have been as severe as I'd originally thought if he didn't bother to tell you about it." Allyssa couldn't discuss what was really going on right now. It wasn't the time or place.

He twirled her around again. Didn't Odar notice the additional guards? He should at least question why so many were present. He couldn't possibly be that oblivious. Why didn't Jarvik tell the prince? Why would he keep the assassin and the travel plans from him?

Prince Odar dipped her backwards, and then slowly brought her back up. "You spoke with Jarvik?" he asked, a hint of jealousy coloring his voice.

"I was speaking with the head of my guard, Marek," she answered, side-stepping his question. "He told me he planned to talk to Jarvik so you'd be informed."

His smile returned. "You know," he said, spinning her around, "you can come to me regarding such matters. You do not need to deal with your guard."

Allyssa wanted to punch him. She wasn't some stupid, naïve girl who had to have a man take care of her. She forced herself to smile at him, ready for this dance to be over. "I will keep that in mind for next time," she replied, a sharp edge to her voice. How was she ever going to survive being stuck in a carriage with this man while they traveled to Fren? He certainly was nice, cordial, and friendly, but he failed to see the obvious and he wasn't quick-minded like Jarvik. Yet, she had an obligation to her kingdom. She needed to speak with the king and queen of Fren and secure those soldiers. If they didn't approve of her, help wouldn't come. Emperion needed those troops to fight Russek.

The song ended. "Your Highness," she said, stepping away from Odar, relief filling her. She turned and found Jarvik before her. Her heart sped up.

"May I please have this dance?" the squire asked, bowing.

Her mother's warning came back to her—she was supposed to put all thoughts of Jarvik out of her mind so she could focus on Odar, her future husband. However, the squire was the prince's best friend and he'd asked to dance with her. It would be rude to refuse him. Glancing at the prince for his reaction, she watched him pat Jarvik on the shoulder and stroll away.

Jarvik took a tentative step toward Allyssa and she smiled at him, letting him know she accepted his offer to dance. *Blimey.* She wanted to dance with him, to feel his hands holding her. He gently placed one hand on her lower back, the other taking her gloved hand and lifting it into the air. A new song began, and the two of them started moving together around the dance floor.

When she gazed into Jarvik's eyes, the music and

people faded away, and all she saw was the man standing before her. Suddenly nervous, she feared she'd step on her dress and fall. However, Jarvik expertly glided with her around the dance floor, putting all her fears to rest. Why did she care what Jarvik thought of her? He was her future husband's squire. She'd be seeing a lot of him and couldn't afford to feel anything but friendship for this man.

Needing to take the focus off her thoughts of running her hands through his hair or tracing the curve of his lips, she asked, "Why didn't you tell the prince what's going on?"

"No need." He shrugged. "He'll find out soon enough."

"But doesn't he give the orders?"

His eyes flickered. "Not when it comes to matters of security. He has confidence in my abilities and has placed me in charge."

Jarvik hadn't twirled her once. In fact, he hadn't let go of her at all. His warm hand was still placed on her lower back. She wished she wasn't wearing gloves so she could feel his calloused skin against hers.

Glancing around the room, she spotted Odar speaking with her parents and wondered what they were discussing. Since he wasn't watching her dance with Jarvik, she felt relieved yet ridden with guilt, as if she was doing something wrong simply by enjoying his company.

"What's the matter?" Jarvik asked, pulling her closer to him, their chests touching and their faces only inches apart. His lips were so close. Her heart beat erratically and she couldn't breathe. How could the squire—a man she had originally loathed—have this effect on her? She was acting like a barmaid.

"Allyssa?" Jarvik asked. "Are you okay?"

Gaining her wits back, she forced all romantic thoughts of Jarvik away. "Yes, sorry. I'm just thinking about the events of the day."

"I know," he whispered. "Me too. But you seem ... off. Are you sure nothing else is bothering you?" His fingers dug into her back.

Her face flushed. *Bloody hell.* It had been easier when she hated him. "I'm concerned about Grevik," she murmured. "I'm supposed to meet *you know who* tomorrow evening, but apparently, that can't happen now. Do you have any suggestions?"

He leaned down, his lips near her ear. "Only one," he whispered. "But it's risky." He hesitated a moment before continuing, "You have the authority—once your parents are gone—to delay our departure by one day. Then I will help you save Grevik on the condition that we do it together. You will not go anywhere near that assassin on your own."

If she didn't meet the assassin, how would she find Grevik?

"You have to trust me," he said.

She nodded.

"Promise me," the squire insisted.

"I promise."

His hand slowly slid up her back, holding her closer. *What is he doing?* She was certain they shouldn't be dancing like this.

The music ended, and a couple of men came up behind the squire to request the next dance. Jarvik didn't even hesitate—he held onto her, not giving anyone else a chance to request her hand. It was considered improper for her to dance with the same man twice in a row unless he was courting her. Yet, she couldn't bring herself to say

anything because she was right where she wanted to be.

The music started up again. It was a slower song, allowing the squire to hold her close to him. She swore she could feel his heart pounding against hers, just as frantic and erratic.

They danced in silence for several moments, her head resting against his shoulder. They turned slightly, giving her a clear view of her parents watching her. Although Rema and Darmik were both smiling, her father's eyes were pinched with worry and her mother kept glancing sideways at Odar. The prince folded his arms as he stood with her parents, staring at her. She lifted her head off Jarvik's shoulder, putting some space between them. She felt cold without his body against hers.

"Why are you willing to help me with Grevik?" she suddenly asked. "I don't understand you."

He sighed. "I shouldn't be helping you," he muttered. "But I know Grevik is your friend, and he's important to you. If he died, it would cause you pain, and I don't want to see you hurting." He gazed down into her eyes. They stopped dancing and stood there staring at one another.

Allyssa couldn't breathe. *Blimey.* She was in love with Jarvik. Quickly pulling her hands free, she stepped back, away from him. His eyebrows scrunched together, questioning her actions.

"I, uh, need to go." She turned and practically ran off the dance floor.

Marek was immediately at her side. "You can't leave," he said. "With the added security measures in place, you can't slip away tonight. I'm sorry."

She needed air.

"The doors to the balcony are open," he suggested. "I'll find one of your ladies-in-waiting for you."

She understood what he wasn't saying—that she needed not only a friend, but to be with a woman. It couldn't appear that there was anything going on between her and the squire. Stepping out onto the balcony, the courtiers present all bowed. Two guards were posted there, and several more were on the nearby rooftops.

"I'd like a moment alone with my daughter," Rema said from the doorway, startling Allyssa.

Everyone except the guards left the balcony, leaving mother and daughter alone.

Allyssa gripped the railing, looking up at the stars and breathing in the fresh air. She didn't want a lecture on propriety right now.

"Are you all right?" Rema asked, rubbing her daughter's back.

"I'm fine," she answered.

"Do you care to tell me what's going on?"

"I'm sorry for my behavior," Allyssa said. "I just got caught up in the moment. I won't let it happen again." She couldn't even look at her mother right now.

Rema hugged her. "I'm proud of you. I know it's not easy having an arranged marriage. The choices you're making are good ones, and I couldn't be happier of the woman you've become. I love you." She kissed Allyssa's forehead. "I need to go back inside so we don't cause an unnecessary scene. You have to have faith and trust everything will work out for the best."

She had expected her mother to be upset with her; instead, she'd been proud and supportive of her. Allyssa watched her mother glide into the ballroom. Darmik took Rema's hand, and her parents started dancing together.

"Your Highness," Madelin said, coming out on the balcony. "Marek said you needed to speak with me."

"Yes, thank you," Allyssa replied. Once she left for Fren, she wouldn't see her dear friend for weeks. She hoped Madelin would be safe here.

Her lady-in-waiting came over and whispered, "I suggest you go back inside and dance with someone. Now. Everyone is gossiping about you and Jarvik."

That was what Allyssa had feared. "Of course," she said. She couldn't afford to have her subjects questioning her actions. Madelin reached out, grabbing Allyssa's hand and squeezing it. Holding her head high, Allyssa went inside with a pleasant smile on her face. A Legion member approached and she took his arm, accepting his offer.

She spent the next few songs dancing with various partners, making lively conversation so no one would suspect her warring emotions. However, no matter how many partners she danced with or how much she laughed, she was acutely aware of Jarvik standing off to the side, watching her every move.

A servant approached with a tray of drinks, offering her one. She politely refused, although she was thirsty. She knew she couldn't have anything to eat or drink unless it went through her food tasters first.

"May I have this dance, Your Highness?" a man asked, bowing before her.

"Of course," she answered, not recognizing him.

A detailed guest list had been made, and no one was allowed to gain entrance if he or she was not on the approved list. He had to be someone of importance to be here this evening.

He carefully took her gloved hand in his, and they started dancing.

"I'm sorry," she said, "but I don't recall your name."

The man smiled at her. "That is because we haven't been formally introduced."

If she had to guess, she'd say he was in his early to mid-twenties. He was of average height and weight with no distinguishing features. He had black hair, tanned skin, and dark eyes. The gentleman wore a tunic with no family crest, but it was embroidered with exquisite detail, indicating great wealth.

"Since we haven't been introduced and we are dancing together, I think now would be the appropriate time for you to tell me your name."

He suddenly twirled her around and when she faced him again, he squeezed her hand tightly as his eyes narrowed. "There's no need for you to know my name," he drawled. His hand painfully dug into her waist, and she knew something was wrong. "I simply wanted to dance with you so we could talk. However, now that I'm with you, you look like someone I recently met." His eyes dissected her face.

She froze. His voice sounded familiar. Was this the assassin? "Tell me your name," she demanded.

"I think not." He winked.

"All I have to do is shout, and you'll be arrested."

"Hmm," he said. "A risky move on your part considering I hold all the cards."

"You're hurting me," she said. "Let go."

His grip tightened. "When the song is over, feign a headache."

Allyssa couldn't help but laugh to herself. That was what she normally did in order to leave a party early to escape out of the castle. However, she had no intention of doing what he said. He was in *her* fortress. There were hundreds of trained soldiers only feet away. This assassin

wouldn't succeed—not if she could help it.

The music ended, and he still held her tightly. "I will meet you in the hallway. Now go and tell that pathetic *guard* who trails you around like a puppy that you are tired and want to retire for the evening."

This may be her only opportunity to kill the assassin. She slowly moved her free hand down her dress, sliding it in one of the folds where a dagger was hidden.

"Very well," she said, trying to stall.

As soon as his hands loosened, she whipped the knife out and plunged it into his side. He grunted, encasing her hand with his. Red blood coated the tips of her gloved fingers. She tried to pull away, but he held on to her.

"That was a very stupid thing you just did."

Her left hand was still free, so she reached down and grabbed another dagger. The assassin noticed her pull the knife out and his other hand snatched her arm, stopping her mid-air. She lifted her right knee and rammed it into him. Out of the corner of her eye, she saw Marek and Jarvik sprinting toward them with their swords drawn.

The assassin's eyes darted around the room. "Nice play, Princess. But this isn't over." He released her and disappeared into the crowd of screaming people.

"Are you okay?" Marek frantically asked when he reached her.

"Go after that man," she shouted. "I want him captured—dead or alive. He doesn't leave the castle."

He nodded and raised his arm, signaling for the guards to keep the doors locked. No one was to enter or leave the room until Marek found the man. Since the assassin was dripping with blood, he should be easy to spot.

Jarvik wrapped his arm around her shoulders. "Let's

get you out of here."

"My parents," she said. "Where are they? They're in danger, too."

"Neco is removing them from the room."

"And Prince Odar?" she asked.

"Is taken care of."

The squire rushed her to one of the back doors where the guards allowed them to pass through. In the hallway, a handful of her guards along with several Fren soldiers surrounded them.

"I'm assuming that was the assassin," Jarvik said as they hurried along the corridor.

"Yes," she answered, glancing down at the blood on her gloves.

"Why didn't he kill you when he had the chance?" he asked.

"I don't know. He wanted me to leave the room, so I stabbed him."

The corners of his lips tugged up. "Glad your survival skills kicked in. I wonder if he wanted to kill you at another location or wait until he could kill your parents as well?"

She noticed they weren't heading to the Royal Chambers. "Where are we going?"

"Somewhere the assassin won't be able to find you."

# Chapter Twenty-five

"Don't light the torches," Jarvik whispered as they entered the library. "I want you two guards with me, the rest of you hide near the entrance so that anyone who passes by won't be able to see you."

"I want to go to the Royal Chambers with my parents," Allyssa insisted. She hadn't seen them since she danced with the assassin, and she wanted to make sure they were all right. "They're going to be worried."

Jarvik took her to the back of the library where the small reading alcoves were situated. He found one and tugged her inside while two guards hid a few feet away. "Sit," he demanded. "Be quiet and don't move."

She slid down in the corner while Jarvik sat next to her. It was going to be a long night if he planned on keeping them sequestered in there. She removed her bloodied gloves and wiped her hands on the fabric of her dress.

He leaned in until his lips were at her ear.

"Since the assassin is here, you can't be with your parents right now. We have to keep you at a separate location. Otherwise, if the assassin found the three of you, he could kill the royal family and throw Emperion into chaos. Neco is aiding your parents in their departure.

They are leaving right now on horseback. Decoys are already in the Royal Chambers. Your father instructed me to keep you safe until the assassin is found. He also told me to tell you that he loves you."

"Why are you telling me this? Why not Marek?"

"Marek is searching for the assassin. The man could have escaped through the servants' stairwell in all the chaos, which means the assassin could be roaming the hallways right now."

"Marek is always at my side—especially in a situation such as this one."

Jarvik ran his hands through his hair. "I know, and I'm sorry." He sighed. "I had a long conversation with your father earlier today. He entrusted you to my care. I promised to keep you safe, and I intend to honor that promise."

She was surprised her father chose Jarvik as her protector since Marek was the one she grew up with and trusted.

"You can ask Marek the next time you see him," Jarvik added. "I am the one in charge of your safety until we return to Emperion and I relinquish the responsibility to your father once again."

She didn't need anyone to be in charge or responsible for her. She could take care of herself.

"There is one problem," he said.

"What?" she asked, wishing Jarvik wasn't sitting so close to her, that his head wasn't leaning against hers.

"Grevik." The squire was quiet for quite some time. "Allyssa," he finally said, "with the assassin showing up here tonight, I think it would be best for us to leave tomorrow night as planned. Staying an additional day is too risky."

She shook her head. "I'm not leaving until he's safe."

"We don't even know where he is."

"Then I guess we better find out."

"Are you always this difficult?"

"You're the one being difficult, not me," she snapped.

"Unbelievable. Your life is in danger and all you care about is your friend. If you die, what happens to the kingdom? Is your friend's life more important than the welfare of your subjects? Where do your loyalties lie?"

She wanted to kick him. After taking a few deep breaths to calm herself down, she said, "What kind of friend would I be if I allowed him to die? I have to try."

"It's not worth the risk."

"Maybe not to you, but it is to me."

His hand came up, cupping the back of her neck and holding her against him. "This is the last time I'll ask you this question. Are you in love with Grevik?"

"No," she replied. "He is my best friend."

He cursed. "At least you're loyal," he said. "Fine. We'll attempt to rescue him. But we're using my plan. Don't even try to argue with me—you already promised."

"What is this plan of yours?"

"We're sending in a decoy."

"He'll know it's not me."

"But if he's at the inn, then Grevik will be alone, giving us the perfect opportunity to rescue him."

She wanted to kiss Jarvik—his plan might work. They just needed to figure out where Grevik was being held.

"I have men searching for him," Jarvik admitted.

A clicking sound made by one of the guards echoed through the room, and the squire stilled. His lips went to her ear again. "Don't move or say a word."

They stayed like that, their heads frozen together as slow footsteps echoed in the hallway. Allyssa had no idea if it was a guest, a guard, or the assassin. Regardless, she didn't move as she held on to Jarvik, waiting for the threat to pass. When the guard repeated the clicking noise, Jarvik released her.

"Close your eyes and go to sleep," he ordered. "We have a lot to do tomorrow, which includes trying to make it through the day without being killed."

When Allyssa opened her eyes, she found herself leaning against the wall with Jarvik's head on her lap. He looked peaceful while he slept; his mouth slightly ajar, his hair messy, and his face vulnerable. She trailed her finger along the side of his cheek. When he nuzzled closer to her, she realized what she was doing and quickly nudged him awake.

Blinking, he immediately sat up. "Sorry," he muttered as he stretched. "Stay here while I go and obtain an update from my men."

He headed over to the front of the library where his guards were positioned by the shelves and desks watching the entrance.

After speaking to them, Jarvik came back over to her. "I must check on Prince Odar, and I need to talk with Marek."

"Did they catch the assassin?" she asked as she stood.

"No. You won't be able to go anywhere without a dozen guards. Are we clear?"

He instructed his soldiers to escort her to her bedchamber. She was only to be granted entrance once it

had been thoroughly checked and under no circumstances was she to be left alone.

The bars of her cage felt like they were collapsing in on her.

SHE SPENT THE REMAINDER OF THE DAY WITH MAREK in the training room. After they sparred, he taught her the smell of the most common poisons, how to tend knife wounds, and other various safety skills he felt were important to know with an assassin hunting her.

On her way back to her bedchamber to dress for dinner, Prince Odar joined her.

"Where's your squire?" she asked.

"Preparing our entourage for our departure next week. He's securing inns along the way for lodging, organizing the plethora of soldiers accompanying us, and trying to decide how many trunks of clothing we can bring." He chuckled.

She suspected the prince knew the truth; however, with so many people nearby, he couldn't discuss their real plans.

When they entered her bedchamber, there was a small box sitting in the middle of her bed.

"Who left this?" she asked the guards stationed in her room.

"It's been there all afternoon," one of them responded.

"It wasn't here when I left this morning with Marek. It had to have arrived afterwards. The five of you have been here all day?"

"Yes, Your Highness."

"I'll check into it," Marek said, coming into the room

behind her. He went over to the box. "Stand back," he ordered as he slowly lifted the lid. Marek hissed at the sight of the box's contents. His eyes darted around the room. "Take the princess out of here," he demanded. Guards surrounded her, and they took her out of her bedchamber to the sitting room.

Marek and Prince Odar joined her shortly after. The prince's face was white as snow, and he swayed on his feet. Marek wouldn't even look at her.

"Tell me," she said, fearing something had happened to her parents.

"I need to speak with Jarvik." Prince Odar hurried from the room, tripping over his feet in his haste to exit.

"Marek," she whispered. "What is it?"

"Give us space," he ordered the guards. When everyone backed away, he said, "I'm so sorry." He clutched the black box between his shaking hands.

"Let me see."

"You don't want to, trust me."

"Then tell me," she begged. Her head started to throb.

"Grevik," Marek softly said. "There's a... bloody finger inside along with a note. It says: *Come to the inn tonight or it'll be his head tomorrow.*"

She grabbed the nearby vase full of flowers and hurled it across the room. It hit the wall and shattered, muting her scream. The assassin had cut off Grevik's finger. She would kill him with her bare hands for doing that to her friend. She started pacing the room. This man was an assassin. She was the crown princess. She could, and would, outsmart the man who had kidnapped and tortured her friend. He should fear her, for he'd crossed the line.

"Assemble the elite guard in the war room," she

ordered Marek. "I want you and Jarvik there as well."

"Allyssa, we need to proceed with your father's plans. We can't deviate from them. I'm under orders."

"I understand," she replied. "However, I am the one in charge right now, and I gave you an order. I suggest you follow it before I throw you in the dungeon; are we clear? And it's Your Highness, not Allyssa."

Marek's eyes widened in shock. She'd never spoken to him in such a way, but if she wanted to save her friend, she had to be just as ruthless as the man she was going up against.

THE PRINCESS STOOD AT THE FRONT OF THE ROOM, ALL eyes on her. Jarvik's lips were pulled tight, as if he wanted to say something or take control. However, he kept his mouth shut and remained seated. Allyssa gave the entire guard Grevik's description, along with a detailed account of the room he was being held in. She dispatched a few of the men to head up searches throughout the entire city for her friend. The remaining men were going to accompany her to the inn.

"Your Highness," Marek interrupted. "Don't you think the assassin is anticipating you doing this?"

She raised her eyebrows, ready to respond, when Jarvik's chair scraped backwards and he abruptly stood. "Your Highness," he said. "I have an idea." He looked pointedly at her, reminding Allyssa of her promise to him last night.

"Very well," she responded. "Let's hear it."

"I'd like to put a decoy in your place. Send her to the inn. We can have soldiers in plain clothing already stationed there as well as along the alleyway where the secret exit is located."

"He'll know it's not me," she said.

He nodded.

"He'll probably kill the decoy," she said.

"Not necessarily."

"A decoy won't be adequately equipped to deal with the assassin," she said. "It has to be me."

"There are women who can fight," Marek said.

"Please, think this through," Jarvik added. "You can't make choices with your emotions."

*Bloody hell.* He was right, and they both knew it.

"I know you're angry," Jarvik continued. "I am too. If we're careful about this, we can get the revenge you seek."

She slowly nodded, reason setting in. "Very well. Can I count on you to organize this?"

"It would be my honor," Jarvik replied. "In return, I need your promise that your father's plan will be put in place—whether Grevik is rescued or not."

She glanced at Marek. He nodded, indicating he agreed with Jarvik.

"I promise."

# Chapter Twenty-six

She stood facing a young girl of similar age, height, and build. They both wore the same outfit—brown pants, boots, tunic, and cape.

"It's an honor, Your Highness," the girl said.

"What's your name?" Allyssa inquired.

"Bri," she replied.

"Do you know how to fight?"

"My father and brother are both in the army. I can fight."

Allyssa studied Bri for a moment. She stood with her feet shoulder-width apart, leaning slightly forward as if she was ready to pounce if need be. There were also a few small scars on her hands, indicating she'd been in some scrapes.

"Very well," Allyssa said, approving of the girl. "The first thing he'll do is remove your weapons."

"I know," Bri replied. "Your men have gone over what to expect and what to do. You can count on me. I promise."

Jarvik knocked and entered the room. "It's time," he said. "The decoy will leave with Marek and a handful of guards—just as you would have done. We'll wait a few minutes and then follow them."

Marek turned to Allyssa. "Stay with Jarvik and do

exactly as he says. I can't do my job if I'm worrying about you."

"I promise," she said.

"As soon as the assassin has Bri, I'll wait for you and Jarvik to follow them, and then I'll trail you guys."

"Be safe," she added.

He nodded and took the decoy, leaving with half a dozen guards.

Jarvik strapped two daggers to his forearms. "Are you sure you won't reconsider? We can do this without you."

"I want to be there," Allyssa answered.

"I know, and I understand why. Sometimes, though, you have to allow others to help you. You have to be able to trust other people."

Sliding two additional daggers in her boots, she said, "You mean like you do?" She adjusted the hood of her cape.

"It was worth a shot," he grumbled. "Fine, let's go."

As they traveled through the city, Jarvik's eyes roamed over every inch of the streets, searching for threats. "You know, I almost locked you in the dungeon tonight."

"Why?"

"For your own safety while I rescued Grevik. Then I realized that if something happened, and your friend got hurt or died, you'd order my execution." He shrugged. "You'd probably kill me yourself. So I decided against it."

She chuckled.

"You think it's funny?"

"No. I like the way you think," she said. "I must say, you've surprised me."

"The feeling is quite mutual."

They turned onto a street a block away from the inn.

Slowing their pace, Jarvik's eyes darted to the rooftops.

"Something's off," he quietly mumbled. "Hide in the nearby doorway."

Pulling out one of her daggers, Allyssa did as he requested. While she leaned against the door, Jarvik stood a few feet in front of her, observing the rooftop across the street.

"What's wrong?" she asked.

"One of my men isn't in position," he answered as he slid in the doorway alongside her.

They stood there waiting for several minutes, neither one of them speaking. Since they hadn't been able to locate Grevik, their only hope was following the assassin to his hideout and rescuing Grevik there.

"Let's go," Jarvik said, waving her forward. "They're moving."

"Is the decoy with the assassin?" she asked.

"Yes."

Allyssa stayed by Jarvik's side as he swiftly advanced through the streets. He kept glancing up at one of his men on the rooftops. They came to the wealthy part of the city where mostly homes were located.

Since there were hardly any people about, Jarvik remained concealed in the shadows of nearby homes and bushes. He squatted next to a tree, pulling Allyssa down with him. "There," he whispered in her ear, pointing ahead of them.

A man wearing a black cape with a woman by his side walked up the pathway to a dark house. Allyssa couldn't tell if the girl was blindfolded or not because of her hood. Jarvik crouched and followed them, Allyssa at his heels.

Instead of going up to the front door, the assassin

skirted around the side of the house. Behind the property there was a smaller house, probably used by servants. The assassin led the woman up a flight of stairs to the entrance of the smaller house. He opened the door, and they disappeared inside.

"Let's go," Jarvik said, pulling out a knife. He raised his arm and six soldiers slid out of the shadows.

As they approached the house, three soldiers took the lead, Jarvik and Allyssa following, while the remaining three soldiers brought up the rear. Clutching onto her dagger, Allyssa tried to calm her raging nerves as she crept up the stairs. At the door, they paused and listened to the voices arguing inside. A female scream pierced the air and Allyssa grabbed Jarvik's hand, trying to steady herself so she didn't burst through the door and ruin the plan. Jarvik held up his other hand and made a fist. Everyone armed themselves, preparing to fight. Already holding one dagger, Allyssa withdrew a second one and nodded. Jarvik pointed at the door and the first three soldiers stormed inside, Allyssa running in behind them, ready to attack the assassin.

As she stepped through the threshold, two soldiers lay on the ground, lifeless, with daggers protruding from their chests. Bri clutched her side, blood oozing out of a knife wound. In the center of the room, slumped over on the chair, sat an unmoving Grevik. Blood pooled on the floor beneath him.

A rushing sound filled Allyssa's ears, and she became dizzy. The remaining soldiers entered and searched for the assassin, who was nowhere in sight.

"Check the floorboards to see if any are loose," Jarvik ordered. "You and you, search the outside perimeter. Hurry."

The room swayed before her, and she stumbled.

Marek stormed inside with the six Emperion soldiers. He ran to Grevik, touching his neck to locate his pulse. Marek lifted Grevik's eyelids and then turned to face Allyssa. "I'm so sorry," he said.

"He can't be dead," she said as she took a step back and bumped into one of her soldiers.

"Forgive me," the soldier said as he lifted his sword with shaking hands and placed the blade against her throat. "The assassin has my family."

"Don't do this," Marek pleaded as he righted himself.

Her soldier wrapped his arm around her upper body, pinning her arms down. She was unarmed since both of her daggers had fallen to the floor when she saw Grevik.

"If I deliver the princess," the soldier said, his blade piercing her skin, "he'll let my family go."

"That's what he told us about this man." Jarvik nodded toward Grevik's limp body. "The assassin didn't keep his word. He's probably lying about your family. Release the princess, and we'll help you rescue your wife and children."

The soldier slowly shook his head. "You don't understand," he said, his voice shaking. "He'll kill them."

"You took an oath," Marek said. "If you take the princess, you'll be a traitor. You'll be hanged."

"But my wife and kids will be safe."

"No, they won't," Jarvik insisted. "If you don't release the princess, your family will be arrested for your crimes."

"No … no …" the soldier cried. "I have to take her to him. He promised."

Allyssa saw the small knife in Jarvik's hand. He shifted his grip, and she knew he was going to throw it at the soldier who held her. However, she had no intention of being the damsel in distress who needed rescuing. Her father was a legendary commander for a reason.

Regaining her wits about her, Allyssa knew she needed to act quickly and couldn't afford to make a mistake since the sword was digging into her throat. Closing her eyes, she took a shallow breath, slamming her heel down on the soldier's foot. At the same time, she shifted her body and swung her elbow into his stomach. When his grip loosened and the blade was no longer at her throat, she whipped out a knife from a hidden slit in her pants, and plunged it into the soldier's side. He dropped to the ground, and Marek jumped on him.

Something warm dripped down her neck to her chest. Reaching up, she touched blood. Lightheaded from blood loss, she staggered and then collapsed.

Allyssa woke up in Jarvik's arms. The dark night sky loomed above as he carried her, his brows pinched together with worry.

"Hurry," he ordered the remaining soldiers. "She's lost a lot of blood. We must take her to a healer." His face blurred as she passed out again.

The next time she woke up, she was lying on a cot in a dimly lit room.

An elderly woman with dark, wrinkled skin hovered above her. "No signs of poison," she said. "Only blood loss. I'll stitch her together and bandage her up."

"Thank you," Jarvik said. "What can I do to help?"

"Give her this."

Jarvik reached down and lifted Allyssa's head. "Drink," he encouraged her. He held a cup to her lips,

and warm liquid slid down her throat. Her eyelids grew heavy, and she fell asleep.

The next time Allyssa woke, the room was dark. She tried to sit up, but a hand reached out, gripping her shoulder.

"Rest," Jarvik whispered. She leaned back against the pillow. "The healer doesn't want you moving too quickly. You must regain your strength."

When she went to say something, her throat seared with pain as if it were on fire. She hadn't realized the soldier's sword dug so deep into her skin.

Tears filled her eyes when she remembered Grevik's lifeless body. A sob escaped her.

"Shh," Jarvik said, rubbing her arm. "It's going to be all right." He brought his chair closer to her cot so she could see his face. "I'm having Grevik's body brought to the castle. His mother has been told. I'll make sure she's heavily compensated for her son's sacrifice."

Tears spilled down Allyssa's face. Her friend was dead because of her. She'd never hear his laugh, see his dear face, or chase thieves with him again.

"It wasn't your fault," Jarvik insisted.

She closed her eyes, wanting to go to sleep so she didn't have to feel the pain of her best friend's death.

When morning came, the sun shone through the room's only window, mocking her. Jarvik slept slumped on the rickety, wooden chair in the corner. Allyssa pushed herself up into a sitting position. The furnishings were sparse, the room small, and no healers lingered nearby. This was not the medical wing of the castle.

Jarvik jerked awake. "How are you feeling?" he groggily asked.

"Better," she said.

"Let me get you something to eat."

"Where are we?" she asked.

Jarvik rubbed his eyes and yawned. "The servants' wing. I thought it would be safer for you here. The decoy is in your bedchamber recovering."

He went to the door, mumbled something to the person standing on the other side, and then he sat down again. "What's that?" he asked, pointing to her neck.

She reached up and felt several bandages covering her skin.

"No, on the chain."

"Oh," she said lamely, not sure what to tell him. "Just a gift." She lifted the necklace the rest of the way out from under her shirt. Strung on the delicate chain was the wooden ring she'd received as a gift. Based on her research, it most likely came from Fren. She suspected Prince Odar had given it to her, although it didn't seem like something he would do.

"You've been wearing it this entire time? A simple ring?"

"Yes," she whispered, her throat sore. "It means something." She wasn't sure how to express that this gift was more valuable to her than all the diamonds and jewels others had bestowed upon her.

"Do you know what it means?" he asked.

"I know there's an old peasant tradition where a wooden ring is given from a man to the woman he wishes to court. If she fancies the giver, she wears the ring on her finger."

"Do you know who gave it to you?"

She fingered the smooth ring, turning it over on her hand. "I'm not certain."

"Then why do you wear it?"

"For what it represents—hope for love that has nothing to do with crowns or kingdoms, but love for love's sake."

Just then, there was a soft knock and one of the Fren soldiers entered, carrying a tray of food.

# Chapter Twenty-seven

The healer removed Allyssa's bandages and smiled. "The wound is closed," she said. "I had to sew several stitches to bind the skin together, but you'll heal up mighty fine as long as you put this ointment on twice a day."

"Thank you," Allyssa croaked. The healer smiled and left the room.

"I want to leave tonight," Jarvik said. "It's too dangerous to remain here any longer." He hauled Allyssa to her feet.

She picked up the can of salve, and they exited the small room located in the servants' wing. Keeping her hood low and her head down, they made their way to the stairwell where they met Marek.

He bent down on one knee. "I'm so sorry," he said. "I failed you."

She patted his shoulder. "You did not fail me. You kept me safe."

He stood tall and stiff. "Let's go to your bedchamber so you can clean up."

Allyssa quickly changed into a dress while her ladies-in-waiting braided her hair and applied dusting powder to her face. Once presentable, she left the decoy, who

was recovering from her stab wound, in the bedchamber while she went to join Jarvik in the sitting room of the Royal Chambers.

"Walk with me outside," Allyssa said to the squire. "We must talk, and I desire some fresh air."

Double the usual amount of guards accompanied them. When they entered the courtyard, the bright sun warmed her skin as she closed her eyes, reveling in the comfort.

"Don't tip your head back," Jarvik mumbled. "You don't want to expose your wound."

She had chosen this particular dress because it covered her neck completely. She took his arm and quietly said, "What needs to be done before I leave?"

"You need to meet with the Legion member who will be in charge until your parents announce their arrival at Emperor's City."

They neared the water fountain so it would drown out their voices. The sweet smell of gardenias permeated the air. "Anything else?"

"Wear commoner clothing tonight. You can bring a sack with one outfit to change into. That is all. When we reach Fren, I'll ensure you receive enough dresses to wear during your stay."

Allyssa trailed her hand over a nearby hydrangea, the leaves wet from the fountain. She couldn't believe she was leaving the castle tonight. She'd traveled throughout the kingdom, but she'd never left Emperion before. The idea of leaving this place was certainly enticing; she just wished it could be on her own accord.

"There's something I must tell you." Jarvik ran his hands through his hair. "I've wanted to tell you for quite some time. It is a secret, and one you must keep until we arrive at the castle in Fren."

Allyssa nodded. "You can trust me."

He took a step closer to her. "When I first traveled to Emperion, I thought it would be best if—"

A soldier ran up to Allyssa, out of breath. "Your Highness," he said, bowing. "You're needed in the Throne Room immediately. Spies from the Russek border have just arrived."

"Of course," Allyssa replied. Knowing she had to keep up the pretense that her parents were still at the castle, she added, "Have the empress and emperor been notified?"

"They have, Your Highness. They are indisposed at the moment, and your father requested you handle the matter."

"They weren't feeling well this morning," she replied. Only the Royal Guard knew decoys had been put in their places. "Inform the Legion I am on my way."

He bowed and left.

"We'll talk later," she said to Jarvik. He nodded, and she joined her guards standing discreetly in the distance.

Sitting tall in her Throne Chair, Allyssa watched as half a dozen men came down the aisle. When they reached the dais, they bowed.

"Are you the spies who just returned from the Russek border?"

"We are, Your Highness," one replied.

"Tell me what news you have learned." These men were all well-trained soldiers handpicked by Neco to serve in his secret guard. Though they were dressed as commoners, they most certainly were not.

"Your Highness," one of the men said as he stepped forward. "A small squad of men from the Russek army has been spotted in the Romek Mountains."

Allyssa abruptly stood. The Romek Mountains extended from the southernmost tip of Fia and into Emperion. "What were they doing?" she asked, afraid she already knew the answer.

"Guarding a cave stocked with supplies such as food and weapons. There were also several boats."

"Anything else?" It was just as she'd feared.

"The Russek army is ready to march into Fia. They have orders to go straight to the Romek Mountains."

She knew exactly what the Russeks planned on doing—using the river that began in the Romek Mountains and ran straight through Emperion, ending at the Great Ocean. "We must cut off their supply chain," Allyssa said. "We can't allow them to use our own river against us."

The men mumbled in agreement.

"Are you ready for another assignment?" she asked. She'd never given orders to soldiers before. A rush of power and excitement filled her.

"Gladly," one of the soldiers answered.

"Excellent. I want you and your men to go back to the Romek Mountains. Dispose of the Russek squad, burn their boats, and destroy their food."

"It would be my honor, Your Highness." He gave a fierce grin in approval.

After dinner, Allyssa excused herself, saying she didn't feel well and hoped she wasn't coming down with the same cold her parents had. On her way to the Royal Chambers, she stopped by the library, unable to resist. There was no harm in taking a book on the journey.

Going to her favorite section, she plucked two books off the shelf and turned, about to leave, when she saw Jarvik standing right behind her.

"What are you doing?" she asked.

"I was passing by when I saw your guards outside." He pointed to the hallway where they stood watch. "You shouldn't be in here alone. What if someone was waiting in here for you?"

"I guess it's a good thing I'm armed."

He chuckled. "You never cease to amaze me." Jarvik took a step toward her. "I need to talk to you," he whispered, nodding down the aisle where no one would be able to see them.

They moved until they were hidden between two bookshelves. "There's something you need to know," Jarvik said. He ran his hands through his hair, messing it up. "How do you feel about the prince?" he asked, putting his hands on his hips.

She set her books down on the shelf behind her. "Why do you ask?"

"A few things depend on your answer." He hesitated before placing his hands on her upper arms. "I need you to be completely honest with me. This conversation is confidential."

Biting her bottom lip, she peered into his warm eyes. "Honestly?"

He nodded.

"Prince Odar is handsome, kind, and everything a

prince should be." Jarvik's hands tightened on her arms as tension radiated off him. "But I am not in love with him. Maybe one day, I will learn to love him. I can't be certain because all I see and think about is you."

His breath caught. "What?"

"I'm sorry," she backpedaled. "I shouldn't have told you that." She tried to leave, but he wouldn't release her.

"Allyssa," he whispered. His hands cupped her face. "I didn't expect to feel anything for you. I thought you'd be just another princess—haughty, arrogant, and uncaring. You turn the very meaning of the word *princess* upside down. I had no idea you'd spark something deep inside of me." His eyes bore into hers. "I knew our kingdoms needed the alliance, but I never thought it would end up like this."

Jarvik bent toward her, tilting his head to the side. When their mouths were only an inch apart, he hesitated. Allyssa leaned forward, anticipating the feel of his lips on hers. And they kissed. Warmth spread throughout her body and she slipped her hands around his waist, pulling him closer to her. His lips trailed from her mouth to her ear to her neck. Returning to her lips, he deepened the kiss. She didn't want him to stop. She forgot who she was, where she was, and that this man was her future husband's squire.

Her hands flew to his chest, and she shoved him away. She was engaged to another man.

"I'm sorry," Jarvik said, his eyes wide. "Did I hurt you?"

She covered her face with her hands, unable to believe what had just happened. She shook her head. "Forgive me," she said. "I got carried away."

He reached out and pulled her hands away from her face. "Allyssa, I feel the same way about you."

"But we can't," she said. "I should never have revealed my feelings for you. I'm sorry, but I'm engaged to your best friend."

"To a man you don't love."

"It doesn't matter," she said, stepping away from him, trying to put as much distance between them as possible. "I won't disrespect Prince Odar that way. I may not love him, but he is to be my husband and I will honor him."

Jarvik smiled. "I've said it before—you are loyal." He took a step toward her, and she raised her hands for him to stop. "There's something I need to tell you," he said.

"Wait." She withdrew the necklace from beneath her dress and lifted it over her head. Unclasping the latch, she removed the ring. "I ... I want you to have this." She held out her hand, the ring resting on her palm.

"Why?" he asked.

"From the moment we leave this library, there can never be anything between us. I want you to have this ring to remember me."

"I'll be seeing you every day—there will be no forgetting you." A smile tugged on the corners of his lips.

"Please," she begged. "I don't know how to be friends with you—I care for you too much. I want you to have this ring as a token of what could have been if my kingdom didn't dictate who I marry."

He took the ring and opened his mouth to say something, but Allyssa grabbed her books and ran from the aisle.

"Allyssa! Wait!"

She sprinted out of the library, not looking back. *Bloody two-bit snake pits.* What had just happened? The feeling of Jarvik's lips was now seared into her mind. She would never be able to forget her first kiss. She didn't stop running until she reached her bedchamber.

Shortly after midnight, Marek led Allyssa to the stables, where a plain carriage that had been commissioned for their journey awaited them. She had suggested they ride horses instead; however, Jarvik didn't want to have to take the time to stop and sleep.

Dressed in the trousers and tunic she usually wore when she snuck out of the castle, Allyssa stood before the small contingent of men—Jarvik, Prince Odar, Marek, and two Fren soldiers she recognized but didn't know the names of. Everyone was dressed similarly to her. Such a small group to travel so far. Fear pricked down her spine.

"Did anyone see you?" Jarvik demanded.

"No," she replied. The decoy was sleeping in her bed. Only the Royal Guards on duty in her room knew she'd left. "Marek and I did as you suggested and left through the laundry chute."

"Very good. We want to travel as quietly and stealthily as possible. No titles will be used on our journey. Allyssa, Odar, Marek, and I will be in the carriage for the first leg of the journey. My two men, Renlek and Dromar, will steer the carriage. When we stop to change horses, we'll rotate positions. Any questions?"

They all shook their heads.

"Excellent. Let's go."

Allyssa climbed into the carriage and slid down the bench so she rested against the open window. She supposed glass was a luxury only the wealthy had, and since they were supposed to be commoners, she'd have to brave the cold air. Odar got in and sat next to her. Jarvik and Marek shared the bench across from them. The lone torch in the stables was extinguished, and Renlek and Dromar steered the carriage out into the dead of night.

Allyssa managed to fall asleep for a few hours. When she awoke, thick clouds coated the sky, masking the countryside in a dull gray. Prince Odar still slept at her side.

"Morning," Jarvik said. He reached under his seat and took out a loaf of bread. Tearing it into four sections, he handed one to Marek and one to her—his fingers gently brushing hers. The wooden ring was on his finger. She felt horribly guilty for having kissed the squire. Every time she looked at him, she envisioned his lips on hers. Taking a bite of bread, she tried to think of something besides kissing Jarvik.

"What's that?" Marek asked. He set his bread on the seat and leaned out the window. Jarvik also stuck his head out, looking for potential threats.

Renlek yelled down, "Someone's coming up mighty fast behind us on horseback."

Allyssa nudged Prince Odar awake while unsheathing a dagger from her boot.

"Only one?" Jarvik hollered up.

"I only see one."

"Stay on course but be ready to fight," Jarvik answered.

"Why not stop and face him?" Allyssa asked.

"It might only be a messenger heading from one town to another. If we stop, we'll gain his attention and if he's later questioned, he'll probably remember our actions as being strange and mention it. If we act normally, he won't

recall us at all."

Marek nodded. "I agree. Remember, don't use names and don't look guilty."

She nodded, clutching her dagger next to her thigh.

"The rider is nearing," Jarvik muttered. "His cape doesn't have any visible markings."

"Still only one horse?" Marek asked, bending over and unsheathing his sword from the scabbard below the seat.

"Yes."

Horse hooves pounded on the dirt road behind them as the rider neared. Allyssa prayed he'd fly past without paying them any heed.

A body fell alongside her window, an arrow protruding from Renlek's back. He tumbled to the ground. Allyssa screamed. The carriage veered to the right, almost tipping. She caught sight of the man nocking an arrow and shooting at Dromar. The second driver toppled to the ground.

"It's him!" Allyssa said. "The assassin!"

Marek climbed out of the window, trying to reach the perch in order to gain control of the spooked horses. Allyssa wanted to order him to stay put, but Jarvik yelled at her to be prepared to fight. Clutching onto her knife, she readied herself. The carriage slowed, and the rider caught up to them.

The sound of metal clinking echoed as Marek fought the assassin. There was an odd shift. She realized Jarvik had exited the carriage and cut the ropes to the horses so they wouldn't crash. The assassin swung his sword, knocking Marek off the carriage. He landed on the dirt road with a *thud*.

"Let's go," Allyssa said to Prince Odar. He nodded

and followed her as she climbed out of the carriage on the opposite side of where the assassin was. Glancing back, she saw Jarvik fighting the assassin with his sword.

"Let's run to the cover of the nearby trees," Prince Odar whispered.

She shook her head. They couldn't go to the forest and leave Marek lying on the ground. Not even hesitating, Odar sprinted toward the trees, not once looking back. She wanted to yell at him but, instead, she knelt next to her friend. His chest moved as he breathed. He was alive then. There was a large gash on his forehead, but it wasn't deep.

Grabbing Marek's arm, she started dragging his body toward the trees, which were a good thirty feet away. Prince Odar had almost reached the cover of the forest. There was a slight *hiss* and then a *thud*. An arrow embedded into the back of Prince Odar, his brown shirt turning red with blood. He fell to the ground, not moving. Allyssa released Marek, stifling her scream. When she spun around, the assassin stood there, smiling at her. Jarvik was at his side, forced onto his knees, a sword to his chest. The squire's eyes were wide with horror at the sight of Odar's body.

"Don't move," the assassin said to Jarvik.

"You killed him," Allyssa said with disbelief. Prince Odar lay lifeless on the ground. How was she supposed to save her kingdom if the prince was dead? Emperion would never receive the soldiers they needed. She glanced at the squire, wondering why he didn't attempt to fight. He reached up, touching his right shoulder. His hand came away bloody.

"I said not to move." The assassin backhanded Jarvik across the face.

What happened to her knife? She must have dropped it when she climbed out of the carriage. She should still have another dagger in her left boot. If she could snatch it, she could kill the assassin.

"Get up," he said to Jarvik. The squire tried to stand, but his leg gave out. His thigh had a gouge in it, blood running down his leg. With the assassin's focus off her, Allyssa reached down and grabbed her dagger. The assassin whipped his head around to face her. She aimed for his chest and threw. He ducked, the knife narrowly missing him. She spun and kicked toward his chest. He blocked the blow and swung, punching her in the stomach. Stars exploded in her vision, and she hunched over from pain.

"Stop your attack," the assassin demanded. "Or I'll kill your friend this minute." He had the sword on Jarvik's chest again. She knew not to trust the word of an assassin. She tried to stand, but her stomach cramped. The assassin hit Jarvik across the head, and he passed out. If his wounds weren't tended to, he would die.

The assassin reached down, grabbed Allyssa by her cape, and dragged her closer to the carriage. He took out some rope, fastened her wrists together, and tied her to the wheel. He jumped on his horse and took off in the direction the other two horses had gone after Jarvik cut them loose.

She wished she could reach Jarvik to wrap a bandage around his wounds to stop the bleeding. Marek moaned and rolled over.

"Marek," she frantically whispered. "Run for help."

He grabbed his head as he tried to stand. "I have to save you," he said.

"No," she said with determination. "I order you to

save yourself. Go and find help. Now."

"I can't leave you here. The assassin will be back any minute."

"If he wanted to kill me, he would have already done it. We'll never make it out of here together, but he might not notice if you're gone."

Marek stood on shaky legs. "Let's at least try to make it to the forest," he said, his eyes filled with desperation.

Steeling her resolve, Allyssa said, "No. He'll just track us, and when he finds you, he'll be sure to kill you this time. If you want to save me, I order you to go and seek help right now. It's the only way."

He looked at her with a torn expression. "I promise to rescue you." He turned and sprinted into the woods. Allyssa watched him until she could no longer see him. Even if help never came, at least Marek was safe.

Jarvik still hadn't stirred. A black bird crowed overhead, and the sky darkened as a storm approached. A few minutes later, the assassin returned with her two horses tethered together behind him.

He dismounted and went toward Jarvik.

"What do you plan to do with him?" she demanded.

"The same thing I am going to do with you." The assassin lifted Jarvik and threw him over one of the horses, securing his arms around the animal.

She thought she was going to vomit. "Which is?" This was the man who had killed Grevik and now Jarvik's life was in his hands. She would find a way to save the squire.

"I'm taking you to Russek. There's someone there very interested in the two of you."

"I don't know who you think I am, but you have made a mistake."

The assassin chuckled. "I don't think so, Princess." He came over and untied her from the carriage. Picking her up, he threw her on the other horse, securing her arms around the animal's neck as he'd done to Jarvik to ensure she didn't escape.

"All of Emperion will be after you. There won't be a safe place you can hide. Especially now that you've killed Prince Odar. Fren will descend upon you for revenge."

The assassin mounted. "I see the decoy has even fooled you," he mused. His eyes darted to Jarvik and then back to her. "I have exactly who I want—Princess Allyssa and Prince Odar—and I'm taking you to Russek."

# END OF BOOK 1

# Acknowledgements

This book would not exist without some key people. I would like to thank Allyssa, Stacie, and Debi for reading (more than once) a rough draft of Cage of Deceit and offering invaluable feedback. This book would not be what it is today without the three of you. I'd also like to thank Beckie for believing in this story from the beginning and encouraging me all along. Your advice on adding more "evil" to the story was just what it needed. Thank you for taking me on as an author. I truly appreciate it.

Writing a book is an enormous undertaking. I am blessed to have a wonderful husband and three beautiful children who know and understand my obsession with reading and writing. Thank you for allowing me to do something I'm passionate about, and encouraging me every step of the way. My eldest son, Nathan, insisted that I specifically acknowledge him for his help and contribution in all things martial arts related. So, Nathan, thank you.

My wonderful sister, Jessica, and my mom, Shirley, have been my own personal cheerleaders throughout the entire process. I love you both dearly.

To everyone at Clean Teen Publishing—I can't thank

you for believing in me and bringing this new series to life. I am proud to be a part of your team. You truly are publishing ninjas! Also, a special thanks to Cynthia Shepp for doing a fantastic job with editing, as always.

I'd also like to thank Leah, Rebecca, Kim, Jan, Mary, Dvora, Jen, Elizabeth, Peggy, Angelle, Cheer, Mary, and Kristy. Your support, encouragement, and advice keep me going.

I need to say a special thanks to two very special people for helping name the book and the series. I appreciate your genius ideas! Mayra, thank you for your help and for allowing me to name a character after you. Teri, thank you for your input and allowing me to use your daughter's name, Madelin, as a token of my appreciation.

I also want to thank Sarah for our weekly writing meetings. It's nice to get out of the house and talk about my characters like they're real people. You've made this journey much more enjoyable. Thank you for everything.

Last, but not least, I need to thank all of my readers. When I first started out as a writer, I had no idea how my stories would touch other people's lives. To receive your fan mail and messages saying how much you love my stories truly warms my heart and keeps me going. Thank you!

# About the Author

Jennifer graduated from the University of San Diego with a degree in English and a teaching credential. Afterwards, she finally married her best friend and high school sweetheart. Jennifer is currently a full-time writer and mother of three young children. Her days are spent living in imaginary worlds and fueling her own kids' creativity.

Visit Jennifer online at

www.JenniferAnneDavis.com